ROYAL

DRESSED TO KILL

ANN DENTON

LE RUE PUBLISHING

Cover by Jodielocks Designs.

Le Rue
Publishing

Le Rue Publishing
320 South Boston Avenue, Suite 1030
Tulsa, OK 74103
www.LeRuePublishing.com

ISBN: 978-1-951714-39-0

To the characters who do all the things we wish we could do ourselves ...

AUTHOR'S NOTE

This book contains a lot of violence and murder since it's about assassins. It has some scenes that may make some readers uncomfortable. It also contains explicit conversations about mental illness and chapter 16 has an in-depth conversation about former suicide attempts. The following items appear in this book: violence, kidnapping, stalking, explicit unsafe sex and language, and other content that may be triggering. There is no cheating or other woman drama in this book.

TARGET ACQUIRED

Royal

*W*hose future is going to be stripped away today?

I sit across from Man in his spacious modern office, noting how white his well-groomed beard has gotten lately. It might be my imagination, but the lines around his eyes look a little deeper. Time's carving him up.

I try to recall how old he is, but he refuses to make a big deal out of his birthday. It's spring though; the birds outside are so loud that it's impossible to forget the season—chattering away like all my pseudo-sisters upstairs probably are, those of them not out on jobs anyway. I'm pretty certain he has a birthday coming up soon.

Perched in silence but for the click-clack of Man's computer keyboard, I yawn and pop my ears, wondering for the millionth time why he hardly speaks. I've known him all my life and yet I'm lucky to get a sentence a day out of him. Shame. He has a nice voice, one that would be good for commercials, though he's such a shut-in that the idea of him at an acting audition is laughable. Maybe he just prefers silence.

What I don't understand is why *I'm* not supposed to talk during these little meetings. But every Belladonna knows about crossing that line from the age of six on: Quiet in the office, thems the rules.

I hate rules and Man's trained me to shuck off society's rules, so I don't really see why I need to follow his.

But I do, at least for the moment, because I love him. He's the best dad in the whole world, even if he hates that moniker and refuses to go by it.

Now that I'm bored, I notice the air conditioner is obnoxiously loud in this space. It's huffing and puffing like the big bad wolf—but it will never blow Man's house down. No, this little cobbled-together family of ours is too much for any wolves. My brain is so random sometimes ...actually, it's not as if there's a wolf bigger and badder than us. If anything, Man is THE wolf.

Click clack.

Click clack.

He's still just typing away.

Ignoring me.

My patience wears thin, and it's only as thick as a fruit rollup to begin with—which sounds delicious right now since I skipped breakfast today.

I wrap my feet around my metal chair legs and bounce them a bit in restless anticipation because Man always loves to draw these moments before an assignment out for dramatic effect. Or I feel that way, at least.

I glance over his shoulders at the wall behind him as I wait for him to *finally stop typing*. Soaking up the details of his space, I play the "what has changed" game.

Honestly, nothing significant has been altered in at least ten years. Is it ten? Yeah, that has to be right. I think it was redecorated when I was twelve … assuming the birthday he gave me is my actual birthday. Nobody knows since I was set out in a box in an alley like an abandoned little puppy.

Oh!

I spot one thing. An old cigar box, which must have sentimental value because I've never seen Man smoke, has moved five inches to the right.

My OCD tendencies twitch with the desire to move it back, the need crawling underneath my skin and pinching my stomach. I have no doubt it was Harlow who moved it; she and I have a constant battle going over where things actually belong. I grimace because I can't move it right now during an assignment meeting. He'd blow a gasket.

I'll have to deal with it later, even though it's going to create a tiny little itch inside my brain all day until I can sneak back and fix it.

Attempting to focus on anything other than that box, I scan the rest of the space.

I used to hate this room; it's so modern and just... square. There are gray fabric squares behind Man's desk that are supposed to be artsy or something. The tiles on the floor are giant tan rectangles. Even though there are curtains lining the right wall from floor to ceiling, they fall in these extremely organized pleats that look geometric with the way the light hits them. It's the exact opposite of everything I love. There are no print patterns, no bold colors, no quirky mismatched mementos. It's ugly.

On the other hand, this room is where I get all my assignments.

That makes it the best damn room on the planet.

I smile expectantly at Man. I try for polite.

He says nothing.

Does nothing but type.

Boriiiing.

I blow a raspberry.

Nothing.

"Are you waiting until my hair turns as white as yours to give me my assignment?" I quip, because I have to. The impulse is as irresistible as breathing. My brain is swelling and it's literally going to explode if he doesn't give me my frickin' envelope.

Still no answer. Not even a glance.

Dammit.

I wait another whole minute before it feels like impatience is going to burst through my skin. That's when I start miming every bored position I can think of. I throw myself back on the chair and fling out my limbs like a toddler. Then I bolt upright and tap my toe. Then I dramatically check my watch—only I'm not wearing a watch. I slowly start to sink to the ground in a boneless heap.

I like to think Man enjoys my theatrics.

At the very least, they annoy him enough that I get my way.

He stops typing, sighs, and opens his desk drawer. I immediately snap to attention and sit upright, heart whacking excitedly at my ribs, like a friend repeatedly slapping your arm with the back of their hand and saying, "OMG! Do you see that!"

Before I can take a breath, I find myself leaning forward over the wide expanse of his desk as he slides the bulging white envelope across the surface toward me. Yes! Striking with the efficiency of a starving king cobra, I snatch it up.

"Woohoo!" I punch the air as I clutch the thick and extensive packet of paperwork in my hand, pulling it to my heart to give it a cuddle in order to make Man roll his eyes. He doesn't.

I don't open it in front of him. I know the drill by now. I'll let him know if I need supplies. Otherwise, it's go time.

I give him a wink before I stand and saunter to the door in my heels, my floaty purple flower print dress billowing out around my ankles. My heart is doing a touchdown dance, I'm so excited. It's been months since I've had an assignment.

Of course, I can't resist the opportunity to turn back and tease him. "You know, *Santa,* if you're gonna make me wait before you give me presents, I expect a candy cane next time."

I point a warning finger at him and cackle before slamming the door shut behind me.

And it might be wishful thinking, but I'm pretty certain that behind the door Man grumbles, "I'm not *that* old, dammit."

1

MISSING THE MARK

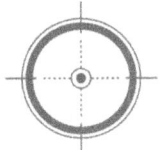

May 17
10:45 p.m.
Bethesda, MD

Royal

T stare through my binoculars, waiting for my target to *keel over and die already*, as I debate what celebratory pair of shoes I'm going to buy myself tomorrow for a job well done.

A good murder deserves a reward, after all.

I've been holding out for some BAPE STAs. I know they're supposed to be low-key white sneakers with black stars but I really want to buy them and get roses painted on the sides by this girl who runs her own Etsy shop. I can't even believe sneaker painting is a real job. That's so damn cool. I almost hired her last month, but I keep delaying and I'm not quite sure why.

Maybe because the paint job is permanent and I can't commit. One day I want stars. Another—astrology symbols. Today—roses. It's the same reason that every time I go into the tattoo shop, I end up turning right back around. Tattoos are forever and I've never been a forever kind of girl.

I make duck lips just for funsies as I glide toward another window in the house I've broken into, stepping around a leopard print ottoman and purple chair as I strive to keep eyes on my target.

I actually really like the place I'm staying. It has a fun eclectic vibe and the owner is out on a girl's trip, according to her emails, which sounds so fun. She and I could probably have been friends.

"Where's my ugly bastard?" I scan his windows again. "There he is!" I coo. He's meandering around his house across the street, a two-story red brick house with ebony shutters and sheer curtains, and fake potted plants indoors. I like to keep my marks in my sight, especially once all my work has ramped up to *the night*. And tonight is his special night, though he doesn't know it.

Tall, with a head full of steel-colored hair, dark eyes, and a darker heart, Yegor Babanin is strolling around in his blue pinstriped suit, thinking he's some sort of a badass as he munches on some French fries left over from the burger dinner he had delivered an hour ago.

I enjoy the fact that this dickhead lives in a nice neighborhood, because it's pretty much silent by ten p.m. Right now, it's quiet enough to hear a mouse fart, which makes all the little bugs I planted in some of his Amazon deliveries (swiping them off his porch before returning them) work that much more effectively.

As he disappears up the stairs, I drop the binocs with a thump against my chest and tap on my tablet to open the app Darcy made for me. That girl is amazing with tech. She even made the background on this app showcase little green aliens wearing bow ties for me, solely because she thought it would make me chuckle. That's a good sister if there ever was one.

I move a slider on the screen to adjust the sound quality on the listening device I placed on his new electric toothbrush. Normally, I keep that one turned down, for obvious reasons, but since he's still dressed when he appears in his bedroom, he's unlikely to use it for a bit. I get a little feedback, wincing and grinding my teeth as the screech whips through my skull. My fingers hurriedly swipe at the app screen until it stops.

Ugh, I can hear him whistling off-key.

He walks across his bedroom head bent over his phone, completely oblivious to the fact that I stopped by earlier and opened all his sheers so I'd have a nice view through his windows this evening. Most men are seriously so oblivious, but add a phone in? Forget it. I could probably cover the floor in tacks and this guy would only notice if one of them actually pierced his shoe.

Going to stand in front of his dresser, he props his phone up, watching a video as he empties out his pockets, just like he does every night. The room itself is fancy but personality-less, decorated in grays (blech)—as magazine-pretty-but-forgettable as it can get.

Despite being Russian, Yegor is really into the American yuppie lifestyle, complete with a Stepford wife who will probably find his body tomorrow after she gets home from her yoga retreat.

I don't really feel bad for traumatizing Katie though. She's cheating on him with her hot-as-hell yoga instructor, probably right this very second. When those two ladies get together, they really go at it. Might even be a love match, though I doubt it. You have to stop to talk for emotional shit to happen, or so I've heard. I bump and run, personally.

Of course, her cheating is nothing compared to what Douchebag Mark Number 72 here has done. He's affiliated with the Russian bratva and sold a family of four into servitude last week, children included.

I glare at him through my lenses as my chest tightens, the knowledge that I couldn't save that family crushing a little piece of me.

If only Yegor knew what was coming for him. He deserves to feel the kind of terror he's inflicted on others, ripping them away from their home countries—selling people like cattle and carting them off to places on the other side of the globe where they don't speak the language and have zero chance of escaping. Slavery. That's his fucking business.

Monster.

I give a disgusted scowl at the "distinguished" lines on his forehead as I watch him loosen his red tie. He's home from a "meeting" tonight at the opera, which really means he sat in a box listening to crap music with another rich and morally defunct bastard who wants a human to be his personal puppet.

"Fuck you, Yegor," I mutter. "I'd wish for your balls to wither but honestly, you're not going to be around long enough to waste a wish on."

Deciding that it looks like Yegor's going to be in this room for a bit, I prop my tablet on the windowsill and drag over a wingback chair with my flower print duffel on it. Then I perch daintily on the arm as I snag a chocolate bar from the snack pouch in my supply bag without looking. Stakeouts always require snacks. I have the one-handed grab-and-unwrap down to a science. I can do it in three seconds flat— I timed it once. Of course, it helps that I always bring exactly five snacks and I alphabetize them so I know exactly what is where. I bring the bar to my mouth and take a bite.

"Just die already," I complain, waving my candy at Yegor like an orchestra conductor.

I really take offense to the fact that sometimes my targets take a long time to go through all the motions I need them to complete before they kick the bucket.

Of course, I could make it easier on myself. Cleaner. A headshot when he's out walking...that's what Tabitha would do with her freaking drones. A little smidgeon of jealousy for the raven-haired Belladona passes through my system, but it disappears quickly because I'm so utterly grateful for Man and my sisters. I can't really begrudge them their success. What's that annoyingly true school marmish saying? Comparison is the death of joy.

Yeah, I can't compare to her. I've done made my bed and decided on my assassination techniques long ago, which is why I'm pretty certain I got picked for this job.

What happens when a well-known human trafficker commits suicide?

Panic among the little spiders in his web.

They start to wonder who betrayed him, who really took him out.

Endgame isn't just about him or the bounty someone put out on his head. We want his entourage to break up, for distrust to run rampant, and the whole stinking thing to fall apart.

This motherfucker is going to look like he offed himself. Of course, those who know him would wonder why since he just made a smooth million of that little family last week and has another client all queued up.

It won't make any sense.

It's not supposed to.

If only he'd *hurry the fuck up.*

Yegor pulls open the top drawer of his dresser and discovers my present.

"Finally!" My chocolate bar-clutching hand victoriously punches up into the sky and my heart rate kicks up. I lean forward on my seat, pressing my binocs a little too hard into the skin around my eyes. This is it.

Yegor pauses and pulls out the bottle of Crown, along with the note I forged from his wife, Katie.

Have a little fun and relax while I'm out of town. XO –K

"Why didn't she get me vodka?" Yegor's brow furrows and I pick up on his complaint through the earbud in my ear.

Freaking Russian.

"Because it's my fucking signature move, limpdick," I inform no one. "Crown Royal. Get it?" I shake my head. They never get it. Neither do the coroners. Of course, I wouldn't be a good Belladonna if they did.

He shakes his head but he still opens the liquor—they always do. Yegor doesn't even bother to go grab a glass, he just takes a swig right from the bottle, like it's mouthwash or something.

Nice.

I shake my head, red hair spilling over my shoulders onto the black jumpsuit I'm wearing for the grand finale. It's the most boring and cliche assassin outfit—I know—but I did spice it up by sewing little black rhinestones along the cuffs. I've asked Man if I could go with a really dark purple instead, but so far, no dice.

Time for me to move.

I shove the wrapper back over my candy bar, stick a Ziplock bag over it, and put it away in my reserved snack pouch before I close up my tablet and slide it into its special pocket in my duffel. I'm just zipping the top closed when I hear an odd thump in my ear.

My pulse triples and tension makes my throat feel thick and clogged. What the hell was that?

I glance around, but the apartment I'm in is empty of life other than the dozen potted plants I watered earlier today.

I turn back to the window and everything happens in a rush.

Boom.

Crash—clink—clink—clink.

The scattered white cracks of the shattered window in Yegor's bedroom block most of my view but I get the full audio version through my earpiece.

Yegor's pained yell ricochets around inside my skull as my blood starts to bolt through my veins, sprinting as fast and hard as it can.

I hear another thump and that's when I see someone else step into Yegor's bedroom. Someone dressed all in black, gun extended.

Oh, *hell fucking no!*

Someone else is trying to take out my mark!

2

CROSSFIRE

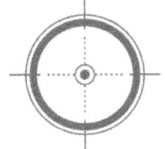

May 17
10:57 p.m.
Bethesda, MD

Royal

S hoving my hand onto the holster on my hip, I retrieve the gun I've only ever fired during practice sessions with Man. It's heavy in my hands, the texture rough against my palms as I raise my arms.

I keep my eyes narrowed while I try to pinpoint my target behind all those damn window cracks.

Goddammit!

I've never had to reveal my position. Never!

Inhaling slowly, my breath is a sharp contrast to the savage hammering of my heart. When I exhale, I shoot, pulling the trigger with more force than necessary. The blast shatters the window in front of me. Immediately, I take a second shot since smashing through two windows will likely send that first bullet off-course.

Potent fury sizzles inside my veins as my ears ring from the shots and the scent of gunpowder lights up my nostrils.

"Motherfucking bastard—" I've hardly whispered the phrase before the shadowy figure across the room groans loudly into my earpiece. I know it's not Yegor because, well, I heard that man's disgusting moans the night before Katie left for her trip. It is a man, however, so I file away that little tidbit about my rival.

Do I feel bad about my first shooting? Not really, since I've been mentally preparing for it my entire life. In fact, I feel a brutal little surge of superiority as I say to the thin air, "That's right. That's what you get."

He's lucky I didn't aim for a kill shot, just his gun arm. But I deliberately didn't shoot to kill because this dude just made my life a hell of a lot fucking harder ... so I'm returning the favor. "Enjoy explaining that at the hospital, turd."

I'm going to have to extend this mission because there is zero chance of it looking like suicide right now.

I hear Yegor whooping like an angry gorilla and a loud crack that sounds as if he's just violated my bottle of Crown by turning it into a weapon.

"You have your own gun, idiot." Now my signature move is going to be splashed all over his carpet.

Dumbasses—both of them.

I slide to my right side and peer through the window next to the one I shot up, trying to get eyes on the scene, but I can't

tell a damn thing with all the cracked glass still left in
Yegor's bedroom window. Tiny slivers have fallen from
around the bullet holes, but for the most part, it's still intact.

Shitcicles.

I grab my duffel, keeping my gun out and ready as I burst
through the door of my borrowed apartment. My pulse is
flying just like the rest of me as I race down the narrow hall
past a startled older woman with a bag of groceries in her
hand. "Police!" I yell at her. "Get inside!"

Whether she listens or even believes me, I have no clue,
because I don't look back. I'm down the stairs and shoving
through the front door, stumbling out into the crisp spring
night air just as Yegor climbs into the driver's seat of his
Mercedes across the road.

Fucking hell.

I don't bother running after him. I already know just where
that cowardly lion is going to go. Instead, I give him five
seconds to peel out into the street, tires screeching, scenting
the air with the perfume of burning rubber before he zooms
off into the night with all the precision of a drunk.

Ugh—now he's going to be paranoid as all get out. Setting
up everything all over again is going to be such a pain.

My head swivels to look at his open front door and adrenaline erupts inside my skull—adrenaline combined with
OCD. I need to go to the scene and clean up any evidence
that I was there, take away any bugs, remove the Crown, the
note …

My feet are moving to the steps before my brain catches up
with the fact that I'm being just a little bit reckless right

now, because underlying all the other emotions, I'm a level of pissed-off I've never fucking experienced before.

Someone just ruined my kill.

My hand tightens on my gun and I slow my feet a little, until my footsteps fade to almost nothing. I focus on the tiny bud in my ear, alert and ready for danger, though the bud isn't picking up any sound right now.

Nerves prickle along my neck as I walk past the long coat Yegor lazily threw on the entry table when he got home from the opera.

Is the would-be killer still upstairs?

Only one way to find out.

Heart wobbling, but fury roaring like a lioness, I plant my foot on the first stair when a shuffling noise behind me sends me whirling, gun lifted, duffel falling off my shoulder and yanking painfully at my elbow joint.

In the front doorway, a tall slender man freezes mid-sprint. He's dressed all in black, though unlike me, he doesn't have on anything tactical. He's wearing a black dress shirt, untucked, and slacks. His dirty blond hair is mussed like he's been running his fingers through it, he's got on glasses and he's wearing a headset with a microphone...

Shit! Shit! Shit! The man upstairs has a team!

I sprint at the newcomer, gun held as level as I can manage until the last second, when I dive right into his torso, taking him down. My knees crack against the tiled entryway with an unholy sound that shoots straight up my spine and manifests as pain. So much blinding pain.

"There's a woman—" the man beneath me says before I force myself out of the haze of total-body agony to shove his motherfucking headset off and cock my gun against the side of his head. I force my body to move enough to trap his arms at his sides, underneath the press of my thighs so that he can't move his hands without me knowing.

"No talking," I growl as I wait for a second wave of racking aches to pass.

Finally, I'm able to focus on his face.

"Shit. You're kinda hot," I blurt out the obvious, but it is kind of a disappointment that I'm going to have to blow this guy's perfect stubbled jaw to bits. He's got the elfin sort of nose everyone wishes they had, expressive eyebrows that are currently raised in alarm, eyes that are a pale sky blue … and that five-o'clock shadow …

I'm seriously tempted to drag my fingers over it—and there they go, moving before I even consciously told them to. His manic pulse is thundering under his skin as I lean forward and scrape my hand up his neck and across the hint of a beard on his cheek. Mmm. I love a man with a little facial hair.

His blue eyes blink at me from behind thick, black-framed, Clark Kent glasses, nonplussed. Startled into submission maybe. "Super hot," I murmur again, because he at least deserves to know before he dies.

"So are you, sweetheart," says a low voice from behind me as I hear the tell-tale cock of a gun before a muzzle presses against my skull. "Tell me, what's your name?"

My stomach tumbles over.

Dammit. I forgot my six. This is why I fucking work from afar.

Agitated dismay rumbles through me as I wonder, *Is this the man from upstairs or another guy? How outnumbered am I?*

Sarcasm beats fear in the rush to control my mouth as I answer him.

"Dixie Normas is my stripper name," I retort.

The huge man behind me lets out a low, rumbling chuckle —the sort of laugh any villain would admire and any girl would fall head-over-heels for. Seriously, his laugh is as smooth as scotch poured over the rocks. Ice-meltingly good.

"You here to strip for us?" he asks, though the gun still pointed to my head tells me he doesn't think so.

"You wish." Not my best comeback, but I'm essentially clenching every muscle in my body right now—the contraction creating a sort of dam that's holding back rising panic threatening to flood my system. I'm just trying to keep him talking long enough to find an opening...

The man leans closer until I can feel his body heat radiating over me, until his lips are right near the shell of my ear and his words float warmly across my skin, making my hair rustle as he murmurs, "Oh, I definitely wish. That outfit makes your ass look amazing."

This is it. Go! I scream at my muscles.

I make use of the hand that was patting the handsome man, palming his cheek and shoving his face sideways to the ground, bracing my weight against him so that I can lever a mule kick backward, hoping like fuck all my combat training sessions with Man paid off.

A horrified guinea pig-like squeal erupts from the man behind me, and he stumbles backward and sideways, feet thudding unevenly.

Relief and a shot of pride are injected through my system in a short, sharp burst.

I did not panic.

I did not panic, and I did not die.

"Jewel shot." Thank you, Man, for drilling that one into my skull.

I release the face of the blond man beneath me and grin down at him as his face rises up to stare at me once again. His cheek has pink lines from the intense press of my hand, his glasses are slightly off-kilter, and his eyelashes flutter for a second, as if he can't believe what's happening.

"Your friend must not have the micropenis I thought he did if he's hurting that bad," I say as I reach down and straighten his glasses for him.

I swear, we share a moment. Just a split-second where his mouth quirks into the very beginning of a grin before he realizes what he's doing and shutters his expression.

Still straddling handsome, I hold up a finger and say, "Stay right there, honey," before I swivel to admire the effects of my kick and train my gun on the armed man instead of the seemingly complacent backup dude beneath me.

I'm not nearly as bad at this badass shit as I thought I'd be. At least my mouth and feet are cooperating nicely. Though my stomach ... it's still trembling like a leaf. But screw stomachs, who needs them?

I spot the other man dressed in black, this time with clothing more akin to my own black jumpsuit. He's still hunched over clutching his junk, gun held loosely in his right hand. Unlike the guy on the floor, this one is brawny and burly in all the right places. He would be handsome too, except there's a goose egg growing on his forehead and his shoulder is bleeding.

Good, so there are only two goons.

I can totally handle two guys at once.

Been there, done that. In the bedroom, but still.

I give myself a moment to take a deep, calming breath and come to a decision.

None of us are going to die tonight. Partially because the hottie on the floor wanted to chuckle at my joke and partially because none of us deserve it. I kill bad guys, not the guys who want to kill bad guys—I decide, making up that new moral code right on the spot because it seems like the right thing to do.

"You're leaking," I point out to the man I kicked in an unhelpfully cheerful tone usually reserved to annoy my sisters.

"You the one who shot him?" handsome asks.

"Of course," I respond as I slowly climb off him, leaving my duffel on the floor.

Handsome's smart enough to stay perfectly still—not tempting fate, or me at all. He's definitely more the behind-the-scenes type.

When I offer him a hand up, he looks startled.

Jewel- clutcher tries to raise his weapon and train it on me but I *tsk*. "Don't bother. I'm not going to kill you and you're not going to kill me."

Handsome with the glasses takes my offered hand and carefully stands.

"Why the fuck is that?" The burly man's eyes meet mine and I'm intrigued by the fact that they're an unusually gorgeous shade of green. Like spring leaves hit by morning light. There's a golden undertone to them that makes them almost cat-like. They're utterly entrancing.

I find myself having to clear away a lump in my throat before I answer. "Because this house is filled with all of our DNA right now and we need to wipe it off the map before Yegor's minions come searching for clues," I contend, offering logic instead of my new moral code as a reason.

The big one glares at me, but Clark Kent plays the hero and raises his hand to stop the other guy from doing something testosterone-y and stupid. "She's right. T thought we had ten minutes at best."

I tilt my head as I stare between the two of them and realize they aren't just partners. "T...who *the fuck* is T? There's another one of you guys? Shit ... they need to redo the light-bulb joke. How many male assassins does it take to screw up a killing?"

Both men stare silently at me until the big one finally growls, "We didn't screw this up, sugar. You did."

I cluck my tongue. "Technically ... you're correct. I stopped you. But you screwed up my assassination before I screwed up yours."

"You're an assassin, are you? That's cute." His eyes trail suggestively over my body in a way that's both electrifying and—at the exact same time—utterly dismissive.

My neck heats and I'm sorely tempted to shoot him again, this time in the dick.

Luckily, handsome senses the tension threading through the air and puts his hands out in a placating gesture as his headset sparks to life on the floor with a garbled male voice. "We don't have time for this shit. We need to get the hell out of here."

I swivel to face the reasonable one instead of the one with a gun.

That's a mistake.

Bam.

My back explodes with bright red, screaming pain. I suck in a breath and tense myself as the agony ripples through my muscles, making them feel like banners in the wind. "Sono-fabitch!" I yell just before I fall to my knees for a second time tonight.

My vision flickers with tiny silver stars.

"Sorry, pretty girl. But there's a bounty on the line. And we plan to collect." The big man casually walks around me, whistling a jaunty little tune, as though shooting me has absolutely zero effect on him. Bastard.

Meanwhile, I'm trying to convince my lungs they still need to breathe, that air is still a priority.

I hear him snap his fingers twice at handsome. "Come on, Avery. We need to fucking move."

"But ... "

Something scrapes against the floor, but I don't see it, because my eyes are closing, braced against the pain—it feels like I've been hit with a hammer.

Footsteps retreat in the direction of the front door—two sets, one heavy and steady, the other light and shuffling, almost as if Avery turns back to look at me once.

A minute or so after they're gone, the pain retreats enough for me to gasp, "Fuckers." Opening my eyes, I force myself upright, even though my entire spine still feels like tenderized meat.

"Damn body armor, ain't worth jack shit," I grumble, even though I know it just saved my life.

I stumble toward my duffel and the motion to undo the zipper nearly makes me keel over because it flexes my back muscles and reignites the fire blazing within them. Burrowing inside the bag, I shuffle through the contents until I unearth a lovely little block of C-4 that Darcy gave me. From apps to bombs, that Belladonna really is the best sister ever.

I need to send her a fruit basket, I decide as I set the explosive on the ground next to me.

Leaning forward again, I dig for the detonator, which looks like a pink makeup compact until I open it. With a tiny snick, the two sides part like a clamshell. The bottom half holds the coiled wires to connect the device to the bomb which uncurl like ribbons when I tug at them. A countdown clock is visible where the mirror would be.

I shove the wires into the C-4, hit the clock to start it, and then grab my bag with a pained grunt. I shove my gun inside before ripping out my earpiece and tossing it on top. Gathering it and myself together, I sprint away.

Three minutes seemed like an eternity when I talked with Darcy about getaway time. Now? It feels like nothing because every single step makes me want to fall to the ground and moan. A thousand knives are being driven into my skin with every damn step.

Adrenaline and stubborn fury are the only things keeping me moving.

Stumbling down the block, I've just rounded a corner when the sky lights up atomic orange, and a sound so potent that it rattles the windows billows out into the night.

I give a little grin as I whisper, "Boom goes the dynamite."

Cleanup done, it's time to pop some damn aspirin.

Then I'm going to find my cowering mark and prove to those fuck- ups that they don't stand a chance at killing him.

Yegor's mine.

3

JUMPING THE GUN

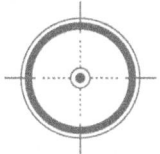

May 20
8:45 a.m.
Marseille, France

Tyler

Turquoise water glimmers underneath boats that sail along the Gulf of Lion. Buildings stack up along the hills, encircling them, and the age of this town is apparent by the eclectic collection of edifices from not only different eras but different centuries. Marseille boasts rubble left from the Romans next to medieval churches, which are bordered by modern shops. I turn slightly in my outdoor cafe seat, away from the colorful collection of buildings, and gaze out across the water at the French equivalent of Alcatraz, the prison where the famous Count of Monte Cristo slept.

The Chateau D'If boasts two round stone towers and an even taller square one, all squatting on an island just big enough to fit the building and a few walls. It glows a warm brown in the morning light and hardly looks capable of containing evil.

I take a drag from my cigarette as I contemplate whether or not I could have escaped from it and made the swim to shore. Once upon a time, when I still wore a uniform, it wouldn't have been a question.

Now?

My eyes drift to my cane, where it rests propped up against the cafe table next to my coffee and untouched croissant.

I'd find a way, I determine before my gaze roams out across the patio again. This time, I don't look at the sailboats or the prison. I focus closer—on the crowd.

Acting like the little bitch he is, Yegor Babanin went straight into hiding after the debacle at his house. He's gone underground.

Luckily, tapping the right phones and greasing the right palms is one of my specialties .

I knew he'd call one of several extraction teams to get him out of the U.S. "safely." Now, I just have to sit here and drink my coffee and wait for him to be delivered like a package at Christmas.

Idiot.

Trusting others with his safety?

A muted sort of disdain rumbles through me, though his actions are not unexpected. That's what these rich fucks do —they get a bit of green and suddenly are too good to do things for themselves, which makes them dependent on others to do it for them. Men like me.

Operators.

If I were Babanin right now, I'd be alone, using the stockpile of personas and cash I have stashed around the globe to hightail it and create a new life. I'd humble myself and become a stock boy at a hardware store—something no one would suspect. These fuckers fall because they become addicted to the prestige, the idea of their own self-importance. They can't give it up. Not to mention their inability to divest themselves of human connections.

They're unwilling to sever ties, even if it's for the good of the other person. Connections have a chokehold on them and blind them to common sense and arrogance won't allow them to admit that they've gone from being assets to liabilities. If it were me ... no one, not even the one family member I have left, would know where I'd gone.

I release a perfect circle of white smoke and revel in the burning sensation inside my lungs as a woman walking a dog passes me. As the minutes go on and American tourists lumber around taking photos and talking too loudly, my thoughts drift back to the woman who put a wrench in our plans.

Her long shapely legs materialize inside my mind.

The hot bitch—Colt called her, the hothead. My stepbrother was a little more restrained in his evaluation: Avery called her our competition.

Competition.

I smirk at the very thought. I'm the best at what we do—or I was when I worked alone. I'm still debating whether bringing a team in was a good idea. The jury is out, given the massive fuck- up the guys made the other night. It's their first job like this, so I can understand their cavalier attitude to a degree. Hell, my first kill was a shoddy mess that took four bullets.

But ... in our line of work, you don't usually get to make mistakes even once. I've drilled that into both their sorry heads so many times over the past few days that I might even have left screw holes from where I bored it into their brains.

Today will either be their redemption—or the parting of ways. I brought them on to help them out but if they aren't helping me ... then this partnership is going to fizzle out before it even gets going.

Can they handle her?

I'm not sure.

I've been looking into this woman.

I pulled her picture from a camera embedded in Colt's gear the other night, glad that I made him wear a bodycam.

She shouldn't have been hard to find but she's practically a ghost. What beautiful woman doesn't have social media these days?

I wonder about her as I stub my cigarette out in the ashtray in the middle of my wrought-iron table and move on to my still-steaming cup of coffee, ready to wash the dark, burnt flavor from my mouth. I love the steady but stable high coursing through my system after some nicotine, the way

I'm able to focus better, but the aftertaste is a definite drawback. I take a sip of coffee that's so warm it nearly singes my tongue as I think about Dixie ... which is the only name I've got for our mystery woman.

There is no ID out there for her. No driver's license, birth certificate—nada. No news articles, not even the self-aggrandizing 4-H or high school track trophy fluff, nothing even when I scraped archived websites that are no longer live. No schools in the area with pretty little redheads looking like her in their yearbooks for the past ten years.

All I've managed to snag are a few random traffic camera shots of her in Babanin's neighborhood the week before his death. The fuzzy photos showed her going up and down his front steps a few times, though his doorbell cam had clearly been wiped.

Dixie's not a novice—I'll give her that.

It makes her more intriguing, though her face alone has the power to fascinate. She has the face of a pinup girl. Perfect proportions, brows with the sort of arch that makes her look slightly naughty no matter what expression her face holds. From the body cam photo I'd printed out after the guys had returned home (and after I'd stitched a complaining Colt back together), I'd realized she had soft cheeks that show just a hint of cheekbone—not the gaunt skeletal things women seem to want these days. And her lips ... Actually, perhaps it was her smirk more than the shape of her lips ... I enlarged and printed the moment after she'd bruised Colt's balls and her superior, gloating grin keeps floating through my head.

Intriguing.

I wonder who she works for and why she was chosen for this job. She accused us of messing up her setup—I'm guessing she was planning to snipe Babanin from across the road, since that's where she shot Colt from.

We swept that apartment across the street from Babanin's place a few hours later that evening, once the fire trucks and emergency vehicles had cleared out after the explosion of his house. Things had been disturbed, but there were no prints, nothing left behind. Very professional.

A pleasurable tingle runs down my spine because the fact that she's competent is as alluring as the fact that I haven't found her yet is frustrating. The two emotions teeter within me, struggling for balance as the all-important question arises once again: Where is she now?

My eyes drift back over the crowd. Babanin's going to be here this afternoon. His little extraction team has orders to drop him here into the care of a "trustworthy" group of bodyguards—Colt and Avery. Colt has complained about the blond hair dye and prosthetic nose he's wearing more times than all the men I served with combined complained about the chow, but he was the idiot who went in without a mask last time—impulsive fucker.

If all goes well, this afternoon will be cake.

All the boys have to do is get Babanin away from the delivery team and take him out.

We'll be done with this and a sweet half a mil richer by morning. I set my coffee down and rip off the end of my croissant.

The only possible hiccup is Dixie.

The little vixen is clearly resourceful. I assume that if I know Babanin is here, so does she.

That's why my eyes keep scanning the crowd as I eat. I've got facial recognition software set to ping me if she shows up on any street cam, but I'm out here myself also doing it the old-fashioned way because two methods are one, and one is none.

One hour later, lo and behold ... what do you know?

There she is—the guys' mystery girl, stepping out from behind a beam of sunlight like an angel.

Though she's dyed her hair brown instead of the flaming red it was three nights ago, I instantly know it's her. I've been staring at her picture long enough that every feature is burned into my brain as firmly as a brand. Dixie—she practically floats up the street with this bouncy, innocent little walk, heels clicking away. Sunglasses shield her eyes but those brows and lips are unmistakably breathtaking.

She's wearing an olive green dress with flowers scattered around it. The neckline plunges into her cleavage in an appealing way, and she swings a wicker bag at her side almost playfully.

Fuck, she *is* hot.

Colt and Ave were beyond right; she's got natural curves that photos don't do justice to, but even more than that, in person, she emits this ... aura. As she walks down the street, stopping every so often to peer into shop windows, there's a joy that just radiates from her. It's like a spring breeze, gentle and playful and light—the kind of thing you want to bask in.

Damn.

Men in the crowd turn to admire her and my vision tunnels, heart rate increasing when one of them touches her. Asks her something. I have the instantaneous desire to grab my fork and stride over there to shove it up his nose, swirling until I can extract his brains like strands of pink spaghetti.

The cold realization washes over me that she's far more dangerous than I believed because shit like that is the sort of thing that distracts a man.

I shove down the swirling vat of possessive anger in my belly and put a lid on it. I let my normal bitterness regain the reins because I know what happens to men who let pretty women like that get under their skin.

Not me. I refuse to be that fool.

For all I know, that man is one of her contacts. I could have just witnessed some kind of handoff. My focus reemerges as she continues down the street, shafts of sunlight catching on the waves of her hair as the sun peeks over the tops of the buildings.

I need to take care of her before Babanin arrives.

I touch the gun tucked neatly into my shoulder holster and the handcuffs hidden beneath my suit jacket. Anticipation drums inside my veins and the heady thrill of the chase amps me up, activating the dark, predatory hunter side of my brain. This is the part of the job I love.

I quickly toss some bills on the table and grab my cane, scooping it up and leaning on it more heavily than I actually need to as I limp after her. People scatter around me, making way for the crippled man, until I'm close enough that I no longer need to pretend quite so hard.

I study the back of her head, wondering what she's thinking about, what her plan for Babanin is, what her plan for after is—knowing I'm going to wreck them all.

The ache that constantly throbs in my right leg is nearly forgotten as I trek down the road—hot in pursuit, while she remains utterly naive.

I don't look at the waterfall of shining hair as it cascades down her back and points the eye directly toward her heart-shaped ass.

No.

Not more than a peek.

I don't draw out the chase a little longer than I need to, savoring it and her.

The fact that she meanders for over an hour ... Fine. I'm as addicted to this predator-prey game as I am to the cigarettes I love. Both of them send my heart into a round of applause, create a standing ovation roaring beneath my skin and I savor it, keeping several paces behind her, riding that high.

I allow an annoying family with a toddler and a stroller to glide between us as Dixie appears to window shop. She buys candy from a street vendor, sucking on a lolly pop in a way that makes a dozen illicit thoughts cross my mind. I'm tempted to use my cane to trip a fucker who passes her and turns, eyes on her ass, clearly admiring the view. I don't, because I'll draw attention to myself, but the grip on my walking stick becomes so tight that my fingers ache.

She moves on, none-the-wiser, and gasps over some shoes. I can hear the tune she's humming as she winds through the crowd, acting like she hasn't a care in the world.

For a second, I question myself.

Is she the right girl?

But when she lifts her sunglasses in order to try on a pair from another street vendor hawking fake brand names, I'm certain. Those hazel eyes belong to Dixie. I look down at my cane and pretend to struggle with an uneven bit of sidewalk when those eyes glance my way.

She'll see the prematurely gray streaks in my hair and my cane and do what everyone else does. Overlook me. Not that she knows what she's looking for because I wasn't on-site, I was backend on the op the other night ... but if she's anything like me, she'll have instincts. Instincts that tell her when someone's watching. When to run.

I *hope* she has those instincts, because there's nothing better than the thrill of a chase when you know your target is terrified and you walk them right into a corner.

I lick my lips, fully aware that I've slowly morphed over the years from a man to a monster. Losing that first bit of humanity—it's painful, horrifying. But each subsequent strip that's peeled away stings a little less, until finally, dark acts become compelling, compulsive, and you start to crave that tiny little ache.

I don't just want to kill this beautiful girl ... I want to break her first.

Looking up, I see she's moved on, leaving the fake sunglasses and a disappointed vendor behind. I follow her svelte form down the curving road, over the uneven sidewalk that is in absolute shambles. The shops get smaller and older, the streets narrower and a bit more crowded. A worker carrying a giant box walks in between us and—damn, I've lost her.

I speed up, heart pounding, as I stop and spin in place—eyes flying in every direction—wondering if I've been made.

Was the moment with the sunglasses my downfall? Should I have grabbed her sooner? Dragged her into a back alley? I swivel my head, heart thick in my throat.

But then I hear a laugh drifting out a shop window ... and somehow, instinctively, I just know it's her. I've never heard her voice before, but the sound itself makes the very air seem to sparkle. It has her aura written all over it.

I hold my breath as I turn to see a florist's shop, buckets of bouquets lining the steps with bursts of color, potted plants spilling out the confines of their terra cotta containers, set on shelves in the display window. It's an explosion of leaves and flowers and the scent in the air is as strong as perfume.

Dixie's back is to me, though she's clearly visible through the arched doorway, and she's caressing the leaves of one of the plants.

This is my chance.

A bright burning need, the closest thing I ever feel to happiness anymore, starts to course through me.

I glance to my right and notice the shopkeeper is rounding the corner with a giant orange watering can in hand, as if he's been around back watering extra plants. He's a balding man with a hawkish nose and a green apron.

With deft precision, I walk toward him. Pretending to trip, I grab his shoulder and stumble forward until I've pressed him against the wall in the small alleyway that separates his shop from the next. There is a row of shade plants out here, lining his side of the alley, and a trickle of water darkens the stones beneath the freshly watered plants.

The shopkeeper utters a startled gasp before I cover his mouth with my hand. Using the other, I yank off the head of my cane. A long needle protrudes from the end of it and I stab a tranquilizer into the man's thigh. He flails for only a few seconds before his bulging eyelids begin to droop and he sags limply against me. "That's it. Go to sleep, buddy."

Wrapping his arm around my shoulder, I drag him further into the alley, my bad leg grateful he's just a slip of a man because his weight causes my tendons to tighten uncomfortably as it is.

I curse under my breath about my idiotic leg slowing me down because Dixie could have just stopped at that place on a whim. She could walk out at any moment if I'm not quick enough—and then this opportunity will be gone.

My eyes dilate and my pulse thuds, senses heightened as I push myself to go faster.

Once we're out of sight of the street and I confirm no one can see us, I strip off the shopkeeper's green apron and prop him up against the wall behind his shade plants, letting his head loll so that someone walking by would think he's drunk.

Then I peel my suit jacket off, tossing it and my cane onto the fire escape landing nearby so that I can retrieve them later. Donning the apron and undoing some of the buttons at my collar, I take out my cufflinks and shove them into my pocket before I roll up the sleeves of my white shirt. I doubt I'll pass for the shopkeeper for too long, but I don't need very long.

I joke with the guys that I'm a two-minute man.

Two minutes to kill.

Lifting my watch to my mouth, I softly say, "Found my phone." That's the code phrase we've devised for her. I hit a green button to send the message as a text to Avery.

As I make my way back to the mouth of the alley to retrieve the orange watering can the shopkeeper dropped, a text buzzes the screen on my wrist and a bubble appears with the words: *Good. Got it in your pocket?*

"Grabbing it now," I reply before I mount the steps.

My knee screams at me, but I tell it to shut the fuck up and paste a fake, welcoming smile on my face. It stretches oddly across my cheeks because it's an expression I rarely make, but also because I've got prosthetics covering my scars. They stretch uncomfortably and make my skin hot beneath them, but I suck it up because I'm not a pussy like Colt.

She's still inside.

Still there among the plants, her figure outlined by a harsh fluorescent bulb that can't wash out the glowing beauty of her silky skin even though it tries.

A tingle starts in my toes and runs up my spine until it reaches my lungs. I release the breath I held unknowingly, the exhalation both a relief and the soft sound of my excitement.

I take a step closer. Turn to water the nearest plant as I give her a soft, "Bonjour."

Dixie's hand drops from the plant as she spins slowly around to look at me, shoving up her sunglasses to perch on her hair. She smiles brightly—making me pause because it's been a hell of a long time since someone's looked at me with such pure joy. Of course, it's not me, she's smiling at. It's the shopkeeper. "This place is just beautiful."

I reply in broken English, because it seems like more fun to keep up the ruse for a few seconds. "You are far more."

She waves a hand bashfully, dismissing the compliment in order to turn back to a delicate bloom nearby. "Please. I'm seriously impressed. I mean—looky at these adorable belladonnas! I love them!" She lovingly caresses the leaves of the little purple-flowered plant beside her and starts cooing at it the way someone else might baby-talk their puppy. "He takes good care of you, doesn't he?"

If this is a ploy, she's very good at it. That smile is as warm as a sunny afternoon—I could feel it on my arms, sinking into my skin. The innocence dripping off of her almost seems genuine. It's beguiling and disarming in a way that makes me feel slightly off-balance. If this girl was a counterfeit dollar, she'd be nearly undetectable.

Nearly.

But I saw what she did the other night. I know she's more than she pretends. She uses this playful innocence the way I use my cane—to get her way.

Fuck, I can practically smell the trickery on her and it's goddamned seductive.

I step closer to her and my pulse pounds in restless anticipation. My fingers ache to touch her. To wrap around her delicate throat. I work to keep my voice from getting husky as I say, "You love la fleur?" I set my watering can down on the shelf beside me so that my hands are free to grab my weapons.

She nods, turning parallel to me so she can pet a hanging fern. "I do." When she glances up at me from underneath her lashes, I notice her eyes are a soft hazel color, warm and green like the plants around her.

I wonder for a moment why she's so good at pretending. Who can fawn over plants like they're children? Is that part of the ploy or a real part of herself that she uses for the ploy? Fascinated intrigue consumes me.

Why would a girl like her go after a bastard like Babanin?

My heart stops beating for a second when I realize ... he probably sold her and her family.

Why else would she have no records?

Why else would she stop my guys from killing him and then storm into his place full of fury?

Yes. It makes sense. She wants revenge.

My stomach tightens with regret for a moment, knowing she's not going to get it.

But now that I've figured her out, I need to know who she's working with. If she's the one sent to do the killing, she's most likely a pawn in a bigger player's game.

A greedy sort of anticipation churns in my lower belly; I'm hungry for details, all the details about her life that I couldn't dig up online. And she's going to give them to me. I'm going to swallow every delicious word that spills from her mouth.

I realize I'm staring at her lips and turn my head shyly, as if I'm the kind of man who's embarrassed to be caught staring instead of the kind of man who's planning to caress those lips with the tip of his gun.

I hold up a hand, gesturing down the row of plants, toward an arched hallway at the rear of the shop. "I keep ... favorite? Is the word, oui? In back."

"Ooh! More in back!" She claps her hands and spins, her skirt flaring out around her calves as she hurries through the narrow hall, not even bothering to look behind her. Unafraid of me. No weapon strapped to her ankles, which I saw during her spin.

Where is her weapon then? There's no space in that dress. Surely, she's not wandering through this city without one.

The plot thickens ...

So does my cock.

I try to keep my expression neutral as I pull the front door shut, turn the "open" sign in the window to "closed," and then follow after my little Dixie chick.

I make my way to the backroom, loosening my apron and pulling my gun from the holster hidden in my pants. I use the pocket on the front of the apron to conceal my weapon while keeping my hand on it—at the ready. My thumb flicks the safety off.

Muscles tuned and tight, my balls tingling, I round the corner into the back of the shop, which is really a long narrow space with an arched ceiling, a wooden table and bench, and a mint-green fridge that looks like a relic from the 1960s. On the table are rows of tiny potted sprouts and a few plants with brown leaves that look like they've seen better days.

Where the fuck is Dixie?

My muscles are coiled, ready to duck back behind the wall —expecting her to be standing with feet planted, arms outstretched, gun pointed right at me.

Instead, I find her purse set down on the table next to her as she grabs a bird of paradise with semi-withered leaves. She whispers to it. "You poor baby. It's going to be okay."

I step closer, away from the protection of the hall, pulse thudding loudly in my ears. I breathe in slowly as I study our surroundings, ensuring there's no weapon within her reach. Can't have her making a fuss, after all.

"Look at this little sweetheart," she murmurs gently, still fingering the plant.

"You want? I am making better. You give me your name. Number. I call you—" I doubt the ploy will work, but I have to try. I need her name the way I need my next cigarette. I crave it. I slide in closer behind her, close enough to feel her skirt brush the front of my pant legs. Close enough to see her pulse in her neck, the soft lines of her soot-black lashes ...

"My name's Royal. And my number's seventy-one. What's yours?" Her soft tone hardens, as does her look when she glances over her shoulder up at me.

A half-second. That's what it takes me to process the fact that I've been made. That she's telling me the truth. A new name. One that actually fits her gorgeous face far better than Dixie. Royal. And that number? That startlingly high number. There's no way it's her number of kills—she's at least a decade fucking younger than me. Early twenties at best.

Red clouds my vision and a sort of battle rage washes through me at what she *might* be saying.

"That better not be the number of men you've fucked," I growl, pressing up against her, letting my weapon and my cock push against the taut curve of her ass. A foreign and utterly absurd sense of possessiveness ripples through me.

"What do you think it is?" she asks, pushing aside one of the broad, yellow leaves of the plant she's been caressing. In the dirt beside the stem is a metallic black circle—a grenade. Her fingers delicately caress and clench down on the pin.

The tightness behind my temples slowly unwinds.

Seventy-one marks.

Seventy-one murders.

That sort of fact shouldn't make a man's dick throb, but I've already admitted I'm more demon than man these days. My dick gives a thump of approval against her heart-shaped ass, a fucking high-five. A rumbling sense of satisfaction fills my chest even as my spine heats up with bone-melting lust as I bend forward, her sweet-smelling hair brushing against my cheek.

"You planning on blowing yourself up, sweetheart?" I whisper into her ear, tempted to bite it. God, she's threatening me—but it's the hottest thing I've ever experienced. I've never had a woman threaten to end me. Definitely not one with the ability to pull it off.

"I was planning on blowing you first."

Shit, she has a smart mouth on her. My free hand latches onto her hip so that my fingers can dig in. "Mmm. Don't tease me."

She turns in my arms to face me, her body brushing deliberately against mine, the grenade gripped in her hand. Blinking up at me with those sinful eyes, arching those suggestive brows, she says, "I'm not joking, Tyler."

I don't know if I'm more stunned by her indecent proposal or the fact that she knows my name.

4

PACKING HEAT

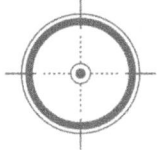

May 20
10:45 a.m.
Marseille, France

Royal

T was just trying to fluster him—but oopsie-daisy—I think I went too far. I'm still learning how to gauge these in-person assassin-to-assassin interactions since normally, I work from a distance.

Note to self: offering to blow a guy probably oversteps the unofficial rival boundaries.

How unprofessional of me, though I can't seem to muster up the energy to care, because this man is fucking hot. Sinfully, deliciously, lickably …

Maybe I should stand by my statement.

Tyler's eyes flare furiously and his free hand digs into my ass as his lips descend on mine.

Okay. I feel better. He's overstepping too.

He kisses me roughly, his lips demanding and devouring, the slight stubble on his jaw scratching deliciously against my skin. He skips all the usual first kiss etiquette, jumping over the hesitation, the soft brush of lips, forgetting the tiny dart of tongue that tests the waters—he dives right into French kiss territory. Ownership. His kiss commands a response.

To my surprise, my body gives him an enthusiastic one. My heart is as perky and bouncy as a cheerleader, even though my hand still has a death grip on my weapon in case this is a ploy. Even if it is, I know exactly why my lungs are breathless and my stomach is flip-flopping. He is a stunningly handsome killer after all.

The gray streaks give me a total daddy vibe, and the suit he wore when he tracked me was—as the French say—ooh la la. Even the whole cane bit gave him a mood, though my research, which started with Tyler's stepbrother Avery—and my subsequent stalking of their whole little group—let me know he's the polar opposite of the posh British look he's got going today. He's just about as red-blooded American as they get.

A Kansas boy, raised on a farm. Soldier with big dreams. War hero. Until he was injured ... my hand not clutching the grenade sneaks up to the side of his face. I grasp it until I can feel the edge of the prosthetic next to his ear.

Using my nails and pulling back from the kiss, I slowly peel the patch up, letting him know that I know about it. His history. How he was captured and held for nine grueling, terrifying days, and how he helped his squad escape, though he insisted they all go first. He was the last man out, which is why the other fuckers nearly sliced his face off.

I trace over the edge of the scar that reveals who Tyler really is inside.

He's a killer. But he's also a hero.

That's one of those things Man has drilled into us repeatedly.

Most heroes aren't comic-book squeaky clean. They have blood on their hands and nightmares behind their eyes. They do what they do because they know other people out there don't have the stomach for it ... but it needs to be done.

Real heroes sacrifice everything from their humanity to their sanity.

Tyler Monroe is one of those men.

He freezes, and I'm not sure if it's because of my touch or because I'm showing my hand, telling him just how much I've dug into him. Dig him.

The dashing veteran with a war medal turned private soldier turned assassin for hire. He's the type of man they should make movies about.

In silence, I resume pulling away the rest of the silicone, and it lifts to reveal a long, jagged scar that mars his right cheek —and it's not a cute little lightning bolt either. It cuts all the way from his ear to his nose and screams dangerous, that this man's been near death and survived.

It gives me pussy flutters. I stare up at him, chest still heaving from the intensity of our kiss, a kiss that's rattled my very foundations.

His dark eyes are unreadable as he awaits my verdict while my eyes scan his face. I toss aside the prosthetic as I lean up on tiptoe. "Don't cover up. Chicks dig scars, honey," I say, before letting my tongue sweep over his scar, tasting his flesh.

"Fuck." He curses and his free hand leaves my ass to grip my jaw, pulling me back into a kiss, one that seems to want to punish me. His lips are angry as they press hard against mine and he steals my breath, swallowing it down as if he wishes he could drink my words to satisfy some aching, thirsty part of himself.

I feel light-headed, and my stomach is all out of sorts like he's just tossed me into the air and I've done a backflip.

I giggle at the mental image and then bite at his lip because I shouldn't be the only one feeling this intensely. If my toes are tingling like I'm balancing on a spindly limb, about to tumble into some dark abyss, I'm sure as hell going to do my best to take him with me. I let my fingers rake over his chest, scrape at his tricep with my free hand.

Pulling back from his mouth to tease him more. I've got this bubbling sort of euphoria inside that I've never had before. It makes me feel giddy and foolish and free. "Is that a gun in your pocket or are you just happy to see me?" Totally an overused line, but one I've always wanted to say.

Life goal: unlocked.

"Both," he answers, before swooping down for another kiss and pressing his dick and the weapon harder against me. He's careful to keep the gun trained on my thigh, right near my artery, even as his pelvis grinds against mine.

Each of us is still very aware of the fact that we should be killing each other right now. Or at the very least—maiming. But ... this impromptu standoff is too fun to resist.

"We are being so impulsive," I murmur between kisses. "I'm never impulsive." It's true. Outside the Belladonna house, I usually don't let myself go. My OCD usually flares up and takes over but something is short-circuiting my normal controlling tendencies right now.

It could be the gun trained on me that's making my pulse skyrocket ... but I suspect it's Tyler. He just exudes this dominant, dangerous vibe that makes my thoughts melt away into nothing.

I embrace the chaos—this strange, messy clash of emotions that splatter across me until inside I'm an abstract mess of feelings.

"Me neither," he retorts, sliding his hand down from my jaw to squeeze my neck lightly before his fingers tease my collarbone and push aside the strap of my dress. It slips down my shoulder and even though no more skin is really revealed by the movement, the glide of the strap makes goose bumps appear along my arm and I feel deliciously naughty.

We're making out in someone's store, mutually assured destruction in each of our hands.

Why have I never fucked an assassin before?

Big mistake.

Big.

One my body is telling me I need to rectify.

Tyler's lips travel from my mouth to my neck and I lean back against the table, tilting my chin upward and just allowing myself to feel.

His hand cups my breast, discovering I went braless this morning. The palm grazing over my stiff nipple causes a zing of pleasure to spread down my abdomen and heat my lower belly.

Mmm.

The ceiling becomes slightly unfocused as his tongue does things to my neck that seem very promising. My entire body is abuzz with anticipation, and I feel a tingle down south that normally takes ages and a shit-ton of work for me to achieve on my own.

Damn. I think I might like this guy a little bit.

But when I blink and my gaze falls to the hallway we walked through, I spy a shadowy figure at the front door struggling with the knob. Flanking him on either side are uniformed French police officers.

"Fuck," I moan. Of course, the idiotic police would show up when I'm about to get the first spontaneous orgasm I've ever had.

Tyler chuckles against my throat, completely unaware that the mood has been ruined.

"Cops," I murmur, pulling back.

"Is that your safe word?" he asks in between kisses down my chest. He's nearly to my nipple and I want nothing more than to let him latch on and give me even more of this mindless pleasure, but I dig my hands into his hair and yank on it instead.

"That would be a shitty safe word," I comment, though I've never actually had one. All of my prior sexual experiences have been rather vanilla. Maybe that's why this feels so intense. I've never ridden the high of danger and pleasure at the exact same time.

I've been missing out.

A throb of longing pulses between my thighs but I attempt to ignore it as I turn his head toward the door until he spots the cops and swears under his breath.

"Guess I'll have to take a rain check on this near-death fuckery," I tell him with a regretful grin.

He snickers. "You think I'll be this stupid twice?"

I give him a single-shoulder shrug. "I know I will be. That was the best kiss I've ever had."

A smirk crosses Tyler's lips even as his eyes narrow in suspicion, but he can believe me or not. That's a him problem, not a me problem.

I move my free hand from his hair down to his chest and push lightly. He steps back but lifts his gun.

I roll my eyes as I straighten up and pull the spaghetti strap of my dress back onto my shoulder. "Please. I wasn't ever planning to kill you, even though, I have to say, your boy Colt pissed me off. You should talk to him about shooting people in the back. I have a massive bruise from his bullshit."

When I reach for my purse, he clears his throat. "Uh-uh."

I sigh. "Fine. You want to grab it and I'll grab your prosthetic? Where's your cane, by the way?"

He's still and silent as I move, carefully scooping up the flap of fake skin where it landed on the table and handing it to him so he doesn't leave evidence behind. Of course, I'm not super worried. The worst we did here was lock a guy out of his store so we could make out—it's not like there's murder evidence all around us the way there was with the rest of Tyler's team at Yegor's house.

Tyler tucks the evidence into his pocket and gestures for me to move to the side so he can grab my wicker purse. He glances into it but doesn't immediately see a weapon, so just ends up clutching it.

"Aww, don't you look domesticated." Why is it so fun to tease a dark and broody man? Maybe it's the thrill of their fury.

Right now, Tyler Monroe looks like he's ready to spank me. I've never been spanked, but a little birdie in my ear is saying I'd like it.

"Are you the spanking type?" I ask casually, as I glance around the room for potential exits. I spot another door that looks like it leads outside but is sure to have cops flanking it.

"Shut up or you'll find out," he growls.

Yup. Definitely a spanker.

Damn. Now I think I might doubly regret the fact that we're about to have to book it in separate directions.

I lean to one side and spot a set of stairs behind the old-fashioned fridge. I use my grenade hand to gesture in that direction. "I vote we go up. But can your leg handle that?"

"I can handle anything. What the fuck do you know about my leg?" He growls as he herds me toward the steps.

"Everything. Just like I know your favorite color is green—nice choice by the way—your high school sweetheart cheated on you while you were away on your first deployment—I'll be sending her a bouquet of roses to thank her for the fact that you're still single—and you love to look at bondage porn."

The muttered curses that echo through the stairwell are delightfully gruff and I kinda wish we had the time for him to shove me up against the wall so his tongue could lash me for all the secrets I just spilled.

But c'est la vie.

We can't get everything we want.

When we're about to round a curve in the stairs, I hear a crash as the front door is smashed open. Wood and glass clatter onto the floor and are accompanied by the bass tones of policemen yelling warnings in French.

My heart starts to race and I spin, ignoring the press of Tyler's gun against my stomach. I yank the pin out of my grenade and launch it down the stairwell. It goes sailing through the room and lands with a plink, before rolling into the hall that leads to the front room.

The horrible, chemical scent of fire immediately fills the air, and a huge plume of smoke discharges.

"I'm sorry ladies!" I call out to all the plants—the poor things. But Tyler and I have to get to Yegor, and neither of us can do it if we're locked away in a jail cell.

Actually, only I need to get to the Russian.

But I kinda want Tyler there now so I can show off.

The other assassin looks a little shell-shocked as his head swivels from the black wall of smoke back to me. "You were only threatening me with a smoke bomb?"

I shrug.

Then I turn and bolt up the stairs with everything I've got, because this is our chance.

The hacking coughs of the police travel through the space as my legs burn and fingers shake from pure adrenaline. Tyler's close on my heels, anxiety shoving at both our backs and pushing us to move faster as yells and footsteps chase after us.

When I come to a window on the second-floor landing, I turn and snatch my purse away from the hot, angry, breathless man behind me. I'm tempted to bite him, just to rile him up the tiniest bit more, but I resist the urge because time is of the essence.

Instead, I wink and dive through the glass. I ignore the tinkling shatter and tiny cuts pricking all over my skin as I shout a quick last few words for Mr. Monroe. "I'll call you!"

5

HALF-COCKED

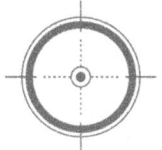

May 20
2:45 p.m.
Marseille, France

Royal

It's hard to focus with a lady boner.

Like, so hard.

I'm struggling, staring blankly at the two chemical compounds that Raven sent with me when I said I had to take this job international. The two little vials from my sister gleam at me in the afternoon light, and the clock in my hotel room is ticking away the seconds because I need to leave here in under five minutes to get set up. But I'm dawdling and dilly-dallying like a twelve-year-old girl because I can't shake those kisses this morning from my thoughts.

Tyler's lips and that furious but utterly hot look in his eyes?

One shower session and two orgasms haven't been enough to erase him from my system. That's a first for me. Normally, I can scrub the scent of a man off me and not have a second thought.

But I googled Tyler's old army picture an hour ago (one that's still left on an archive site) and just ... stared at it.

Who does that with someone that's not a mark? I mean ... if you aren't planning to kill the person then why? Why dig up every little detail of their life?

Originally, when I looked up this little group, who've been mentioned once as Triple X, I thought I was getting to know them so I could outwit them.

But today my head has gone in a dozen different directions— none of them productive. I've grown light-headed and swoony fantasizing about Tyler being stuck in this tiny hotel room with me and pinning me up against the wall, banging me so hard that the staff come tell me the other guests have complained.

I've imagined him grabbing my throat and kissing me while his handsome stepbrother, Avery, who is only a few years older than me, kneels just behind my spread legs and eats me from the back.

I've even thought about absolutely ridiculous scenarios like the two of us out at dinner together, on a normal—*blech* —date.

I think his kiss might have broken my brain.

I sit down on the twin bed with a huff and a bounce as I glance out through the lacy curtains at the winding road for the millionth time and wonder what he's doing.

No.

No. I have to get my tranquilizer darts loaded and get into position ASAP ... but all I really want to do is moon about and touch myself again. Stupid Tyler is too fucking hot for words and my entire body wants to sink into a boneless puddle over him.

Under him.

On him.

Behind him if he'd let me.

I want all the prepositions.

And propositions.

Yes, please.

"Fuck off, dumb butt." I curse at myself for being so annoying under my breath.

I lift the vials up to the light and study them again, struggling to remember what my sister told me. Raven and her blue-black hair and nerdy-chic look pop into my head and I can just see her rolling her eyes at me for being so scatterbrained.

"Dammit," I curse under my breath because I can't remember which one is the knockout mixture and which is the dirty bomb. Her dirty bomb is world-famous. Or it should be, I always tell her.

But it's not the one I want to use today so I need to make sure it's not the one I load.

I grab my phone and dial, resting it on my ear as I pull open one of the darts, ready to fill it as soon as she tells me which color to use— blue or purple.

Raven answers on the third ring. "Yolo!"

"You're such a weirdo."

"Which of us had a full-on conversation with the hydrangea bush outside last week?" she counters.

"You said you'd deleted that video," I assert with suspicion.

"I lie sometimes."

"I hate you." She's one of my favorite sisters and she knows it.

"I'm going to go switch your pillows while you're gone," she threatens.

My throat tightens up and I point an aggressive finger at her even though she can't see it. "Don't you dare." She knows how I get about things out of place. Even the thought of one of my pillows being in the wrong spot makes the nerves on the sides of my eyeballs start to twitch.

"Maybe I'll call Harlow and ask her where the plates should go in the kitchen," she adds, piling on.

This bitch knows all my buttons.

Harlow and I have an ongoing war about how things should be organized because she's just as particular and picky as I am. Only, she's utterly and completely wrong and always puts things away improperly.

Raven's threat boils my brain like an egg—it's bouncing, my skull cracking at the thought of coming home after this job to find the kitchen and my bedroom in utter disarray. "Dammit! I'm the weirdo, okay? Me. I'm weird. you and your medical dramas are awesome, and I really need to fucking know what kind of darts you've given me again."

"Doctor Ramona is so pretty ..." She gets off track until I clear my throat pointedly.

"Oh, the vials? That's easy! They're color coded—the—and the—"

"Wait. What?"

"The—" She cuts out.

I pull my phone away from my ear and stare at it. We're still connected, but I can't hear anything. "Hello? Hello?"

I don't hear my sister's voice, but my phone does start to buzz in my hand.

Fuck my luck.

That's my alarm. It's time to go.

My phone dies just then—because some swoony idiot forgot to charge it. I hiss at myself, shoving my phone in my pocket because there's nothing else I can do right now. I'll have to settle for less-than-perfect today. I lick my lips as I load two darts, one with each chemical compound, trying to ignore the fissures forming inside my chest at the fact that every-thing isn't absolutely aligned, pre-planned, and perfectly set out.

Stupid Tyler.

Yes, I'm blaming him and his kisses for this.

I allow anger to expand like smoke inside my chest, hoping the emotion clouds the burning need to always be perfect, always get things right. Today, right is a luxury, not a given.

Swinging my dart gun onto my back, I glance in the mirror to give myself one last check. Yeah, I look hot. I've got a new bodysuit, since Colt ruined the last one, and while it's still mostly black, the seamstress made a concession and my right sleeve is royal purple, which I thought was a nice touch. The purple offsets my pale skin and my dyed brown hair is back in a braid to keep it out of my eyes. I take a deep, reassuring, calming breath before I stalk to my reflection. "You've got this. You'll just have to wing it. And if you accidentally use the wrong dart, just shoot Yegor twice."

"UP ON THE rooftop assassins pause, Out jumps bad old Yegor Claus," I hum a little tune that's completely off-key and off-beat as I get my dart gun all set up. Yegor's due to arrive in approximately four minutes in a bakery shop van.

I feel like I should make some punny remark about how Yegor's pancake is about to be flipped. His buns are done. He's going to be eaten alive or something ... but I can't come up with anything good. Nothing that zings. I'm blaming Tyler for my lack of witty repartee. I blow a raspberry at him, wherever he is, which I know must be close.

He picked this location after all. It's actually a pretty good one. The winery across the street is on the outskirts of town and so the nearest police station is about ten minutes away. Even though it's daylight—which will make Yegor feel more comfortable about the handoff—there are few witnesses around. And those who are present stumble out of the winery drunk as skunks and oblivious to the rest of the world.

I'm on top of the blue-painted metal roof that belongs to a pretty empty office building across the street. The top two floors aren't even currently rented, which sucks for the land-lord, but is great for me. The landscaping here clearly show-cases how little effort the owner is putting into the building. Trees and shrubs are all overgrown and I have to walk the roofline a bit to find the perfect place for my shot, but I do find one and settle in, carefully setting down my duffel beside me.

If I'm getting set up for this handoff, so is Tyler. An antici-patory tingle wriggles down my spine and I can't tell if I'm excited or afraid to have such a competent rival.

"Just focus on you, girl," I pep-talk myself as I arrange all of my items in a neat spread along the roof and slide my dart filled with a shining purple liquid into the chamber.

It's bright this afternoon, which is generally a bad thing for assassins, because it hinders the whole low-key, don't-get-caught thing. But the warmth means my fingers won't lock up while I wait to take my shot the way they did the last time I was in Belarus on a job. Gloves do absolutely nothing against sub-freezing temperatures.

Of course, where there's an upside, there's always a downside.

The clearest shot I've got to hit Yegor in the parking lot means I've got to lie prone on this roof. This metal roof. I'm going to burn my tits off while I fire darts at this motherfucker like he's a cocaine-addled grizzly bear. But ... it is what it is.

Maybe I can get Tyler to kiss my boobs better later. If he'll forgive me for ruining his assassination attempt and taking that bounty away from him.

Ugh. This attraction stuff is complicated.

I sigh, the reality that I might not get to suicide this mark and use my signature drink washing over me. It's a disappointment that settles like a stone in the bottom of my belly and sits there heavily. It makes my controlling tendencies flare up like a rash. But it's undeniable. This job is different. And the fact that other assassins want in on this mark really cramps my normal style. Of course, the fact that they make my ovaries cramp up in delight gets them slightly off the hook. But just slightly.

I pull a dark navy hoodie on and bring the hood up over my hair to hide it and help me blend into the rich blue color of the roof. Finding just the right shade for the sweatshirt and getting it rush-delivered took two hours earlier, but I like things to be perfect.

Disguise in place, I splay out on my stomach. My dart rifle is in hand, backup dart carefully laid right beside my weapon for easy reloading.

Thank goodness my boobs aren't huge or this would be hella uncomfortable. My sister Karma would never be able to pull this off. Her boobs are massive. Of course, killing people with baked goods sounds a lot more comfortable than just about anything I've done for this job thus far. Maybe I did pick the wrong type of murder.

I blow out a gentle breath and see a small white van with a green logo on it and every muscle in my body clenches up. It trundles on past and I glare at it for making my sphincter clench.

Damn all these high-stakes, high-adrenaline red herrings.

"This is why making it look like people kill themselves is better," I grumble to myself. Mock suicide assassinations are slow and meticulous, not nausea-inducing like this wait right now.

I try to ignore an itch that rudely starts up on my elbow. Doesn't my body know that we're currently otherwise engaged?

It would be just my luck that I'd reach around to scratch it and Yegor would show—speak of the devil. There he is. Another van, this time a black one with a white croissant logo set inside a circle, pulls slowly up to the parking lot.

A man in a suit steps out and he does not have the appearance of a baker. Nope. He didn't even try to fit into the role. He's wearing a black suit thickened up by a bulletproof vest underneath and his Matrix-style wraparound sunglasses look horrible, though I'm a tiny bit jealous of them at the moment because the glare off this roof is annoying as shit.

He peers around the parking lot, which is actually for a winery that orders the bread in order to make patrons soak up some of the booze in their bellies. In the distance, a tour bus unloads and college students pile off, loud and rowdy— and I use my sight to scan over them. Almost immediately, I spot Colt trying to blend in among the group.

Ahh, so there's the first member of Triple X trying to make their move. I wonder what the game plan is and why Colt is over there with the kiddos trying to blend in. Too bad for him he's so handsome. Even with the wig they've shoved on him and Hollywood's universally overused disguise of a ball cap and sunglasses, that muscular build of his is a dead giveaway. Don't they realize they should try to change his body shape? Give him a beer belly or something?

I shake my head, though Man's probably a better teacher than these guys have gotten. From the looks of things, they're winging it.

Tyler's killed a string of assholes since he took on this whole for-hire gig, but Colt is fresh out of a mercenary group and he's not quite got the hang of the whole subterfuge bit, obviously. He could definitely have used my help. I'd have made him wear a pregnancy belly with a pouch inside it for a nice nine-millimeter and grafted on a double chin. No one would ever have suspected it was him, though I'm pretty sure the grumpy man would have had a few deliciously choice words to say about it.

We could have argued before Tyler told him to shut up and do as he was told before sweeping me backward into one of those dancer dips and kissing the shit out of me.

Sigh.

Missed opportunity.

I keep scanning, looking for Tyler's limp or Avery's shy gait. I might not recognize their faces if they're wearing prosthetics, but people have a lot harder time changing how they move. I lick my lips as I try to focus on one of the guys on the tour bus who seems to be hanging around behind all the others.

Is that him?

Tyler?

A scuffle starts up among the kids just as another strange, soft sound echoes behind me—but both those things happen just as a new car pulls up to Yegor's van.

My pulse taps so rapidly it could win a typing contest. I hold my breath just in an effort to slow it down, though my thoughts start racing just as quickly. Everything becomes supersonic inside my body, while the world around me seems to slow down.

Thoughts tumble one after the other through my brain as I spread my feet out across the roof, using two beams to brace myself for the shot.

Is Tyler driving? Are they still going through with the idiotic handoff plan? I give a discontented little grumble as I prop myself up on my elbows and use my sight to zero in on the back door of Yegor's vehicle. I am not going to let this handoff happen.

The door to the new, sleek black car starts to open. Tyler steps out, his hair dyed full white for the occasion, his scar covered back up, wearing yet another suit for this handoff, a blue one this time. His cane is noticeably absent.

Inconvenient parts of my anatomy remind me of their existence as I try to focus on what I'm supposed to do. But it takes a long, drawn-out moment before I can get the scope to move away from Tyler's face. And even once it does, my breathing is short and shallow, not the deep meditative sort of breathing Man has taught us we need when we're trying to shoot long distances.

"Focus," I scold myself as I breathe in for a four count and slide my finger down until it rests directly on the trigger.

Where's the stepbrother?

Smash.

A huge weight crushes my spine and all the air is squished from my lungs in a giant gasp as something lands on top of me.

Holy shit!

As if I've just walked into a giant spider's web, panic coats me and clings to me and feels impossible to shake. So instead of trying to dispel that energy, I use it, rolling onto my back, though it's a struggle and my hood slides down halfway over my eyes in the process. The person holding me sticks with me, reaching for my weapon, trying to yank the barrel away from me. Shit. No. If I lose that, I'm done. I plead with my body not to give up the struggle as I writhe underneath this person—who I'm guessing is fucking Avery —hoping to buck them off me and make them tumble down the roof.

A hand comes to my neck and squeezes, the pressure setting off a demon inside of me who kicks and bites and scratches. Instinct writhes inside of me, wild and unforgiving as I try anything and everything to break free.

I manage to clock the man above me in the nose and he curses. "Fuck!"

After that, though, his hands stay off my neck and he tries a new approach. "Tyler told me to try not to kill you, so don't make—"

His words are worse than when he was trying to choke me out because little bitty fireworks immediately erupt in my belly. Tyler Monroe, admitted assassin, told one of his crew to try not to kill me?

Shit.

He must really like me.

I become filled with sparkles and tiny booms of delight. The color bursting behind my eyelids isn't solely because of my lack of air anymore.

Avery yanks on the gun, making it slip in my grip, and reality barges rudely back into my daydream, smashing it down. "Dammit!" I clench my abs and sit up, one hand clutching at the gun while the other reaches down to pinch whatever bit of his dick I can find.

Newsflash: there's a lot.

I hide how impressed I am, focusing on the weapon because I have zero doubts right now that Tyler's about to escort Yegor to his car, if he hasn't already left.

Motherfucker. My pulse surges at the realization that I'm almost out of time.

Avery howls when I twist his dick through his pants and I barely manage to keep hold of the rifle with one hand, swinging the butt of it upward and clocking his backlit figure in the jaw before deftly maneuvering it back around into position and pressing the trigger at close range, nailing this motherfucker right in the gut.

"Oh shit!" Avery's soft voice fills the air as the dart drains into him. The sheer terror of the prior moment recedes as I realize that I just wasted a motherfucking dart on him and now I probably have mere milliseconds before all my hard work and planning is stolen out from underneath me.

I roll away from him, scrambling to find the other dart. There! I spot it only three feet away. Thank goodness the roof isn't steep or it would have rolled right off!

Dammit!

I have to reload quickly.

My hands are rocked by adrenaline-filled tremors as I slide open the gun and splay out on my stomach across the hot roof, the second dart in my fingers.

I load it as quickly as I can, glancing more than once at the scene down by Yegor's van. The parking lot is empty of tourists now, except for Colt, who's crossing the parking lot, head on a swivel for witnesses. The back doors of the bakery van are both open. A bodyguard is standing next to him and Yegor's climbing out himself.

Fuckity fuck!

I'm about to lose my chance. If he slips away now, Tyler will put a bullet in his brain in under five minutes.

No.

I don't want this fucker to die so easily. And I don't want him to die at someone else's hands, no matter how hot said hands are.

My heart booms inside my chest as if someone's cranked up the bass on a really terrible, angry song. Shakily, I raise my gun a second time. I look through the sight.

Yegor's idiotic bodyguard is blocking my shot.

"Sonofabitch!" I curse as I glance over my shoulder at Avery, wondering why he hasn't charged at me like a raging bull yet.

Avery's curled on his side, eyes closed, a tiny bead of drool perched on the corner of his lip.

Crap. He got the knockout potion.

Well, fuck all my plans. I've got to try something. Anything's better than nothing at this point.

I look down the sight a final time and press the trigger, shooting the dart right at the bodyguard.

Every function in my body hits the pause button as I tense and wait—hoping against hope—and the motherfucker moves just in time for my dart to pierce Yegor through the motherfucking heart.

"Hell yeah!" I punch the air with my gun for a split second, before realizing that's a shitty idea.

Shitty idea.

I crack up.

Shitty. Shitty. Shitty.

I use the gun sight to look close up at the scene in the parking lot once more. The bodyguard is yanking the dart out of Yegor's chest. The Russian mafia kingpin's face has turned a strange shade of red. He lurches forward, hunches over, grabs his gut ... and his bodyguard jerks back.

I can't hear anything this far away, but by the way the bodyguard recoils, I know Raven's dart has done the trick.

Her dirty bomb gives instant diarrhea.

This asshole isn't just full of shit. Now, he's covered in it.

I chuckle. "Go ahead and collect him now, Tyler."

Tyler's head swivels suspiciously, as if he's looking for me, but he doesn't hesitate. He practically shoves Yegor into the backseat of his car as Colt darts over. Both of the Triple X men jump into the front of the car and the vehicle peels away across the asphalt with a screech of tires I can hear even from this distance.

But when I see all the car windows roll down from the stench, all I can do is glance over at a sleeping, sighing Avery and smile.

Because this game isn't over yet.

6

FRIENDLY FIRE

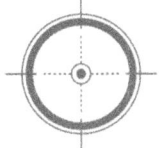

May 21
7:15 a.m.
Marseille, France

Royal

I 've never had a man tied up and nearly naked on my bed before, but I think I might like it.

This job is unlocking a whole new set of kinks for me.

Avery is stretched out on my hotel bed sans covers and his lanky form is nude but for some green boxer briefs that leave nothing to the imagination. His pale skin is lit by the warm light of a frosted glass bedside lamp—and staring at him is a scrumptious sort of indulgence I've never really allowed myself before.

Normally, I go to a bar, find a suitable bedmate, get to his apartment and rip off his clothes in relative darkness, then complete a couple orgasm exchanges before I head out. There was the occasional threesome but still, that was relatively anonymous and always about the O.

This situation is obviously a bit different. I had to strip this man to check for weapons and wires. And I may have had a peek inside that underwear to be sure he wasn't packing any weapons away in there because the bulge was ... well, unrealistically large.

Avery's packing a weapon all right ... but only the kind Mother Nature gave him.

I considered getting him dressed again but there is something to be said about the psychological advantage of him waking up and feeling vulnerable. Plus ... it's becoming a fascinating sort of debauchery for me that's sending a racy thrill up the small of my back.

I've never let my eyes drift over that attractive V near a man's hips before. I've never leisurely studied a guy's happy trail or the way the dark hair contrasts deliciously against his stomach. I've never let my fingers trace over a man's toned calves or circle his nipples while he's been passed out.

I don't actually touch those spots, just imagine I do as my eyes map little circles over his skin. But after a low-sleep night, the imagination can be quite potent.

In my head, he likes nipple tweaks ... I hope reality matches the version of him I've been building up because that version is hella hot.

I can't wait to hear Avery breathless, panting, screaming my name when I actually put my hands on him. I want to see the look of utter subjugation in his eyes. I lick my lips in anticipation, wondering if this morning, I'll get to live out my dream.

But I might not get to play.

It's all going to depend on him and how cooperative he is.

And I'm going to have to think through how I'll do it, because yesterday I texted Tyler from Avery's phone to tell him that I had his stepbrother.

You touch one fucking hair on his head ... the return text had read, which let me know I'd hit the jackpot and made the right call about this kidnapping.

You touch one fucking hair on Yegor's head without me ... I'd sent back before I forwarded calls from Avery's phone to my burner and abandoned his cell inside a small stone church, tucked it under a pew.

My phone had buzzed nonstop for an hour until I silenced it.

I smile as I picture Tyler tracking his stepbrother's phone down yesterday, arriving just in time for evening Mass. I hope that's what happened—that he was swarmed by a group of old ladies on their way to pray while he was silently praying for my death.

I love when little ironies like that collide.

Meanwhile, I'd huddled up here last night, watching over Avery's prone form, eating some divine French onion soup that had me opening the window to air out the room after because it tasted a whole lot better than it smelled.

Still smelled better than what Triple X had to deal with. Haha. That image of Yegor bending over and shitting himself is going to live rent-free in my head forever.

After dinner was over, I'd spent several long hours staring at the door I'd locked and barricaded with a dresser, gun at my side, ready for anything. For Tyler and that big brute Colt to burst through the door all riled up with testosterone ... my anticipation devolved into full-on daydreaming about the two of them tag-teaming me as the hours wore on and I heard nothing but the sounds of life drifting up to me through the open window: pigeons cooing, people chatting, cars honking, seagulls squawking until everything grew still and the city fell asleep. Only the distant sound of the waves told me that the ocean itself was still awake.

Well, the ocean and me.

When I'd finally decided Avery didn't have an under-the-skin tracking device and Tyler wasn't going to burst through my door all hot and bothered (sad day) I'd stolen the covers and a pillow from the bed and slept on the floor ... well, for most of the night anyway.

I got chilly around four a.m. so I did sneak onto the mattress for a mini cuddle session to warm up.

I may or may not have woken up this morning with my thigh draped over Avery's legs and my arm wrapped around his slim waist, the steady beat of his heart soothing underneath my cheek.

I may or may not have laid there in the dark for an hour after I woke, just enjoying the warmth that radiated from his skin, the surprising comfort of having a male pillow whose lungs rose and fell beneath me, the baffling and unexpected sense of calm that emerged after sleeping next to another human being for the first time ever.

Those things may or may not have happened.

A lady never tells.

And while Belladonnas might not technically qualify as ladies, we know how to keep secrets. Especially precious ones.

Now, as the sun starts to make the window gleam like a video-game jewel, I recline in the small chair in the corner, one elbow resting on a little round table set with an electric tea kettle and a basket of fixings in order to make a morning cuppa. I got my early morning deliveries an hour ago, tipping big for them. Everything's all set up for playtime. I just need Sleeping Beauty here to wake.

The birds twitter outside, providing background music as I finish counting Avery's freckles while I wait for the knockout solution to ebb from his system. The counting is an activity I started last night between sessions of staring at the door.

"Two thousand seventy- one." Those are all the freckles easily visible on the front of his body, though very few are on his face.

Finally, Avery comes to with a groan, his head turning sideways in an attempt to nose his own bicep and probably go back to sleep. The fact that he can't move his arm seems to rouse him. His soft blue eyes open and I admire the way his lashes brush against his cheeks as he blinks slowly, staring at the handcuffs that link him to the metal bedframe of my twin mattress.

I chuckle as he glances over at me, handsome face alarmed. His expression reminds me of how I imagine nature enthusiasts actually look like after getting lowered into the ocean and coming face to face with a shark.

"So, are you a shower or a grower?" I ask conversationally, glancing down at his boxers before grabbing the teacup I've been sipping from for the past hour. "Because, if you say grower ... " I whistle. "Wow. I mean that thing already looks like it could do damage. Python!"

"Are you insane?" Avery's voice comes out as a hoarse whisper.

"Well, sanity is kind of a sliding scale," I tell him, wavering my free palm in the air in a "so-so" gesture. "So ... maybe a bit, but not *too* crazy, you know?" I'm not sure he's comforted by the smile I give because he starts to pull at his handcuffs, straining hard against them, making the bed knock into the wall.

"Hey, calm down," I say, standing and shushing my prisoner like a real guard would. Boom. Got this kidnapping thing on lock.

His nostrils flare and I can see the muscles in his neck straining when he retorts, "Calm down? I'm fucking naked and handcuffed to a bed, you psycho!"

Or maybe not.

"Lots of guys pay good money for that," I retort cheekily.

"I don't pay for sex."

"Well, I'm not selling it," I chirp haughtily as I flip my hair behind my shoulder.

He stares at me for a long moment, and I assume he's sizing me up. His look definitely feels like an analysis, like he's running little calculations and if/then scenarios in the back of his pretty brain, trying to weigh his chances and all the possible outcomes.

He swallows and lowers his gaze, letting it deliberately sweep over my bare legs and then leisurely travel up my body. Awareness prickles through me and his stare plucks at my nipples, sharpening them to points.

That's when he softly says, "Maybe you should be." His tone does a complete one-eighty from a minute ago, going from angry to sultry and his facial expression is the same, as if he used that long moment of perusal to transition from panicked to bedroom eyes. "Clearly, you like what you see or you wouldn't be asking about my dick."

Not untrue.

"Why don't you come over here and finish what you started … ?" he suggests slyly, glancing pointedly at his boxers.

I press my lips together so I don't laugh because he *is* super hot. But it's abundantly clear that he's been in this world far less time than I have and he needs practice at this manipulation thing. His blatant attempt to take control of this situation is not going to work.

If we're going to psychologically fuck each other … it's going to be me pegging him.

I've never actually tried pegging before.

Pretty sure I'd like it though. Dressing up is fun.

I play along for the moment, building him up so I can knock him down. Sauntering forward a few steps before I stop and cock my hip, I drag my eyes over his toned body before staring into his baby blues aggressively. "Yeah. You want me to see how hard I make that big dick of yours?"

"First I want you to get up here and ride my face, let me suck that pretty clit until I've made you scream at least three times," he counteroffers.

Fuck. Now, *that's* tempting. He might not be subtle about his subterfuge, but the man can dirty talk.

"If I did that, my thighs might accidentally choke you out." I state as I take a sip from my teacup.

"Best way for a man to die is with his tongue inside a hot pussy and a woman howling his name." The words roll smoothly off his lips but are followed by a minuscule look of surprise, as if he just shocked himself by saying those things aloud.

That's it, Avery. Embrace your bad-boy self.

My lady bits are applauding this naughtiness and about to strip away my logic and give him his way. But I can't have my ovaries running this show. The last time I gave them their way, I ended up fucking a circus performer.

Nothing ruins an orgasm like having a bear growl in your ear at the last second because their idiot trainer forgot to lock them up.

Never again.

I need to let Avery know he isn't holding the reins, even though his plans and my daydreams aren't actually that far apart. There's no way I'm letting my captive top me from the bottom.

I set my teacup down on the bedside table and lean in close, breathing heavily, staring down at him, and dragging my palm deliberately over one of his peaked nipples before whispering, "Sorry. I have other plans for you. They do involve bodily fluids, though." I pull back and wink, letting that little double entendre settle underneath his skin.

That seems like it's just a smidge too much for him to handle because his face pales before he starts thrashing against his restraints again, calling out, "Aidez moi!"—the French phrase for help me.

Oops.

Just like Avery, I'm still learning how to walk this tightrope, balancing sexy banter with threats. Mightta tipped just a weensy bit over the edge there.

In my defense, it's a really thin line to walk.

So thin.

Like tiptoeing on dental floss.

Since my teacup is still near at hand, I decide that I should tone down this whole scene a bit by doing the polite thing and offering him a drink. Maybe it will quiet him. At the very least, the distraction should break his wild, panicked bucking that's making the bed squeak and the wall rattle, and hopefully keep the hotel staff away for a little longer.

If we do get kicked out of here for wild bucking in that bed, I'd prefer it be a mutual thing. On my terms though, of course.

Staring at him all morning long has my hormones buzzing like bees around my head. His dirty propositions didn't help matters. It's hard to think straight with that white noise of horniness blaring between my ears, but I make an effort. I hold the cup out to him, a pretty little painted pink mug filled with chamomile. "You want some tea?"

He does lie still, but only so he can pin me with a violent glare. "So you can poison me again?" His eyes are dilating, the black pupils swelling up to overtake the beautiful blue of his irises. Avery's breathing is shallow and his gaze flies around the room in search of some way out—as if I'm sloppy enough to leave an opening like that.

The fact that he doubts me and my abilities—after I got his ass off the roof and through the city all the way to this room undetected—is a little offensive, as is the fact that he isn't blatantly checking me out any more as I bend toward him. What, if it's not part of his game, I'm suddenly not hot enough?

Rude with a capital R.

I'm totally hot right now.

I'm sans bra, with a shirt that barely covers my lady bits and I've brushed my teeth and put on lip-plumping Chapstick. I even spent half an hour fixing my hair into "effortless" beachy waves. I look fucking good.

I pull my cup back and sip my tea as I fight the urge to pour it on him for his obnoxious theatrics when he starts testing the limits of the cuffs around his ankles without even trying to peek at the hem of my nightshirt. "You really need to get out more if you're going to get offended over a little sleep dart," I finally say, proud of my self-control, even though my delivery is through gritted teeth.

"You really need to get out more if you think you need to chain a guy up to get him in bed."

I raise a brow and some of my fury ebbs away a little bit, receding like the tide. Somehow, in a roundabout way, I think Avery just gave me a compliment. And this time, he wasn't pairing it up with a bedroom-eyes look or anything that seemed like an attempt to actually seduce me. I think it might have just slipped out. Hmm.

He might be half-forgiven.

It definitely erases some of his failure to ogle me, which I quickly attribute to the distress of being kidnapped instead of a lack of attraction to me. I hope.

Time to turn this panic train back around so that it heads towards Seduction Station.

"Oh, I don't think that. Not for normal guys at least." I turn and go set down my tea at the table in the corner, deliberately bending over a little so that my t-shirt rides up and gives him a glimpse of my ass cheeks spilling out of my silky bikini briefs. My heart quivers in my chest and a tiny thrill races through me when I hear Avery suck in a breath behind me.

Okay, yay. He's off the naughty list because that was definitely a sexy breath catching in his throat.

Will the wild plan I've been hatching in my devious, deviant mind since last night actually come to fruition?

Please, oh please, yes.

I turn around and slowly pull the oversized white tee I'm wearing off. I've only got on lacy white panties underneath and my nipples stand at attention as Avery's gaze rakes over me, his teeth grinding together and his throat bobbing as he swallows.

My eyes trace over his shoulders, which are broader than his hips by several inches, even if he's not as muscular as his step brother. There's something about Avery that just draws me in—and has from the first moment I saw him in Yegor's house. It could be the quiet vibe that seems to radiate logic and confidence, the blond hair, the way he's quirking one eyebrow in disbelief (like he's done in tons of the photos I've stalked and like he's doing right now), the fact that his former girlfriends used to post about how meticulously clean he is, or maybe it's purely the size of his dick, which appeared to be at least seven inches while resting.

I take a slow, deliberate step closer, making sure to sway my hips and keep our eyes locked together in an exquisite show-down. "But you aren't a normal man, Avery Monroe. You're part of Triple X. You're dangerous." He sucks in a breath at the word *dangerous*, and my lower belly heats beneath his gaze as his eyes travel down to my panties.

Goose bumps start to pebble along the backs of my shoulder blades and a buoyant feeling fills my chest.

Yessss. Does he see where we should take this little encounter? How we should make the most of it? He proposed it earlier but he wasn't serious then; that was just life-or-death babble. A little "don't kill me" bargaining.

Does he still want it if all that negotiating is off the table?

I bite my lower lip.

God, he's handsome. I wonder if any woman has ever called him dangerous before. From my research, I know he's single now, but he's dated three older women; there's a chance here that I might not be his type. But part of me wonders if his type is less about age and more about control. "I have to protect myself against you, even though I want you," I add, in nearly a whisper.

"What?" his tone is confused but his gaze is hungry, his fingers clenching into fists where his hands are restrained against the head of the bed.

"You could hurt me," I shrug one shoulder and take a step closer. "You tried to push me off a roof earlier."

"What?" His eyes widen and a look of dismay crosses his face. "I didn't! I just tried to take that gun—"

I shake my head at him in mock disappointment. "If you would have told the truth just now, I would have let you go. But trying to downplay what you did ... " I cluck my tongue. "I'm going to have to torture you now."

He immediately stiffens on the bed, though I notice his cock looks thicker and perhaps a tiny bit longer than before.

Does he like things rough?

I move around the bed, letting my fingertips trail lightly over his calves, even that tiny bit of touch lighting up my brain, which is currently as brilliant as Times Square.

"I think you're going to like torture though," I tell him with a little wink, smiling wider when he swallows so hard that the gulp is audible.

"I'll be right back." I pat his knee twice and then turn and saunter toward the attached bathroom. "I just need to get a few things ready."

"Wait. Wait!" he yells after me, but I simply give him a mysterious smile as I grab the bathroom door and slowly close it behind me, letting the door's thump punctuate my last statement.

Twenty minutes later, after Avery's exhausted his voice trying to bargain with me and calling for help, I leave the bathroom, all my preparations complete.

I glance over at him and see a sheen of sweat coating his forehead, no doubt from the anxiety of wondering what kind of cruelty I have in store. His eyes snap from my nude breasts up to my face and he swallows hard when he sees the determined look in my eyes. His chest rises and falls rapidly and I can practically hear his sprinting heartbeat from where I stand.

"Slow down, Ave. We haven't even gotten started," I coax him to take deep breaths by doing it myself. "In and out. In and out." Then I head casually over to my dresser and grab a length of chain.

His abs contract and his body grows rigid.

"Not a whips and chains guy? You might be in the wrong line of work," I quip.

"Might be," he says breathlessly, a little edge of that panic back in his voice, though it's not nearly as strong as when he was trying to knock down the wall with his wiggles.

"Relax," I coo at him the same way I talk to my plants. "Everything's going to be okay." Meanwhile, I round the bed and stretch one thick chain between his feet, connecting it to two loops on the cuffs clapped around his ankles. "What ... what are you doing?" His eyes follow me, dropping to my nipples at least twice before he seems to remember the severity of the situation.

"It's a surprise," I tell him with a wink, which results in a shaky chuckle tumbling from his chest as I return to the dresser for the next item I need.

"I'm not much for surprises," he admits.

"Are you sure? I thought you surprised Melanie with a puppy for her birthday." The name of his last girlfriend rolls off my tongue with a little bit of wistfulness because I've never gotten a puppy.

His face pales ten times more than before. "We aren't still dating. I haven't talked to her for more than a year. She doesn't even know anything about this or what I do. Don't hurt her!"

God, his panic on her behalf is both adorable and infuriating because I can't think of a single of my hookups that would do their best to protect me from a hired killer if their life was on the line. Or even if it wasn't.

I've been scraping the bottom of the barrel.

Damn.

I stand there, having a moment, mulling over the fact that I've solely fucked losers up to this point and resolving to change that fact, when Avery lets out a panicked sound. It's barely more than a shaky exhale, but it brings me back to the present.

To the fact that this very sweet, nearly naked man in front of me is waiting for me.

I round the bed, moving closer to the head, to where his hands are bound, each hand enclosed in a separate set of cuffs that are linked to the bed frame. "My sister loves torture." I don't mention Ivory by name, because I don't want him digging into her any more than he wants me to know about Melanie. "She loves all kinds of torture. Physical. Mental. You name it, she's done it." I pause and wait for Avery to glance up from my bare breasts and meet my eyes so that he'll understand how serious I am. "Now, I don't want to use her methods, but if you force me to, I will. Is that understood?"

A sharp swallow and a single nod are his response.

"Good. Now, I'm going to remove one of your cuffs, help you sit up in bed, and then cuff your hands behind your back. You will not try to move on your own. You will not try to use the opportunity to escape. Your feet are still chained to the bed. So don't do anything stupid that will get you hurt, okay?" My voice cracks a little as I make the threat; I find I kinda don't want to make it. This is why it's better to work behind the scenes and never come face-to-face with anyone. I'm getting attached.

I blow out a breath as I hold up a key, my nerves rattling just as badly as a prima donna about to step out on stage for her first beauty pageant.

Ohhhh, this could go so badly. So so badly. I left my gun on the table. Deliberately. Hoping like hell I could trust Avery with this and believing it because it's his first real foray into the assassination business. He'd been caught up in some weapons trades before this, but Tyler had scooped him out of that line of work—I assume because no one had Avery's back there. But even though this is only Avery's first attempt at the kill-for-hire thing, I shouldn't underestimate him. I'm trusting him because I want to believe he's trustworthy.

Jesus, Man would have my head if he knew I was doing this.

It's so utterly stupid.

Carefully, I kneel on the bed at Avery's side. His eyes drop to my nipples for a split second before coming back up to study my face as I lean forward and unlock his left cuff from the railing, leaving the handcuff cinched around his wrist.

My throat is dry. So damn dry. My eyes burrow into his as I try to tunnel into his brain and figure out what he's thinking.

He stays perfectly still, doing the same, and the intensity of our mutual stares is dizzying until I murmur, "Put that hand on the bed behind you and push yourself up to sitting."

He does, the bed quaking under him, making me very aware of how long his torso is when he suddenly looms over me where he sits.

"Good boy," I whisper, leaning close to his ear, letting my breast brush lightly against his arm. I catch the sound of his tiny inhalation, lean back and note the spark that flits through his eyes before he tries to hide it. I take both those sweet little secrets and tuck them into my memory as my excitement starts to rise once more, outweighing fear.

Confidence buoys me as I decide this is going to work. I let my fingertips trail lightly over Avery's forearm and the delicious veins there. "Now put that hand behind you in the middle of your back. And wait."

My stomach morphs once again into a hot, writhing mess of need as I stand and carefully circle the bed, keeping eye contact with Avery as I go. This time, however, my eyes burn with lust, trace fiery paths up his skin, and clearly communicate everything I'm thinking.

By the time I reach his second hand, I'm pretty certain he's well aware of my interest. Based on the fully erect state of his absolutely monstrous dick—I think there's at least a sixty percent chance he's interested too.

Cuffing his hands together behind him goes like clockwork and then I release his feet from the bed so that he can walk using the length of chain between his ankle cuffs.

"Come on, handsome." I tell him, helping him stand. I usher him into the bathroom, my footsteps nearly inaudible compared to the rolling clank of his chains. He complies, but stops, stock still in the doorway, staring.

His eyes are wide and disbelieving as he looks at the free-standing tub, which is filled with steaming water. White rose petals float gently on the surface. Behind the tub, the countertop and shower floor are covered in dozens of flickering candles. Next to the tub is a breakfast tray set up with tarts and croissants and other baked goods.

"What is this?" He stutters, tone utterly boggled.

"Well, my sister recommends starting with water torture. But I think there's a better type of torture out there."

Avery's nerves are back. He presses his body against the doorjamb as he looks back over his shoulder at me and asks, "And that is?"

I pair a soft smile with my answer. "Kindness."

DOUBLE-EDGED SWORD

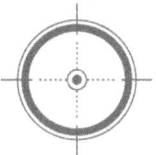

May 21
7:45 a.m.
Marseille, France

Avery

I'm not sure if this is the worst thing that's ever happened to me or the best. Royal was right when she called this torture—there's no better word for what's going on inside my mind right now.

Is there anything more amazing in the entire world than a gorgeous, nearly naked woman feeding you? On the flip side, is there anything worse than knowing she's an assassin who could kill you at any second?

My brain is spinning in circles right now as it tries to reconcile those two simultaneous realities and the only thing I'm sure of is that the scent of roses will forever bring me right back to this moment. The question of how long I'll get to remember things at all is still up in the air, hovering like the shimmering steam around us, silently suspended but with the thick power to infiltrate my lungs and make it hard to breathe.

I'm seated in the tub, and Royal hand feeds me the final bite of the world's most amazing fruit tart. As I suck the last bit of custard from her fingers a tiny bit drips onto my chest above the water line.

She stares at it, then at me, batting those long lashes of hers as she bites down on her lower lip in a way that makes my cock twitch under the water.

When she leans forward and her finger swipes across my pec, scooping up the tiny drop of custard, I'm left spell-bound, my heart jackhammering against my ribs.

She lifts her hand and glides her finger across my lips before pushing the digit inside. I let my tongue swirl across her fingerprint, wiping away the sweet custard at first, and then just suckling.

From the angle where she's kneeling on a bathmat just outside the tub, I can see the deliciously full shape of her breasts but the side view hides her light pink nipples, creating a profoundly erotic and teasing sight. I lash her finger gently with my tongue and can't help but imagine that I'm sucking something else. From the way her nostrils flare and she bites down harder on that tempting lip, she's imagining it too.

What are we doing? We should stop.

Neither of us does.

Instead, she pumps her finger slowly in and out between my lips, and my entire torso is pervaded by desire.

Disappointment rolls over me when she slowly withdraws her finger. I even use my teeth to gently scrape the sides as she retreats, in an effort to continue this sick game, whatever it is.

I don't think I've ever been involved in something so diabolically addictive.

My eyes remain glued to her as she turns, and I can't help but stare at her perky breasts when they finally come into view in profile as she reaches for the soap and a sponge. She grabs the two items before standing, her magnificent ass on display close enough that I could lean over and bite it.

The desire is so overwhelming I find my mouth opening and teeth snapping before I'm fully conscious of what I'm doing.

When she glances back, I simply hold her gaze.

We're teetering on the edge of something I don't understand here.

She fed me in relative silence, our looks questioning one another's intentions, expressions speaking more loudly than any words could have.

Nudity and attraction seem to be weapons she wields just as easily as a gun, and it makes me nervous.

Why did she shoot me down before only to bring me in here and build all this sexual tension? I don't understand.

This is outside my realm of expertise. So far outside that it might as well be in a different galaxy.

Growing up, I hated school and liked computers and money. I was drawn to hacking, then to the logistics side of illegal arms deals in the U.S.—but all that shit is done with men. Brutality and logic. Simple.

When Tyler recruited me to join his op after a bad deal singed my rep in the weapons business, I assumed that this would be more of the same. Violence. Hatred. Death and cash holding hands.

I've never dealt with such softness before.

I can viscerally feel her sweet looks cutting through my defenses. It doesn't seem to matter that I intellectually recognize that she's manipulating me; my dick still does a happy dance and knocks all my inhibitions down like dominoes.

It's particularly awful because I don't know her intentions.

Does she want to partner up? Or is she just toying with me before she kills me, like a cat batting around a mouse?

It's driving me mad with both lust and utter self-loathing.

Because for some idiotic, masochistic reason, I want her attraction to me to be real.

I want it to be real because she's the most beautiful woman I've ever seen and right now I'd give my left nut to have half her strategic skill.

She's so damn perfect, and I barely know a thing about her, other than the name she gave Tyler yesterday: Royal.

A name that only exists in whispers in dark web circles, information scarce and fleeting as if everyone's too scared to talk about her.

I don't want to be scared of her. I want to whisper her name in her ear and make her smile.

How pathetic is that?

Here she has me captive, and I'm not just a fucking prisoner, she has me captivated as well.

It might have been better if she'd just fucking shot me.

I stare up at her, gaze raking over her perfect form, that silky hair, aching to trace her flared hips, the tiny rise of her belly, her trim waistline, all of it—any of it. My eyes practically plead to let me touch her. I've never fucking hated handcuffs more.

She soaks in my agitated adoration with a beatific smile that would fit right in with any of the religious paintings in this ancient city. A veritable goddess of war.

Her voice is soft and calm, drifting over my skin like a caress when she says, "You can say no. But I'd like to wash you since you can't use your hands at the moment. Is that okay?"

Fuck.

Fuck.

She's asking for my permission? I'm completely at her mercy and I'm fully aware there's a loaded gun in the next room. A gun she hasn't touched but could get at any moment and we both know there's no way I'd be quick enough to stop her.

But she's asking me for permission? I squeeze my eyes closed as I try to process the myriad of emotions assaulting me right now, the largest of which is distrust. This has to be a trick.

"Avery. I'll be nice. I promise."

I open my eyes and try to pin her with a glare but I can't muster one up. I want to tell her that she's being too nice and that's a problem, but my tongue is stuck to the roof of my mouth, as if my hormones want to prevent me from saying something that might make this whole situation backslide.

Encourage her, My dick chimes in, becoming sentient and offers his wisdom. *Get her to climb in here with you. Play the nice game back.*

For once, he doesn't have a terrible idea. Either that or I'm desperate and at the end of my rope so even bad ideas seem better than no ideas.

Intent on my new course of action, I muster up a shy smile and nod at her.

I don't expect her to climb into the tub.

I'm rendered absolutely speechless when she leans forward and puts weight on my shoulders, those breasts dangling right in front of my eyes as she steps, one glorious leg at a time, into the water. Her climb in gives me a full, unobstructed view of her gorgeous body, all the way down to those lacy white panties, which have a very obvious wet patch on them. The sight sends my pulse into hyperdrive.

I quickly divert my eyes, but the damage is done and my lungs are suddenly unable to function properly.

Dammit.

This woman definitely knows what she's doing and she's definitely not playing fair. But her eyes, when I finally meet them, radiate a soft innocence, instead of the sultry seduction she absolutely knows she's pulling off.

Fine.

She wants to play nice?

I can play nice.

So fucking nice.

"Um, you want to sit? I can move," I offer, trying to channel some inner sitcom clueless dad energy.

She gives a lopsided grin that's so adorable it could melt ice cream. "Thanks. That's sweet."

I slide my legs toward my chest, water sloshing inside the tub as the chain attached to my ankles clinks and drags across the bottom. Royal settles in across from me, sinking into the water, obscuring my view of all her naughty bits—thank fuck.

The soap and washcloth, which she kept in one hand as she got in, now both are dunked beneath the water before emerging so that she can rub them vigorously together and work up a lather.

I let my gaze wander around the room instead of landing on the way she's pressed her breasts deliberately together or how they're jiggling from her efforts.

"So ... um. It feels strange to let you wash me when I don't even know anything about you. Can I ask innocent questions?"

"Is there such a thing?" She returns before giving a tinkling little laugh. "Sure. Why not? But I may not be able to answer."

"Favorite song?"

"Anything by Bring Me the Horizon," she responds quickly.

"No way. I love them too." I blink, stunned and yet pleased by the coincidence. "Good taste."

"Thanks. My favorite is Doomed."

For a second, I think she might be fucking with me, throwing out that title, but she blushes shyly as she sets the soap on the ledge of the tub and then, slowly, almost cautiously leans forward. "Is it okay if I start with your chest?"

I nod once, trying not to look down as she leans even further, not to notice how her body is curling over mine, or the feel of her fingertips through the warm sudsy rag as she drags it in soft circles over my skin.

I stare at the small window on the far side of the bathroom, trying to breathe slowly and evenly, trying not to inhale the soft scent of her hair.

Nice. We're playing nice and it's all just a game.

She moves from my chest to my arms, massaging my triceps as she washes them, lifting my hands and carefully dragging the rag over each and every finger.

I think I'm going to explode.

"Um ... so, what's your favorite pop?" I ask. "That's innocent enough right?"

"Pop? Soda pop?" she giggles, the rag pausing dangerously low on my abdomen.

"Yeah," I lick my lips and focus on one candle in the shower that's flickering, just barely hanging on—exactly like me.

"Such a Midwesterner," she croons as she drags the rag back up to my shoulder so she can glide it over my neck. She slips in the water a little, causing her thigh to graze my shin.

I've never felt skin so soft.

"I like root beer floats," I blurt out, trying to mentally picture one and get my dick to deflate in my underwear a bit. If she leans over any farther, she's definitely going to feel it and I'm pretty sure that will change the parameters of this whole "nice" lie we have going.

"Root beer floats are good. Orange Crush floats are better," she challenges as she slides the rag down my side, skimming a ticklish spot.

I jerk and writhe instinctively, causing her giggles to escalate into full-on belly laughs as a whole tsunami builds and rolls across the tub—a wave that bursts up the tub wall and catches her in the side of the face.

Her jaw drops and she stares at me for a moment, one half of her face dripping wet, hair soggy, and eyelashes beaded with water droplets. "I'm ... uneven." Something about her thin tone and the way her gaze becomes unfocused and distant tells me those two words are the truest thing Royal's ever said to me.

They aren't part of the game.

I see her stop breathing. Just stop completely. Almost as if she's starting to panic. As if being uneven is somehow a trigger for her.

I'm not sure exactly what's wrong, but I know something is causing this gorgeous, competent woman to begin to spiral before my eyes.

The sight hits all my protective instincts at once and I spring into action immediately. "Well, let's make you even then," I declare mischievously, bucking harder, and creating a second wave. Tangling our feet, I force her to fall forward and get wetter.

She ends up splayed across my chest, and even though I laugh heartily, I'm absolutely aware of every inch of our skin touching, and painfully aware of the handcuffs biting into my wrists behind my back when I want nothing more than to have my hands on her right now—though I honestly couldn't say if I'd use them to splash her more or strangle her.

"You!" Her outraged tone is playful as she wipes the water from her eyelashes. She uses my body to lever up and gives me a solid glare before cupping water in her hands and throwing it at me.

I barely close my eyes in time before it splashes against my face. I think she might have gotten a rose petal in there too because it feels like something's sticking to my cheek. My eyes pop open to see a cat-got-the-canary grin spreading across her face and the fire back in her eyes.

For some reason, seeing the fire there warms my belly.

"Hey! Unfair. I don't have hands!" I pout, keeping the game alive.

"Life's not—"

"Oh no you don't! Don't say it!" I writhe madly, creating waves that splash water onto the tile floor, making Royal slide and giggle as she tries to find purchase on something other than my slippery skin.

Mad laughter erupts from her as her arms swoop in waves, countering my attack and forcing some of the water back in my direction. I duck, dodge, and shit-talk her until I'm laughing so hard that my ribs hurt and the tub is half empty.

"Truce?" I gasp breathless at Royal, who's somehow sprawled halfway onto my stomach, swiping at her eyes again.

"Truce." She glances up at me and her voice gets husky and I think her answer might apply to more than just our little splash session.

It suddenly gets quiet enough in the bathroom that I can hear the distant sounds of traffic, and I recall that there's a world outside the two of us. For a second, I'd forgotten.

Royal stares at me for a long moment, considering, tilting her head.

"Tell me what's going on in that beautiful mind of yours," I prompt.

"This is my first kidnapping. I never knew they could be so fun," she admits.

"Your first *and last*," I growl, a sudden possessiveness erupting in my chest as wild and unpredictable as arcing electricity.

"What?"

"Nothing," I say, exhaling harshly and trying to hide my confusion over these sudden emotions behind a charming grin. "You're gonna have a hard time getting rid of me if *this* is your idea of kidnapping."

She dusts her shoulders off playfully for a second before swallowing hard and turning those big hazel eyes on full blast in my direction. "Does that mean you might be up for sex?"

Best. Kidnapping. Ever.

I don't ever want to go home.

TRIGGER FINGER

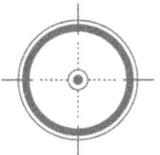

May 21
8:20 a.m.
Marseille, France

Royal

When a guy agrees to sex, it's always a good feeling, but when he whoops and says, "Hell fucking yes!" that good feeling multiplies by a factor of ten or whatever the mathy saying is.

Avery is so adorably enthusiastic that a little balloon filled with glee inflates inside my chest and I have to swallow a squeal. My heart speeds up to a frantic pace and my body tenses in excitement for what's about to come. Little shivers of delight travel down my spine and tangle in my lower belly, heating up.

"Okay then." We grin at each other like fools; it's hard to believe we were rivals-slash-enemies just a few measly hours ago. Right now, I'm pretty certain I'm living through every single high-school romance movie I've ever watched all at once smashed together. "We should chat logistics."

"I vote bed, not tub," he states.

"I mean about your cuffs. I want to trust you ... but, I also kinda want to control you." And I also kinda don't trust him even if I want to. I don't say that part aloud, but I figure it's a given in this whole dueling assassins sitch.

"Anything. I'll take anything you want."

He's so perfectly eager to please and give me control. I credit my torture techniques. Kindness has broken his will and turned him into my willing sexy-times playmate.

I'm gonna recommend kindness from now on to all the girls. It really does a number on men.

Who knew?

"First, we gotta get out of here." I stand, dripping water all over, and reach for the handcuff key, which I hid on the tray behind a jar of jelly just in case things went in this direction. I try very hard not to notice what a mess we've made of the floor or how twelve of the candles were wiped out by waves.

Fuck. A little tingle starts in my fingertips—the desire to clean.

I don't want my horny vibes ruined by my OCD right now, so I fix my gaze on Avery's face. His handsome face, that great jaw.

"I'm going to move your hands to the front and cuff them there, okay?" I tell him. "Then, I'm going to take you up on all those naughty things you offered earlier."

"I love this plan."

I laugh. "I think you'd love this plan if I told you I was going to make you lie over hot coals—"

"Nope. I'd agree to it so I could get laid. But I wouldn't love it. There's a difference."

When I'm done chuckling and rolling my eyes, we exchange another sappy set of smiles. I don't know if I could force my face into a frown right now even if I tried. It feels impossible.

"Lean forward."

He does as he's told, and I admire the toned muscles on his back as I undo the cuffs. "Take a minute to stretch," I instruct, reaching in to knead his neck, which I'm certain is sore from being stuck in the same position all night.

"Yes, that, right there," his appreciative moan when I hit a knot and start working it makes my core tighten in pleasure. That's the sort of sound I want to hear in just a minute when we're finally in bed.

Sooner than I would have expected, he thanks me for the massage and stands slowly, using the sides of the tub to push himself up, without letting me cuff him again.

I watch the beads of water sluice down his body, my heart rate fluttering like a bird taking flight when he turns and looks down at me.

The air crackles between us.

Vulnerability is probably etched all across my face because he could kill me right now. Reach over and grab my throat and just end me with the hands I just freed. My nerves prickle, perversely enchanted by the thought.

But Avery gifts me with a soft look and simply asks, "Hand me a towel?"

Our fingers brush when he takes the towel from me, and the tiny touch sends fire streaming through my veins.

He shucks his boxers, sliding them down his legs until they pool at his ankles, covering the chain between his feet. They'll just have to live there now because we've absolutely reached the limit of my trust boundaries, but also partly because I'm too entranced by the sight of his dick to worry about other practical things.

As dicks go, his is dicktacular.

It's long and thick, the base nestled in well-groomed hair, the shaft a soft rosy pink topped by a huge bulging cap. I lick my lips, because I'm so ready to feel that cock that I've daydreamed about inside of me. Waiting for him to dry off is the most delicious kind of erotic agony.

He grins tauntingly as rubs himself off with the towel, well aware of the fact that he's currently performing his own form of torture because he takes his time, slowly rubbing it in circles over his pecs, around his nipples, down his abs, swiping it across his back and over an ass that I might be able to bounce quarters off of.

By the time he dries his legs, and finally his dick, I'm openly panting.

Finished with the towel, he gives himself a few long strokes with his hand as he watches me.

Then, like the neat freak he supposedly is, he carefully folds the towel, laying it over the side of the tub before facing me, eyes scanning down my body with very obvious hunger. "I like my women wet, but ... you sure you don't want to dry off?"

If I did that, I'd have to take my eyes off him. My confidence in our sexy-times truce is already stretched as thin as it can go. I shake my head, though my fingers twitch and I avoid the mirror because I wouldn't be able to handle the mess I probably look like right now.

He nods as if he knows exactly what I'm thinking. But then he bites his lip and smiles before asking, "Ready to ride Big Thunder Mountain?"

His words immediately crack apart the gnawing need to fix my hair that was building inside of me. "You did *not* name your cock that!" I screech, half out of mirth and half out of horror.

"Nope. But it made you laugh," he retorts smugly as he sits on the ledge of the tub and carefully lifts his feet out of the bath, chain clinking and clanking clumsily. I watch him carefully blow out all the candles in the shower, and the few left still flickering on the flooded floor.

"Safety first," he states.

Safety.

"Fuck. I forgot condoms." All that shit I ordered—candles, breakfast, flowers, even contact solution for him because he didn't have on his glasses. What the hell was I thinking?

He stops and stares at me and I stare back at him, both of us pondering for a second if we're going to do the responsible thing and call this off. The tension ratchets up tighter and tighter until I don't know if I can breathe.

"Fuck it," I say. Sex with him is already unimaginably stupid so doing it unprotected is just the cherry on top of my idiot sundae.

He strides toward me with a hot look in his eyes, one that's a little wild and unhinged and utterly sexy as hell.

I stiffen, fear getting the better of me for a millisecond, wondering if I've made the wrong choice, if he doesn't actually suck at the manipulation game but earlier was all a ploy to make me think he sucked so that I'd develop a false sense of confidence.

My brain builds a wild conspiracy theory in less than two seconds and populates it with a million tiny people, all of whom are screaming that I'm a fool and he's going to grab me and smash my head into the sink.

He reaches toward me, and it takes everything in me not to duck or recoil, but to stand there and stare him down as if I'm not scared—as if I think I'm still in charge.

His hand passes by my neck and every hair on my body stands on end.

But he merely grabs a second towel from a shelf on the wall next to me, bringing it to his chest.

In under two seconds, I morph from stiff as a board to boneless jelly and I have to fight against the desire to expel a relieved breath. I don't want him to know just how scared he made me. I don't want him to know he has that kind of power.

I need to maintain my illusion of control, even if he's just made me aware of how much that is a delusion.

Our eyes trace lacy patterns over one another's faces, before meeting in an intense stare that I don't understand. I try to translate the look he's giving me, but I don't have words for it. I try to name the emotions swirling through his eyes but they're unnamable. I try to decipher his intentions, but I can't.

I'm simply lost in his gaze.

And then, my captive takes my hand.

My throat closes completely as he leads me back to the bedroom and stops to sit down on the mattress while I'm still standing. He places the towel on the bed beside him and, with a quick glance up at me first, almost as if he's asking permission, he dips his head toward me.

His lips brush my abdomen, right near my belly button, and my heart jumps up into my throat.

One kiss.

That's it.

He gives me one perfect, utterly submissive kiss.

Then I watch as Avery reclines back against the bed reaching for the second set of cuffs, the ones left dangling from when I freed him earlier and cuffed his hands behind his back with a single set. He grabs the lone silver circle still attached to the frame and fishes the other circle up from where it fell behind the pillow. Snapping the free side over his free wrist, he traps himself. Willingly.

Shock rolls through me at the sound of that click, at the metallic glide of the cuff as it slides down the metal post of the frame.

He's given me back control.

Given it to me when he could have taken it.

He's giving *himself* to me—in more ways than one.

My mouth opens and closes and opens again. My thoughts —my feelings—I'm trying to process all the implications of his actions, but I'm stuck. I'm a computer screen that's frozen, a car that won't start, the faucet that won't gush water. I'm a vending machine with a bag of Skittles trapped against the glass, refusing to fall.

Until it hits me.

I've been defeated at my own game.

Avery just won the kindness war.

I'm not even mad about losing.

"You can dry off now," he nods his chin toward the towel he carried in here and laid beside the bed.

Fuck.

Can he earn bonus points even after I've already lost?

I want to jump his bones.

Damn the itch underneath my scalp that tells me I need to dry off and fix the corner of the fitted sheet where it's come undone from his bucking earlier.

I quickly satisfy those aching physical needs before I strip off my wet panties, folding both items and putting them in a neat stack near the bathroom door, which I dutifully close. That room doesn't exist for me anymore.

I have to do that all the time at home, with my sister's rooms, which are utterly disgusting hair-raising pigsties.

I have to lock them away so that I don't go insane.

Turning around, I feel better, as if a weight has been lifted from my chest. In fact, staring at him makes me feel weightless.

I look at Avery and promise, "I'm going to give you the best orgasm you've ever had."

"Yeah?"

I prowl towards him, arching an eyebrow. "Yeah. I'm going to make sure you see stars."

"You're threatening me with a good time, but um...where's the follow-through? My dick's waiting." He makes his dick twitch against his belly.

Goof.

I climb onto the bed with a grin, straddling him, lowering my center so that it presses right against his hardness. God, he's so thick and warm and just the feel of him against me makes my body heat.

"We'll get there. But you promised me you'd make me scream three times first," I challenge, throwing his earlier bribe back at him as I lean forward.

"I'm a man of my word," he says, though his words and look are gentle instead of hard, mellow instead of daring. His eyes trace my face with a look that feels like velvet rubbing lightly over my skin.

I'm so glad I'm a huge fucking idiot.

So glad I took this chance.

I stare at his eyes for a second, trying to understand what he could possibly be thinking, before I give up, tilting my head and closing the distance between us because I can't wait another millisecond to claim him.

I kiss Avery for the first time, giving him an open-mouthed, soft kiss that's the opposite of all my naughty teasing because I want to remember my first kiss with this man as sweet for some reason.

I've never cared about that before, but to be honest, the hours I've spent *thinking* about kissing Avery are probably more than all the hours I've spent *actually* kissing any one guy in my entire life.

I've had a long-ass wait leading up to this kiss and I want it done right.

As I press my lips to his, I cup the sides of his cheeks and the tiny bit of stubble he has from one night without shaving is minimal; it tickles the palms of my hands.

My tongue swoops across the seam of his mouth, and I'm all aglow with this giddy delight that I didn't know could accompany kissing. I've only known kisses—after that first exploratory kiss—to be hormone-driven precursors to sex. A quick system check to ensure all engines are go. But this kiss opens a whole new set of possibilities, an entirely new definition.

Merriam Webster watch out.

Avery's mouth is gentle under mine but still participative. He's docile yet receptive, his tongue placidly stroking mine back. He kisses me almost leisurely, like we have all the time in the world. This kiss doesn't feel like foreplay. It's not an appetizer —he treats it like the main event. It's magical in and of itself and I'm astounded. Kisses before have been sloppy, naughty, disappointing, or hotter than Hades. I wanted this one to be sweet. And it is. But it's also somehow so much more than that.

This kiss is reverent.

I feel like I'm discovering the beautiful serenity of Yellow-stone when all my life I've been vacationing at theme parks. There's no noise, flashing lights, stomach-dropping sensa-tions or fancy tricks. There's just Avery and me, existing in the same space, breathing one another in. There's some-thing magnificent about simply appreciating a moment and allowing it to exist, not rushing it in order to seek thrills. About simply appreciating another human being.

I press closer to Avery, letting this kiss soak into my very bones.

Why this is so emotional, I don't really understand, but a tear forms in the corner of my eye that's completely absurd because it doesn't fit with what I'm feeling, which is tender wonder.

Too intense.

This is too intense.

I start to pull back from the kiss, slightly panicked. But Avery, as if he's a damn mind reader, immediately changes the tone of the kiss. His tongue gets more aggressive. His teeth start to nip. His free hand comes up to press against my lower back, just above my ass, the metal of the unused cuff dangling against my hip and his pinky finger teasing my cleft. A tiny shiver of pain glides through me because of the still-healing bullet bruise from his teammate.

Ok. This.

This I can handle.

I wrench my lips away when he's mid-bite, partially because I love the sting and partially to regain control because I feel like I'm spinning wildly through space without gravity to hold me down.

"Did I give you permission to touch me?" I growl, pulling back and giving my best dominatrix impression. I'm not sure it's any good, because that's not the kind of porn I normally watch, but I give it the ole college try.

I narrow my eyes and keep from smiling and everything, though I think my lips twitch up a couple times and ruin the effect.

His hand immediately drops but the expression on his face doesn't seem to be disappointed. The expression on his face is Christmas-morning-perfect-gift awe.

Yeah. I'm pretty sure Avery likes his women heavy-handed.

"You can touch me," I clarify, leaning back down to nip at his lips because I want to drink that expression right from his face. "But you only get one finger. Your trigger finger."

"That sounds like a challenge," he murmurs, leaning forward and nuzzling my neck.

"It is. Think you can handle it?"

"Oh, I know I can." He brings his pointer finger back to the seam of my ass and traces down gently before his finger glides further and finds the bottom edge of my folds. I'm soaked for him and there's absolutely no hiding it. "Mmmm," he murmurs.

"Lay back now. I want to fuck your tongue," I order.

His hand drifts to the side as he complies, arranging himself farther down on the pillows so that I'll have plenty of room for my knees.

I crawl up over him, surprised by how much the sight of his arm chained to the bed turns me on.

I glance down at his face one last time, but his eyes are purely focused on the prize and he's licking his lips, either in anticipation or else to get ready to do a damn fine job of pussy eating.

Definitely don't want to ruin his headspace.

Ha.

*Head*space.

I wrap my fingers around the iron posts of the headboard, suppressing a little grin about my random thoughts.

Then I lower myself onto his face.

His tongue traces up my center and the heat and friction instantly sending pinpricks of pleasure through me. Avery's tongue gets up a rhythm that leaves me dazed, unable to focus on anything other than the feel of him.

My hips start to gyrate of their own accord, moving back and forth as my knuckles cinch tighter around the bars I'm clasping.

Yes..

Oh yes.

Yes!

Avery's lips find my clit and he sucks it into his mouth, at the same time using that single digit to trace along my seam. He completes several circuits that have me shaking my head and gritting my teeth and muttering, "Fuck. Fuck me. Fuck me."

I'm really articulate when I'm horny.

Sue me.

Avery doesn't seem to mind that I've reverted to elementary-level communication skills. Like the good lover I suspect he is, he complies with my request. He uses his single finger to penetrate me. He pumps in and out of me, my wetness making his glide easy, the steady motion of his finger heating me to nuclear-fallout levels as he strokes over and over, back and forth.

My body starts to jerk, and the wall grows brighter before my eyes; everything lights up as my senses go into overdrive and an animalistic, mindless fervor overtakes me.

I come undone, my head falling backward, my gaze rolling up to the ceiling as my breath escapes in short pants and fierce howling sensations race across my spine and through my mind.

When my body calms and my muscles unclench, Avery slows for a second. I move to slide down, out of position, but his face chases after me, lips latching on harder to my clit, compelling me to freeze as my lady bits stretch in a way I didn't know could feel so good.

He starts the process all over again and I'm helpless, unable to defend myself against this delectable assault as he forces another orgasm to wrack my body until I'm humping against his mouth, writhing on his face as one of my hands abandons the bedframe in order to tweak my own nipple.

The spinning vortex of a second orgasm is always more intense than the first and I'm swept up into it, sounds torn right from my vocal cords and flung into the air at random as I abandon all conscious thought and my mind flees my body to float on some other plane of existence.

After I crash down, feeling as scattered as a debris field after a tornado, I shove my palm to his face, forcing it to the side.

"No more," I rasp, in an effort to defend my overly sensitive nerve endings.

"But I promised three," Avery's tone is smug, as it should be.

"Look. You win the trophy. First place. Okay? Best pussy eating ever," I tell him, hissing as he slowly extracts his finger from inside of me. "I need a lil' break." I struggle to use my limp limbs and sore hands to climb down from my riding spot. My left palm has an imprint from the pattern on the headboard bars and my legs are just about as stable as flan.

Do I begrudge his chuckle? Not at all. Nope. I'm totally in post-orgasm derp. Goofy grin. Half-formed thoughts.

"Derp is the best," I murmur, nosing him dreamily.

"What?"

"Let me kiss your pussy-licking mouth," I tell him, tapping his cheek so he'll turn his face toward me.

He indulges me and we exchange some sloppy kisses for a minute, where I taste how hot he got me. My body slowly recovers enough for my hands to become semi-functional again, and when they are, I trail them down his body, tracing over that soft happy trail I spent so much time admiring. "Your turn," I say, as I grip his shaft.

"Hey, what about the one finger rule? Shouldn't that apply to you too?"

"Tell me you want a blowjob without telling me you want a blowjob," I tease, grinning up at his pretty face.

"Fine. I want a blowjob."

I snicker as I maneuver myself around so that I'm on top of him again before kissing my way down his torso, deliberately stopping at a few of my favorite freckles along the way.

Then I kneel between his knees and admire how he looks, stretched out before me, hair floppy, completely comfortable in this moment despite the fact that later we're going to have a lot to unpack.

But if he can shed all those rivalry worries, shuck them off and shove them behind a door marked "not now" then so can I.

Leaning down, I take the head of his cock into my mouth and swirl my tongue around. Smooth, silky, and hot—his dick's temperature runs warmer than most of the other guys I've been with and I have to say, that makes my thighs tighten in anticipation. I'll bet he's going to feel so good once he's inside of me.

Popping off the head, I lick the underside of his shaft and am rewarded when I hear a faint moan of appreciation. That prompts me to palm his balls with one hand, circle the bottom of his shaft with the other and then take him into my mouth, bobbing up and down as he arches up slightly, lifting off the sheets. The chain rustles against the mattress behind me and I think he's flexing his feet.

That's right.

I'm toe-curlingly good at this.

All too soon, Avery's hand is reaching down, stroking my hair, and his words are drifting over me. "Come up. I need to fuck you now, Royal. Come up here and ride me."

I swallow him down one last time, pushing myself as far as I can go, which isn't all the way down his shaft—tapping my tongue along the underside of his cock, trying to tempt a tiny bit of precum out of him.

My efforts are rewarded when a salty taste fills my mouth, though suddenly his free hand is on my shoulder, roughly pulling me up.

"Don't. Want. To. Come," he rasps, as if each word is hard to form.

Apparently, he gets a pre-orgasm derp—how cute.

I grin and climb up over him, my hands dipping, imprinting on the mattress as I loom over him on all fours, gazing down into his luminous blue eyes for a moment before I use my right hand to reach behind me and grab his dick. I pump once before slowly aligning his body with mine and then I sink carefully onto him.

Fuck.

"God, yes. You feel so good," he whispers.

"I feel what?"

"Good."

I agree with him, the stretch is epic. But I want to coax more dirty words from the man who rattled off so many earlier.

"What feels good, Avery?"

"Your pussy."

"Full sentences," I coach.

"Your pussy feels so good on my cock that I'm ready to explode. There are stars behind my eyes and it's taking everything in me right now not to grab onto your hips and hold you still as I fuck you deep as I can get—so that I come inside you and breed that fucking cunt." All of that filthy talk spills out in a single stream, leaving both of us breathless at the end.

Damn boy.

That's what I'm talking about.

If I wasn't already soaked, I would be now. His dick slides in nice and deep and I don't give myself time to adjust because I want to ride that edge of pain and pleasure this morning. I start to move immediately, rolling my hips and rocking back and forth on his cock as a small breeze darts in through the open window and wraps around our heated bodies, pebbling our skin.

His free hand comes to my hip, simply stroking softly, until I start to fuck him harder, with more abandon. As my breasts start to bounce, his gaze becomes glued to them. His hand darts up and he cups the right one, feeling it slap against his palm as I move. I use his dick, his balls, his pelvis, grinding against him as I seek out another orgasm.

There. I get an angle and a rhythm that works just right and the inside of my mind spins like a kaleidoscope—the world starts to change shape. The shadows along the walls, the bedframe—the entire room becomes a blur as I strain toward that distant feeling which glimmers just beyond my reach.

I start to breathe shallowly as I move faster and faster.

Then Avery drops my breast and his fingers magically reappear near my pussy, I don't know how—I'm too far gone to notice details. But he swipes along either side of my clit, lightly brushing the sensitive bundle of nerves.

I come with a scream and start to clench around him.

"Fuck. Fuck. Fuck! Where do you want me to come?" he asks frantically as his hips start to piston underneath mine.

"Inside me! Come inside me!"

"But—"

"I want you to breed me like you said. Hold me and shoot deep and hard into my pussy and fill it with your cum until it's dripping out on either side of your dick."

"Are you—"

"Fucking do it, Avery!" I growl, my hand reaching down to mingle with his and rubbing my clit in order to draw out the tingling, sparkling, radiant orgasm still flickering inside me.

His hand goes to my hip in a punishing grip and his fingers dig in so hard that I know I'll have bruises there later, but it only makes me grit my teeth in satisfaction as his breath catches and he strains against me—silent as he comes.

I use my muscles to clench down on him and draw his orgasm out, watching the way his mouth falls open and his eyes close as he savors the sensation—feeling a tiny bit of pride, and maybe even something a bit softer, at the fact that I'm able to unravel him.

When he finally slumps back down to the bed with a sigh, I follow him, pillowing my cheek against his chest just like I did last night. Just like last night, I listen to his heartbeat. Only now, it's wildly thudding against my ear.

I have my first ever post-sex cuddle in a twin bed with a man I've taken captive. And even though he's the one tied to the bed, I feel like I might be the one who just got put in chains.

That sex was...

That sex was...

There are no words.

"Are...are you okay with what just happened?" he asks, hesitantly.

"Shouldn't I be asking you that question? You're the kidnapee."

"I'm fine. But the end..." his tone is still so thoughtfully, respectfully worried.

Avery is too much of a gentleman for this assassin shit. And I'm a terrible kidnapper because I don't even have the heart to torture him. "I'm on the pill. Normally I use condoms too, though."

"Oh. Oh good." His hand comes up to wrap around my back, extra handcuff sliding along with him as he strokes my spine. "Yeah, we'll do that next time."

He said next time.

Next. Time.

I turn my face further into his stomach to hide the smile that arches across my lips, as bright and brilliant as a rainbow.

LOOSE CANNON

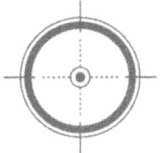

May 21
9:30 a.m.
Marseille, France

Royal

I t's time for ... *Let's Make a Deal.*

Brought to you by our local sponsor, the Belladonnas. Want to get out a dirty stain on society? Then you want Belladonna Fresh, the newest, most advanced formula of assassin out there. Belladonna cuts the crime in half the time—I should have gone into marketing. If only Man didn't want to keep his whole operation under wraps ... Think about the potential. He'd call it cheesy but cheese sells. Those annoying jingles you can't get out of your head? Case in point.

Sigh.

I stare at the screen of my burner phone. I've gotten side-tracked again in my attempt to decide what to say to Tyler, my brain wheeling off in random directions instead of focusing.

Cleaned up (Avery was a gentleman and took point cleaning up the bathroom and making it habitable again so I could step inside), in new clothes rush delivered right to my hotel door, and reclining against Avery's chest—it would seem like the perfect morning.

After all, Avery looks insanely cute in the baby blue polo, khakis, and boat shoes I got for him. Perfect tourist look. Meanwhile, I'm wearing a floral, mock neck bodycon dress that hugs my curves, along with some strappy sandals with just a smidge of heel. I want to look good for the upcoming prisoner swap but the shoes are a compromise because I still need to be able to run.

Just in case.

My so-called prisoner stares out the window as we cuddle, listening to some angry French people chattering on the street below, the speech too rapid to sound like anything more than undulating noise to me.

Meanwhile, I'm regretting that all the years of training in our mansion didn't include hostage negotiations. But...what kind of assassins take hostages? Why take one when you could just kill them? Easy peasy.

Except the thought of a dead Avery makes me feel nauseous.

I'm going to have to bumble through arranging this meet-up, just like I've been fumbling through this whole assignment.

I chew my lower lip to the point of pain as I start and erase several messages.

I don't have a great opening line.

Hey, let me in on this kill because I slept with your step-brother and want to do you both at the same time ... just doesn't have a convincing ring to it.

But the clock is ticking.

Tyler's only going to wait on Yegor for so long before he guts him and just straight up comes after me.

I decide to start simple.

Carefully tapping at the screen and rereading it twice to make sure I don't have a super helpful autocorrect error, I text:

Hey. It's Royal. We met at the flower shop the other day.

WTF? Where is he? Tyler's return text is almost immediate, and I have to say, it's a little aggressive. No hi, how are you, it was nice making out with you. Where are his manners?

I mean, Avery seems to have them, so I can't blame Tyler's stepmother.

Maybe some men are born with good dicks and others are just born dickheads.

Yeah, that seems like it could be a thing.

I'm gonna call it a thing.

I'm gonna put a bullet in your brain. His next text is even more hostile.

I'd rather you shoot something else inside me. ;)

SHOW ME FUCKING PROOF OF LIFE.

Damn. Not even two seconds for playful banter? He must really be wound up tight. Tyler needs to have a morning jerk-off routine. I do. It really helps clear your head for the rest of the day.

Of course, hot sex does that even better.

"Your brother really loves you," I tell Avery, scanning over the angry text a second time.

"Nah, he drags me along because he doesn't think I'm competent enough to keep myself alive." His shrug makes his body undulate underneath my head. "Guess he might be right." His tone holds a bitter sort of resignation.

I turn to look up at him. "Hey, I know a few things you're very competent at." I wink, earning a soft smile and a caress on my lower back. "Besides, I got lucky with that dart. You nearly had me."

"I'm glad it all worked out," he responds, fingers digging into my hip a little.

Oh, Avery. So sweet. I smile and turn back around, nestling into him. But he's wrong. It hasn't all worked out yet because I'm pretty sure his brother's going to try to slit my throat. And not by stabbing me in the mouth with his dick.

I decide that the best course of action is to soothe Tyler's worries about his stepbrother so that we can skip over all this worry drama and get to real talk.

"Smile for the camera," I tell Avery, before lifting my phone and taking a selfie of the two of us snuggling, no cuffs in sight because I took them off after that amazing round of sex. Apparently, I'm that girl. I can be sexploited.

He's good. I send that text along with the picture.

"I'm better than good," Avery reads the text over my shoulder as he reaches up to play with my hair, twisting it around his finger. "I can't wait to see this when you go back to the natural red."

I tamp down on the fluttery euphoria that erupts whenever he mentions some little future interaction between us, which he's been doing for the past hour during our random wandering conversation, but every time I seem to get a handle on it, he brings something else up and *pop*, it comes back just like a weasel.

I force myself to stay focused on work, because I've probably already pushed out the timeline with Yegor as far as Tyler's willing to go. *We need to meet.*

I want to hear his voice first.

Oh, Tyler's being bossy.

But I gave him what he wanted. It takes me a second, and then I realize ... I wonder if he's pissed about that picture. Is he jealous?

A sense of anticipation has me tightening my grip on the phone and I can't decide if what I'm feeling is a bit of fear or attraction at the prospect that Tyler might be harboring a little covetous fury. I rub my thighs together and heat flares to life between them—providing me with a very clear emotional winner.

Yeah.

Jealousy is hot.

His mouth's a little preoccupied right now, I text, hoping to get a rise out of the other assassin.

"You're poking the bear." Avery comments, and I can just tell he's shaking his head at me.

"Think if I get him pissed enough, he might *eat me*?" I tease back emphasizing those last two words, before clarifying exactly where I stand for Avery, because it's only fair. "Heads up. I want both of you."

"What?"

"I want to fuck you and Tyler ... at the same time." I look up at him then, my cheek pillowed on his chest.

He stops breathing. Avery becomes still as stone and just as quiet.

Am I asking too much?

He avoids eye contact as he tries to process what I've just thrown at him, gaze flitting from the ancient TV I haven't bothered to turn on, to an ugly print of Paris, over to the window.

Crap.

Is he one of those one-girl forever, happily-ever-after believers?

"Hey, no pressure. If you haven't done the threesome thing before, I get it. I'm not talking guy on guy action, though. Of course, you might not be into spit-roasting—"

"Fuuuck, Royal. Stop talking or we're gonna have a second round of unprotected sex again right here right now," he groans, abandoning my hair to run his hand down the front of his face.

Relief glides through me, though his words do send a little spark up from my pussy that I have to tamp down, because right now, I need to light a fire under Tyler's ass, not one in my loins.

I press my lips together to hide a smile and turn away, giving Avery time to process what I've proposed. I'm not sure if he's fully on board with the reality of the threesome situation, but at least the fantasy of it is hot enough to make him threaten me with sex. That's a good sign.

My eyes go back to the screen, to find that Tyler has sent me a series of texts.

You're fucking hilarious.

You'd better not be touching my brother.

DO YOU HEAR ME?

Ohh, I get all-caps tingles. He's mad.

You'd rather I touch you? I type.

The phone rings ominously and when I check the caller ID it says Unknown. That's a lie. I know exactly who's on the line when I answer.

I hit the green button to accept the call and breathily say, "Y-yes? Yes! Yes!" Pretty sure my fake-orgasm skills are on point because I think I can hear Tyler punching something. A table. A wall. Maybe even Yegor.

Yeah, he jelly.

"Goddammit, give the phone to my brother."

I chuckle, amused with myself. "Fine. But after you have proof of life, we have some important matters to discuss."

I sit up and turn on the bed so that I'm facing the headboard before handing the phone over to Avery. I can't hear what Tyler says, but his anger is loud enough to blare through the speakers.

"Yeah ... No. I'm fucking fine. Better than ... yeah. None of your business." Avery's expression goes from calm to annoyed to downright pissed off.

That's when Tyler really raises his voice, and I can hear every single word. "YOU FUCKED THE ENEMY!"

Nope. Not gonna let him chew his brother out like that.

I snatch the phone away from Avery's ear, noting the burning pink color of his cheeks, before putting it to my own. "I'm not the enemy. Merely a rival. And need I remind you whose tongue was down my throat the other day? Don't act like you're any better."

"I'm going to wrap a rope around your neck—"

"Change neck to wrists and you've got yourself a deal," I quip.

There's no noise for a moment, then a rough clatter interspersed with static hits my ear. I cover up the microphone and exchange a glance with Avery. "Pretty sure he just threw the phone," I state happily.

He shakes his head. "You really don't want to get him this mad."

I waggle a duck-lipped expression back and forth as I pretend to consider his advice. "Pretty sure I do."

He clucks his tongue in response.

I hang up before I explain, "Men who are mad make mistakes, sweetheart. And I want him to make mistakes."

"Why?"

I don't tell Avery, because I don't quite think we're in one another's inner circles. I mean, he's been in *my* inner circle ... but the other kind, the mental circle ... takes a little more than an orgasm.

I text a meet-up address and time to Tyler, licking my lips in anticipation.

Because somewhere in the back of my head, I still kind of want to claim this kill for myself. Not for the money, or because Yegor deserves it, but to see the look on Tyler Monroe's face when I do.

God, that fury would be volcanic. It would be natural-disaster-level animosity.

It would be so fucking hot.

POWDER KEG

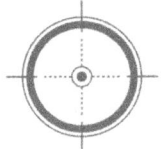

May 22
10:12 p.m.
Marseille, France

Royal

I t's twenty minutes until Tyler arrives and I feel all kinds of girlish first-date/last-date jitters. I'm super excited to see him, but not exactly certain I'm going to live through the encounter.

My fingers waggle back and forth nervously in my elbow-length black gloves as I rearrange the table for four set out on the deck for the eightieth time—straightening a silver spoon.

Deep breath, girl. You've got this.

God, I hope I've got this.

I better have this, or I'm not the only person who's going to die tonight.

I've done my hair in big loose curls, and I changed from my dress into something more suited for the four-bedroom yacht I commandeered about an hour ago, Avery providing the assist.

He's actually quite the eye candy in the suit I had delivered to match my dress.

I figured if I'm going down tonight, it's going to be in style.

If Tyler's going to make me a corpse, at least I can be a pretty one.

Gosh, sometimes I have such bad ideas.

Maybe I should have let this kill go—but walking away would leave a permanent itch inside my brain. I've never not finished a job before. And I really do want to see Tyler's furious face when I steal the kill out from under him ... but only if it's a furious pre-fuck-me face, not if it's a pre-murder-me face.

I'm worried about the latter right now.

One kiss does not allies make.

On the flip side of that, a kidnapping and six rounds of hot sex, because we kept getting distracted whenever we touched yesterday, does seem to have made allies out of Avery and me. More than allies. Who would have thought —forty-eight hours ago--that would be the case?

I look over at the handsome assassin next to me and move toward him, needing the reassurance of our connection. I lift my fingers and fiddle unnecessarily with his tie and pocket square, which perfectly match my dress.

We look amazing together.

And we worked in such unexpected synchrony earlier today. I was a little shocked, because I've always worked alone. Always. That's how Belladonnas are programmed to work.

I started out worried, because I'm very particular about how things should be done, but Avery was very easy-going and yet methodically did as I asked. From the quick robbery at the museum, to the visit to the costume shop, all the way to taking over the *La Sirène* here, he's been stunningly helpful.

He totally distracted the sweet old lady who was waiting on the dock with some suitcases while I snuck onboard and knocked her husband out. Then he chloroformed her gently before we tied them up and left them in the cabin of a different ship.

Their new boat is a little smaller than this one, but we need the space more than they do. I hope we do, at least.

I smooth down the green silk gown I'm wearing, though my opera gloves dampen my ability to tell whether I'm doing much good or not. My hair—at Avery's insistence—is back to red but not a natural color—that would require more than a quick box at the local grocery store.

"Stop fidgeting. You look amazing." He comes over and plants a gentle kiss on my forehead.

He doesn't help my tummy flutters—nor does the fact that both of us might die if I don't pull this negotiation off just right.

No pressure.

No thick guilt clogging the back of my throat with a horrid, acidic taste. But I have to do this. I have no choice.

"Avery, you know you're special, right?" I tell him, taking a step closer. The sun is setting, painting the water and his blond hair orange, casting a magical glow around us and I soak in his handsome features as I trace a finger over the strong line of his jaw. The boards underneath our feet tilt back and forth, rocked gently by the peaceful waves.

He kisses the tip of my nose. "So are you. Don't worry. I won't let them hurt you. This is the start of something good."

He's so confident the guys will want to work with me. Or at least let me live for his sake.

I'm not; not at all.

All my cocky confidence during my phone call with Tyler yesterday has leaked out of my pores.

Head swimming, I turn and grab the unopened wine bottle. Fuck waiting. I need to be drunk for this. I struggle with it for a second, trying to manually remove the cork, before Avery sweetly takes the bottle from my hand.

"Here. Let me. I'm sure they have a wine opener in the galley." He strides off and I watch the way his shoulders fill out his suit.

If only things were different.

God, his pickle has left me in such a pickle.

If I weren't attached, this would be easy. But now ... I kinda want things I've never wanted before. Like a team. Regular fuck buddies. And all the sweet tender looks from Avery that make me feel as fluffy and light and airy as cotton candy.

But Man has taught me to be a realist. My happy ending is only one possible outcome here and not even the most likely one. I have to plan for contingencies.

And I need to make sure I get this kill more than I need anything else.

The second Avery's out of sight, I reach into my glove and pull out a tiny bag containing several dozen belladonna berries I gathered the other day at the flower shop. Thanks to Harlow, I know all about these pretty little babies, which also go by the name nightshade. Unfortunately, I haven't mastered growing a plant myself yet, they're tricky little sweethearts and take a tender touch. My travel schedule for work doesn't really let me give them the attention they need.

But one day ...

If I live through the night, that is.

I quickly dump the bag of berries over the salad from the catered meal I had delivered. The rest of the food is in covered dishes, but the smell of the duck confit drifts out from the plates and mingles with the saltwater scent of the sea.

I have to hedge my bets if Tyler proves to be an asshole.

Be a hot, throbbing dick and not an asshole, I plead to the sky as I mix the berries in with the blueberries already in the salad. *Let this work out. Let him give me the kill and he can take the cash.*

I've just tossed the bag overboard and am standing at the railing, staring at the marina when Avery returns with the open bottle and a wide grin.

He pours me a blood-red glass and hands it to me with a flourish that tells me he waited tables at some point. "Madame."

"Merci." I take a big gulp. The wine immediately warms the back of my throat.

Avery looks down at me with concern. "Don't be nervous."

"Is this what it feels like meeting the family for the first time? Like you're facing a firing squad? I feel terrible for anyone who's ever done it," I exhale and try to use slow, deep breathing to calm my heart—which is currently ricocheting around between my ribs. "Of course, their firing squads aren't so literal."

"Look. Tyler focuses on marks. He doesn't just go around murdering random people." Avery's hand comes to my upper arm and his thumb traces a gentle line there, trying to soothe me.

I glance up at his soft expression and melt a little inside. I love how we met ... to be honest, it might be the only way we would ever have gotten together because it's just not my M.O. to date and do all the ooey-gooey stuff, but right now I hate how we met because it might make us both very dead.

"Yeah, what about Colt?" I query. From what I know about the third member of their merry little band of killers, Colt is cocky and slightly unhinged. I know he was in basic training with Tyler and they were deployed together for a bit, though they were in different squads. Whereas Tyler's group got sent to Iraq and captured, Colt's was sent into the mountains of Afghanistan to rout out groups who were hiding in caves and firing on planes. I couldn't find documentation after that, not until his dishonorable discharge for punching a Captain. The reason why is a mystery.

Beyond that, Colt doesn't have social media—which is smart but also frustrating. It makes it impossible for me to dive into his head and determine his likes and dislikes from a distance. How am I supposed to judge him if he isn't posting about his favorite meal or the one time a drive-through worker was an asshole to him?

"Hmm," Avery's reticence is not at all comforting. "Yeah. Maybe you should shoot him again. Just a little though."

I bring a hand up but stop before I bury my face in it because it will smear my makeup. I can't be distracted by stupid OCD things like uneven eyeshadow tonight, not when Avery basically just admitted that the one guy on their team who actually shot me is going to have zero qualms taking me out.

"What do you know about him?"

"Um. Nothing useful," he tells me.

"Anything. I'm desperate," I urge.

Avery rubs the back of his neck as he stares out across the water and thinks. "He likes the Cowboys and hates onions. Has a bike."

"A bike? Like a spandex, Peloton-lover kind of bike?" The mental image I'm suddenly in possession of is like, super un-hot. The idea of Colt in a bike helmet and those tight shorts is labia-shriveling.

"No. A motorcycle."

I put a relieved hand on my chest. "Oh, thank God. I thought I was gonna have to cross him off the to-be-fucked list."

He chuckles before glancing down at me and doing a double take. "You're serious?"

"Well, I mean, wouldn't it mess up Triple X mojo if I slept with only one or two of you?" I click my tongue.

He stares at me for a long moment as if he's not certain whether I'm joking or serious.

"Are you picturing it right now?" I murmur, stepping closer to him, so that his thigh is between my legs and the silk of my dress glides luxuriously over my skin. "Colt holding me in place, fucking my face while Tyler spits on his dick and finger fucks my ass to get it ready for him? You, underneath me, bucking up into my pussy...all of you using me for your pleasure at the same time. And then all of you eating all the cum dripping out of me after...giving me orgasm after orgasm until you're ready for round two?"

I brush my gloved hand over the front of his trousers. He's hard as a rock. I can't blame him. My panties are now a sodden mess and I wish more than ever for that slim hope I'm holding onto to come to fruition because damn, I'm good at painting a dirty fantasy.

I take a deep breath and step back, leaving both of us panting. "I want that. But...it's not up to me whether it happens." Not completely anyway, though I'll do my damnedest to make it happen.

I glance over at the dock again and see a shadowy figure approaching.

Great.

Dammit.

Yay but also, I might puke.

Tyler walks with a slight limp, though his back is ramrod straight and proud. He's wearing an all-black suit tonight, paired with a black shirt, and it only highlights how he's gone prematurely gray.

He hasn't covered up his scar, which means he's not here to play games.

Or ... maybe because I told him I liked it. I do like it. I love the way the shadows catch on it and give half of his face a dangerous, almost skeletal vibe as the sun starts to dip below the horizon.

I bite my lips in anticipation as he spots us on the deck of the yacht, where Avery and I are standing in a puddle of light by the round dining table.

While I love seeing Tyler ... I hate the fact that he's here alone.

My throat dries out and I set my wineglass down on the table as I try to work through the implications of what that could mean.

The fact that Colt, a wildcard in this whole poker game we're playing, isn't with him is good for me. Unless, of course, Colt's up in some sniper position somewhere.

Of course, someone would need to babysit Yegor. I cross my fingers and hope Colt got that lucky job instead. Running my tongue across the front of my bottom teeth nervously, I watch Tyler board the ship and Avery go to greet him.

I should have bought four more bottles of wine for tonight.

I stay put, letting them converse quietly, not wanting to put Tyler on his back foot and make his hackles rise immediately. It takes everything I've got not to duck behind the table myself and take up a defensive position. All my years of training scream that I should have a gun on me right now. But I don't.

When Tyler's dark gaze flits over to me I know it's time.

Time to act.

Act tough and calm and confident.

I stand as still as a statue, trying to find my poise.

Avery claps Tyler on the shoulder and then leaves to go do all the things we'd previously discussed, the boring tasks to unmoor the ship and get us moving while Tyler stays, at a distance, just staring at me.

Dammit. He's not coming over here.

Heat rises along the sides of my neck and unfurls along my cheeks, and I feel like we're in an old cowboy western for a moment.

A standoff.

My nerves only double when Tyler slowly removes his jacket and I see a gun in his shoulder holster as he strides slowly closer, eyes scanning my body—in appreciation or in a search for weapons, I can't tell.

I reach up slowly and he immediately drops his suit jacket and grabs his gun, drawing it, aiming, and cocking in under ten seconds.

Fuck.

He's so good at that and it's super hot.

I have to lick my lips, but the bolt of attraction surging through me does good things to me. Great things for me, because it unlocks my muscles and allows me to finally move with confidence. For my sluggish brain to finally start thinking again.

"I'm just going to show you that I don't have any weapons on me," I say breathily.

"Nice and slow," he instructs, gesturing with his gun.

I keep reaching up nice and slow as I hear Avery start up the engine, the purr of the yacht rumbling up through the soles of my heels.

Carefully pulling aside my hair, I undo the button that holds the halter top of the gown together at the back of my neck. My dress falls into a green puddle of silk at my feet. I'm only wearing lacy white panties, my elbow-length black gloves and my black heels as I step out of the pool of fabric. My nipples pebble from the light breeze in the air and the ice-cold look in his eyes.

I wonder what he sees, what I look like, fire-red curls falling down my back, milky skin exposed to him, standing under the deck's spotlight as the moon rises overhead. I hope he likes the view.

"See?" I softly hold up my hands, palms up. "Nothing." My heart leaps into my throat, making a valiant effort to escape my body as I slowly spin and give him my back to show I'm not hiding anything. My palms instantly coat themselves with sweat and my thighs are quaky.

I don't know that I've ever felt this vulnerable in my entire life. I swear that my entire back is covered in goosebumps and my pulse is less of a thudding beat and instead more of a rush of river rapids barreling toward a waterfall right now.

I suck in a deep breath while my back is to him and rapidly blink away the nervous tears that have spontaneously erupted in the corners of my eyes. Buck up, body. It's show-time. Nervous meltdowns will have to wait.

Finishing my turn, I bat my eyelashes at Tyler and manage what I hope is a sultry grin. "Satisfied?"

"Far from it," he growls, voice laced with an emotion I can't decipher.

With Tyler, I find it hard to tell the difference between his desire and his fury. I wonder if he does too.

I walk slowly to him with all the nonchalance I can muster, holding his dark gaze and feeling the tension caress my skin as if it's a physical entity. Every step makes the antagonism more palpable until it feels like I'm wading through it, this animosity mingled with attraction. Stopping in front of him, inhaling the spicy scent of his cologne, staring up at his stubbled jaw, I want nothing more than to reach up and run my fingers along it, drag them over the rapidly beating pulse in his neck. But I don't touch him.

Instead, I bend at the waist, letting him have a moment to ogle my ass while I carefully sweep his jacket up before sliding it on over my shoulders.

Something feral lights up in his eyes as I cover myself using his clothes, his jacket hiding my nipples but still showcasing the center of my chest, the soft curves of my breasts. His tongue darts out to the edge of his lip, almost like he wants to salaciously lick them for me—but he cuts the motion off. Stops himself from enjoying it.

"Don't play the honeypot. You're better than that."

I roll my eyes at Tyler and stride back over to the table, increasing the sway of my hips just to provoke him. I yank out a seat and sit down, glaring at him. "I'll quit if you quit."

"What?" He moves his gun to the side, looking genuinely confused.

"Please. The all-black suit? The cologne? Leaving your scar out the way I like it so you look all dark and dangerous? As if you didn't know what you were doing. I'm sure at least ten women eye fucked you on your walk down here." Jealousy creeps into my tone as I think about how I'd like to take a big red "Taken" stamp to his forehead.

That brings out a smirk, but he quickly wipes it away. "I told you not to touch Avery. You disobeyed me."

Hmmm. First off, why does he think he's the boss of me? Unless ... he wants to be. Oh, I think that little streak of jealousy is back, rearing up.

It's disturbing how much I like the fact that he won't drop the subject of me and his brother, even when we have so many others to talk about. Like where the fuck Yegor and Colt are. My eyes scan the dock, looking for shadows, though I don't find any human shapes among all the pricey boats. "You're welcome to spank me for being naughty, but I didn't do anything he didn't want me to." I put my feet up on the table and cross my legs, trying not to smirk at the fact that Tyler's eyes can't help tracing a path along the line of my body.

I pick up my glass of wine and drink as Tyler stares sullenly at me while Avery navigates our yacht away from all the other docked ships and cuts through the water.

"I should make my brother shoot you."

"Too scared to do it yourself?" I taunt.

He simply steps closer and grabs a chair at the table, the one next to mine, the one that will give him a prime view of my legs. I let his jacket fall open so he can get a glimpse of the panties he won't admit he wants to see. Hiding my smile, I take another sip of wine.

I swallow.

He swallows hard.

I swallow again and make a show of rubbing my right foot up my left leg...just for fun.

"Cut the crap. What is it you want?"

"Dinner before negotiations or it'll get cold. Avery said you liked duck, so I had it delivered."

The yacht makes a slight turn, and we're both distracted for a moment by the sight of Marseille. I turn my neck to get a better view as we leave the city on the edge of the sea behind. It's timeless in appearance, with so many stone buildings and terra cotta roofs scattered around. The basilica on the hill with its golden, eleven-foot statue of Mary reaching far above anything else in the city, looks nearly molten in the dying sunlight.

"Damn, that's a beautiful sight."

I glance back over to find Tyler staring at me. "What, you don't think so?"

He puts his elbows on the table and tents his fingers. "I'm just inclined to disagree with you on any topic."

I laugh. "What you mean is you adore our playful banter."

"Is it playful if I plan to kill you?"

"If you'd planned to kill me, you would have."

"Maybe I like drawing it out."

"You'd better like drawing *it* out. I require at least two orgasms before you get to come." I kick my feet off the table and sit up straight, giving him plenty of time to hide the smile that crops up on his face.

"I don't think you deserve any."

"Who *deserves* orgasms?" What a ridiculous notion. Nobody deserves cake but like hell if you can keep me from eating it.

"Good girls," he rasps as if he has an intimate knowledge of what that phrase does to me.

Holy shit.

I wasn't even aware that I liked that phrase, but my spine tries to melt on me right then and there and the heat between my thighs becomes dangerously intense. I have to subtly grab at the table so that I don't sink to my knees and beg him to call me that.

Instead, I avert my eyes, trying desperately not to notice how stiff my nipples are against the inside of his jacket, trying to fight my body's urge to breathe shallowly. "I think you might like bad girls better."

"Do you?"

"Yes." Fuck. That was too breathy. It was a dead tell. He'll know he's winning. Do. Not. Let. Him. Win.

"You're wrong."

"I think you'd rather have a bad girl who'll let you fuck her pretty little mouth while your stepbrother rails her pussy—"

Tyler's up and out of his chair, his hands around my throat in less than a millisecond. "I'd be the one owning that pussy—"

I grin up at him mockingly, knowing I made him break first. Even the sharp click as he cocks his gun and presses it against the base of my chin doesn't wipe the smug grin from my face.

"Fucking impossible," he grunts, uncocking his weapon and glaring at me as he takes his seat once more.

I shouldn't gloat.

I shouldn't gloat.

"I win." I give him a naughty little wink as I pop out my tongue. God, fuck, the intensity that sizzles between us is addicting.

"Get the fuck over here," he growls, setting his gun down on the table next to him.

Ohhh, does this mean we're going to make out? I desperately want a repeat of what happened in the flower shop. But I glance up at Avery, who's in the wheelhouse, to make sure he's okay with this.

"You don't look at him for permission. You look at me." Tyler's tone is low and deadly and makes all the hair on my arms start to rise.

"Bossy."

"Because I'm in fucking charge."

"You can be in charge of fucking. I'll allow that," I murmur, as I leave my chair and take two steps toward him.

His hand whips out faster than I can move and smacks me on the ass before pressing on my lower back and urging me to straddle him.

"Brat," he mutters.

"Yes, I'm quite the handful," I tell him as I draw his free hand up underneath his open suit jacket to cup one of my breasts.

His hand is so warm compared to the wind created by the speed of the yacht cutting through the water. His skin is the perfect texture, just rough enough to be manly, not enough to grate against my skin. My nerves crackle red hot.

He doesn't kiss me. He bites. His teeth dig into my lower lip as one hand presses against my back to hold me in place. His other hand squeezes my breast while his thumb sweeps out to flick across my nipple.

Holy bejeezus.

I'm a dandelion blown apart and fluttering in the wind.

And then, just as quickly as he starts, Tyler stops, dropping all points of contact at once and leaving me dazed, confused, blinking dumbly at him.

"I win."

Oh, I want to smack that smug look off his face but at the same time, my grin is stretching ear to ear.

"One round to each of us then." I begrudgingly accept his win because if he'd told me to unzip his pants and slide my panties to the side just now, I totally would have.

Jerky jerk with the self-control.

Why can't he just fuck me like a normal guy?

But then...it wouldn't be nearly as intriguing or special.

Tyler's a certain brand of cruel.

And I'm addicted.

Even when he smacks my ass and says, "Now turn around and feed me, woman," I can't get pissed about the chauvinism, because I don't believe it. It's all part of the game, an attempt to rile me up so he can get another point.

Screw that.

I spin around on his lap, making sure to rub my ass tauntingly against his erection as I play the ditz, pulling the lid off the duck and showing it to him. "Mr. Monroe, I've got duck, salad, and tarts for dessert Of course, you could always just eat this tart." I crack myself up, though Tyler doesn't seem amused.

"Salad. You eat some first."

Ohh, so he's going to make me his poison tester. Ha. Well, joke's on him. I've been building up immunity since I was eight.

I serve us a big plate of salad as Avery brings the yacht to a slow halt in the middle of nowhere. I feel more than hear the anchor lower, before he strides out to join us.

His eyes glance over my change in attire and my spot on his stepbrother's lap, but he doesn't say anything. He just pulls out a chair, pours himself some wine and then serves himself salad.

I consider making eyes at him to tell him not to eat it, because my heart starts to pound...but I can't trust Tyler yet and so I can't warn his brother and tip him off. Tyler's still holding out on the Yegor front and for all I know, he could walk away with Avery and signal Colt to shoot me in the head.

I stay silent and take a bite of salad—the belladonna berries a bright burst of flavor on my tongue, contrasting the oil and vinegar dressing.

"Your turn," I carefully load a bite for Tyler and am sure to include at least two berries in it. I turn slightly to make eye contact with him as I feed him.

He wraps his lips around the fork suggestively, gaze burning into mine.

I turn away as he chews and load another bite for myself, trying not to notice how Avery's completely devouring his salad. But I can't ... I just can't. "Hey, save room for dessert," I tell him.

Our meal continues for a few more bites, me feeding Tyler more and more Belladonna, my worry for Avery ratcheting up in my stomach until I'm wound so tightly that I think I might explode.

At the end of my rope, I finally turn to Tyler and ask, "Ok. I can't do it. Where is Colt and where the hell is Yegor? You were supposed to bring him."

Tyler smiles an arrogant, infuriating smile at me. "You're cute. You actually expected me to comply with your demands?"

God, I want to hit him. Just smack him across the face. "I don't want the money. You can have it. I just want to have the satisfaction of humiliating that fucker—"

"Well, you're going to have to learn to live with disappointment." Tyler's nonchalance as he leans around me and picks up my glass of wine to take the final sip nearly breaks me.

He won't even fucking compromise? What the hell? Then why bother showing up?

My fury lashes out like a flaming whip. "We'll fucking see about that." I move to stand as he sets down the wine but he easily yanks me back down with two hands on my hips. One of them snakes up to clasp my neck again, squeezing deftly over my raging pulse.

"The only thing you're about to see is stars."

Tyler keeps a firm grip on my neck, sliding his fingers deftly over to my windpipe and cutting off a bit of my air as his other hand slides down to the front of my panties.

Oh. Those kinds of stars.

Dammit.

I don't fight because every second with this man has me on the edge of spontaneous combustion. I want to finally tip over the edge.

"Admit that I've won," he growls in my ear as his finger circles my clit.

Excuse me?

"Never," I can barely speak, barely breathe, as a red haze filters over the edges of my vision. I'm so damn angry at him that I could spit. He thinks this is over? It isn't even close to over. But the potency of my temper is nearly matched by the swirling heat between my thighs, especially when Avery shoves aside his dinner plate and leans forward so he can watch his stepbrother play with me.

Goddammit.

Both of them are laser focused on my body, on watching me erupt in pleasure—

I don't want to lose like this!

I try to think of unsexy things—things that don't make sense like electrical circuits or carburetors—but lack of oxygen makes it difficult to hold onto any singular thought for long. I'll grasp onto a concept only to fall back down into lust, my animal drives taking over as Tyler's fingers swipe up and down over the soaked gusset of my panties, tracing either side of my swollen clit with every pass.

"Fuck—"

"Yeah, that's it, Royal. Are you going to come for me?"

"You!" I writhe up, trying to escape his hold, but Tyler's too strong. He simply moves his hand from my clit to wrap around my waist and keep me trapped on his lap, his boner digging suggestively into my ass. I'm confined, forced to feel every inch of his firm muscles, forced to endure his hot breath against the shell of my ear.

Worst of all is when Avery says, "Please. Royal. Let him ... God." His head tilts back and I watch his Adam's apple bob as he realizes just how hot he finds his brother manhandling me.

I'm so worked up, I could come at the slightest touch, but it's as if Tyler knows. His hand stays firmly on my waist, though the one on my throat plays—loosening his grip and then tightening it again. God, I love/hate him so much right now.

"You're going to find, I always win, little girl," Tyler derides me.

I debate smashing my heel into the top of his foot, but I doubt that would get me either the orgasm or Yegor. I still want both.

Patience.

I need patience.

He starts to nuzzle my neck as a sound catches my ear. It starts as a soft whir but quickly grows louder to a sharp buzz, then becomes a steady thump-thump overhead. My gaze lifts to the star-sprinkled sky and I see the black shape of a helicopter approaching.

What the hell?

A brittle, anxious sort of anticipation fills me, particularly when Tyler's muscles relax beneath me and his chuckle ghosts across the soft juncture between my neck and shoulder.

A sickening realization hits me. This helicopter isn't a coincidence. Whatever it's here for, it's part of Tyler's plan.

Chills creep over me and I stiffen.

I glance over at Avery, to see if he was aware of this. but he's staring at the sky with a surprised and slightly confused expression. "Did Colt fly the helicopter?"

Fly the helicopter?

Colt can fly a helicopter?

That would have been fucking nice information to know, *Avery*.

Motherfucker.

Tyler's hand moves back between my thighs, a power play. I move to close them, but he jams his hand between my legs before forcing one of his knees between mine and wedging them apart. His hand resumes leisurely stroking, but I'm already so close after what he did before that it takes everything I have not to tumble right into bliss. My jacket falls completely open and my breasts are exposed to the night air, nipples puckering delightfully as Avery groans at the sight of them.

Pure spite keeps me from orgasming when Tyler's fingertips brush over my clit through my absolutely drenched panties.

"Watch, baby. I want you to watch."

The helicopter tilts and I realize the middle door of the helicopter has been left open, shadowy seats just visible. A figure with a bound torso slides across the floor and falls out of it, legs flailing through the sky.

Tyler's fingers pinch my clit and I buck against him, exploding into electric shock waves of pleasure just as the body splashes into the ocean.

For a second, I stop breathing. I see nothing but white.

When my senses flick back on, I find myself limply slumped against my rival.

The bastard has the audacity to lean over and nibble on my ear before whispering. "Say goodbye to Babanin. Check and mate."

11

DODGING A BULLET

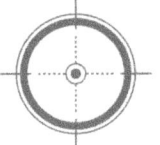

May 22
10:35 p.m.
Mediterranean Sea

Royal

rgasms are supposed to be followed by a happy boneless high, not the urge to strangle the man who just gave them to you.

But nothing about Tyler and me is normal.

The second he releases me, I stumble to my feet, seething.

Oh, I so do not regret poisoning that bastard.

I'm about to give him the tongue lashing he deserves when the annoying whir of the helicopter doubles and I watch the bird fly closer, hover overhead in an ominous looming way that creates a horrible wind—the kind that tangles all of my careful curls.

To my shock, the craft smacks down on the upper deck above us, the weight and impact of the massive chopper causing the ship to bob in place so much that I have to grab onto the table in order to remain upright.

What the hell?

These assholes are decimating every single one of my well-laid plans.

My fury must be clearly written on my face because Tyler smirks at me as he brings his fingers to his mouth. Instead of savoring my flavor, he simply taps his lips thoughtfully.

"I was going to let you take the first shot at our little fish, but you don't look like you're in the right mindset to handle a weapon." He turns to Avery. "Colt has spearfishing guns. Why don't you go help him?"

I clench my fists, ready to stomp my foot and scream—wishing like hell that I'd taken Man up on his offer to teach me how to fly a helicopter. Planes I know. But helicopters are different beasts, moving in all directions. And they're loud, not stealthy. I literally never thought I'd need to know how to fly one.

More fool me.

Now, I'm stuck on a boat with three assassins who stole my mark and my only way off seems to be swimming for it.

The itch of imperfection creeps up behind my eyes, cackles in my ears. My skull starts to throb.

The whir of the blades slows and the slap of the ocean against the side of the boat becomes prominent once more as does a distant stream of cursing from Babanin, who must be bobbing in the water right now. Tyler's smug face is as loud and obnoxious as the clash of symbols, making me grit my teeth.

I should have kept a gun on me.

My whole 'disarm them by being disarmed and sexy' strategy was shit. Utter shit.

I wrap my arms around myself because if I don't, I might just burst into tiny sharp little bits like glass.

What was I thinking?

I stew as I pace near the table, trying to figure out a way out of this impossible mess, while Tyler pulls out his phone.

WTF? Is it selfie time? *Me and my bros. On a weekend fishing trip. #friends*

Grabbing the bottle of wine is the only viable solution I see at the moment. I'm going to drink the rest of the fricking bottle so that I'm drunk enough to cope and then break it so that I can slit Tyler's dumbass, arrogant throat.

He takes my kill, I kill him ... if I kill the killer it's the same as killing the mark, right?

My itching brain likes that idea. My heart doesn't.

The first swig burns when I swallow and a little droplet spills onto my lips. I have to swipe my hand over my mouth to wipe it away

That's when I hear Tyler curse.

"Motherfucker!"

I glance up to see him swearing. Just above him, I see Colt's massive, muscular form leaning over the railing of the upper deck. The other assassin is dressed for battle, with a bullet-proof vest and all-black gear on, including a black beanie. Black grease is smeared under his eyes, which glow, almost cat-like in the moonlight—the yellow-green color emphasized. He squints as he aims a spear gun loaded with a nasty-looking spear.

"Stop!" Tyler's yell pierces my ears with its harsh, abrupt command.

But Colt fires just as the word erupts into the night, the bolt slashing through the air. I watch it stream through the sky like a silver streak of light before it plunges into the water just beside a thrashing shadow.

A scream erupts from the bobbing figure in the waves.

Studying Yegor, surprised he hasn't sunk, I spot a lifejacket peeking out from underneath the ropes that bind him.

So ... they didn't want to just drop him off and be done with it.

They wanted to terrorize him a little first.

My anger at Tyler eases up a fraction of a percent, because Yegsy really deserves the worst.

"DON'T FUCKING SHOOT!" Tyler bellows.

"What? Why?" Colt's tone is utterly offended as if he can't imagine any scenario in which he didn't deserve to torture the Russian.

If I didn't want this kill for myself, I'd agree with him.

"Someone else just claimed the fucking bounty," Tyler's free hand is clenched into a fist and his eyes are as dark as the grave as he stares up at Colt.

"FUUUUCK!" The huge man's reaction is bigger and angrier than I expect. He smashes the spear gun into the railing, which vibrates with his outrage. "I need that goddamned money, man."

Instantly, I see my opening. My in. My slim shot at making this kill my own again. A way to win over Colt.

Spinning, I hurtle across the deck as fast as I can in my four-inch heels on a ramp, shedding Tyler's jacket. I reach the swim platform at the very base of the yacht and dive into the water.

Frigid, icy cold sears my skin as I surface—the water can't be warmer than sixty degrees. Shit.

I blink, trying to wipe the water from my eyes and ignore the painful screeching burn from the salt. Then I scan the waves as my teeth struggle not to chatter and all the heat is leached from my body by the greedy ocean.

There!

I ignore the shouts coming from the yacht as I fall into a loose freestyle stroke, kicking and cycling my arms, breathing steadily.

Yegor better not fight me, that little fuck.

Should have thought of that before I hopped in.

Too late now.

The ocean waves aren't high, but they do make the going slow, constantly trying to nudge me to the shore instead of my target.

My lungs start to feel the strain and my arms start to burn because apparently Yegor's farther away than he looks from the deck of the ship. I feel a tweak forming in my back from the bullet-bruise Colt gave me when he shot me.

The trip back to the ship is going to suck.

When I do reach Yegor, I find him floating on his back. Breathing hard, I grab onto the shoulder of his life jacket and then do the same, going belly up for a moment so that I can catch my breath.

If they wanted to, the guys could easily end us both right now.

That actually seems like the easier option than swimming back.

Man's voice drifts through my head. "The easy way is rarely the right one."

Fuck him.

Fuck them.

I want hot chocolate and a bubble bath.

I get neither. Instead, I get to flip over to my stomach as the wind decides to smack my ass with a horrible, cold gust. And then I have the privilege of dragging a heavy, smelly, pleading Russian along as I swim the million yards back to the yacht.

I might dunk Yegor under the water when his whining gets a little too much to handle.

There are only so many times you can listen to someone beg for their life before it becomes annoying.

I mean, seriously, who beyond a four-year-old thinks a crying fit is going to get them their way?

Fuck the hell off.

By the time I reach the swim platform, my arms have become limp spaghetti, my legs are burning, and I'm seriously irritated by the fact that I have to keep this man-baby alive for the next few days.

I try, but I'm out of juice. I don't have the ability to haul Yegor up.

So instead, I turn to face all three members of Triple X who are standing side by side on the platform, all armed, looking like a firing squad.

"Little help?"

Avery takes a step forward, but Tyler holds up a hand to stop his stepbrother.

"What the hell are you doing?"

OMG.

He wants to debate this now? While I'm naked, frozen, and about to collapse and become shark bait? Of course, he does.

How silly of me to expect him to be reasonable. That man doesn't have a reasonable bone in his body.

"If we bring a *live* Yegor to the man who posted the bounty, then he'll realize that whoever claimed it was a liar."

Avery's skepticism comes across, even though he tries to speak gently to me. "It was posted on the dark web."

"Yeah, it was fucking anonymous. The money's gone." Colt's still practically smoking, the inferno of his anger palpable, his fingers squeezing at the air as if he wishes he was throttling someone right now.

"Maybe for you all it was anonymous. But my sister figured out the bounty was posted in Morocco." Thank you, Darcy.

"By who?" Tyler asks.

I shake my head as I grab onto the ladder in order to keep a wave from shoving me right into the side of the bobbing ship. I don't have the strength left to pull myself up, though.

"That's my leverage. No way I'm telling you until we get there. We'll get to the guy who posted the bounty, show him Yegor's still alive, and he'll be pissed enough to tell us who collected."

"Yeah, then fucking what?" Colt looks like he wants to punch something.

I pin him with a glare. "Then we finish the job, track down the liar, and collect your fucking money." I'm careful to say your because at this point I don't give a shit about the dollars and they clearly do.

Beside me, Yegor starts to thrash. "I can pay more. Whatever the bounty is—"

I grab his hair and shove his head under the water, a surge of annoyed adrenaline giving me strength.

This is going to work.

This has to work.

I can still get this kill.

And maybe...still get Tyler and Avery to tag team me.

The guys exchange glances and I swear a silent conversation goes on between them. Colt and Tyler are both angry while Avery's expressions are softer. The looks get tossed around for a minute before I can't stand it any longer.

"Or, option two, I can just drown right here from exhaustion while you make up your minds." I tell them in a dry tone as I let a spluttering Yegor resurface.

Colt surprises me by stomping in my direction and extending his huge hand. I gratefully take it and let him do most of the work pulling me up. But I mean, he does get bare breasts pressed against him as I shiver and try to steal his body heat—so he gets something out of the deal.

"Dammit, you're getting me wet," he complains.

"That's my line," I joke through chattering teeth.

The delivery is good enough to make Avery chuckle and shake his head before he hurries over, concern lighting up his light-blue gaze.

"Here," My handsome former captive comes forward and gives me his suit jacket.

I reluctantly release the mountain that is Colt in order to wrap it around myself.

The huge dude then bends and hauls Yegor out of the water.

"Go lock him in a bedroom," Tyler orders.

Colt slings the Russian over his shoulder like a sack of potatoes and stomps off.

"Let me get you into a warm shower," Avery slings an arm over my shoulders and starts to escort me up the ramp. Even though I'm wracked with shivers so painful I think I might crack a rib, I can't resist the urge to turn around and stare solemnly at Tyler.

"Tied the score."

I grin at his resulting glare before letting Avery play the gentleman and scoop me up to carry me off.

God, it feels good to snuggle into his warm chest, looping my arms around his neck, and just let down my guard for a second. I've probably used more adrenaline tonight than most people do in their entire lives.

Exhaustion starts to creep in and my eyes start to flutter shut.

But then Avery stumbles.

My fingers dig into his shoulders as I glance up, suddenly fully awake again, studying his eyes as his face contorts in pain.

Avery sets me gently down on my heels and immediately turns toward the wall next to us, leaning his forehead against the window.

Shit.

Behind us, Tyler starts screaming.

I hear a series of thuds and Colt comes bursting out from wherever he was inside, the door smashing into the wall behind him.

His green eyes grow wide in disbelief as he stares at the other two members of Triple X, gaze flickering from where Avery is slowly sliding down the glass window over to Tyler who's punching and kicking at the sky, fighting a monster that isn't there.

"What the fuck is going on?" he yells, full beast-mode activated. Every single one of his six foot three inches radiates panicked fury and he looks like he has the power to smash a hole right through the wall of the ship. Or me.

I want to curl into a tiny little ball, just shrivel up and float away, as I reply, "Oh. Um. That would be the poison."

12

MOVING TARGET

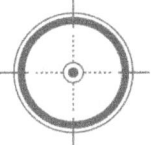

May 22
11:27 p.m.
Mediterranean Sea

Royal

T've read about men roaring but I don't know that I've ever actually experienced it until now. Colt lets loose a feral noise that vibrates the very air and hits my ears with all the impact of a cannon shot. Seriously, that sound should come with smoke effects.

Except, it's not really all that funny because his ire is aimed at me.

My nerve endings are telling me that running away would be the best option right now. Pretty sure my muscles agree with them, as tightly as they're bunched, ready to spring into action and carry me far far away from Colt's anger.

He swoops forward and I can't help but think what might be my last thought—people are wrong about what the Grim Reaper looks like. He's not some skeletal dude in a cloak. He's Colt Brenner in tactical gear. And this man doesn't need a scythe, not when hands that I swear feel the size of baseball mitts clamp down around my wrist and drag me to him.

One of my sister's gave me a panic button as a gag gift once. I'm mentally slamming it repeatedly right now.

In all my missions, this one is definitely the closest I've come to direct violence. Even with Tyler, I didn't have the same visceral level of fear that's currently turning each of my vertebrae into a block of ice. Choking fright makes my throat start to close as Colt pulls me right up to his chest and I have to tilt my head up to look at him.

Promises immediately drop from my lips, one after the other, like a prisoner trying to plea bargain with the head bitch in a prison—which is a situation not so far off from my own. This luxury yacht might be a bit plusher in terms of accommodations, but I'm pretty certain I'm about to wish for a jail cell.

"I have an antidote. I swear, the goal wasn't to kill you guys, it was just to disorient you all enough that I could take—"

"Fix it," he barks.

I nod too many times, head bobbing up and down with a nervous sort of enthusiasm that borders on crazy. "Yeah. Sure."

Tyler lets out a fierce growl and both Colt and I turn our heads to see him execute a roundhouse kick against one of the side rails. I flinch in sympathy because I'm pretty sure he just fucked up his foot.

Colt's fingers dig into my wrists so painfully that it feels as if he might want to twist my hand right off. My knees start to buckle from the deep-seated, dark pain that flares across my entire arm all the way up to my shoulder.

"I need to go get the antidote from my bag," I squeak, unable to do anything to shield the hysteria in my vocal cords from bleeding through.

Colt releases my wrist, which just causes another throbbing surge of agony as blood flow resumes to my limb.

I hesitate. "Um, you might want to grab him before he breaks something or falls overboard," I rush out the words as I spin and scurry away from Colt, shoulders hunched because I swear I can feel his visceral desire to smash my head into a wall until it cracks like a watermelon, spilling red liquid all over the floor.

Dashing inside, past the sunken living room with the gaudy chandelier, the acrylic clear pool table, through the over-sized galley, I get to the hallway leading to the bedrooms. A wet trail glides along the carpet, like a slime trail left behind by a giant snail. The first bedroom door is open, and I dart inside to find Yegor wriggling his way across the gray carpet, one foot twisted oddly behind him as if Colt stomped on it and broke it so the Russian couldn't run. Our prisoner is making his way toward the bathroom—no doubt to look for something to cut the ropes binding him.

Motherfucker. As if I need to deal with this bastard trying to escape right now.

Can't he tell we're in the middle of a crisis?

"Nuh-uh-uh." I wag my finger at Yegor, who turns his dark, pleading eyes in my direction.

"Please! No! I can—"

I yank the gold bedside lamp off the nightstand, ripping the cord right out of the wall. With a swing my sisters and I have all practiced in case of emergencies, I bring it down onto his skull with a smash.

I can't help the giddy pun that escapes me then. It just pops out—the result of nerves or anxiety, I'm sure. But I stare down at Yegor and giggle. "Lights out, motherfucker."

Then I drop the lamp and hurry to the next bedroom, where Avery and I dropped our things earlier. With shaking hands, I grab my go-bag, my duffel, the beat-up carryon I use on every job. I unzip it and dump the contents right onto the bed.

The sight of the mess makes my lips twist and a familiar itch crawls across the inside of my skull like a spider, but I do my best to squash it. "Later," I promise myself. "I'll clean it up later. It needs to be reorganized anyway." I speak aloud in order to alleviate some of the pressure in my chest, to make myself feel better about the pile of chaos on the downy white comforter.

Quickly, I run my hands through my stockpile, searching for the velvet pouch. It looks like a makeup bag to the everyday traveler, but the contents aren't filled with makeup at all. I have a nice little collection of poisons and medicines hidden in lip gloss and mascara tubes, homemade pills made out to look like eyeshadow pallets. I spent years creating and cultivating my collection, and now, when I unzip it, I hurriedly cast all those painstakingly beautiful items aside to reach for what looks like a compact. Opening it, I toss aside the "for appearance's sake" sponge and peer down at a black disk that resembles some sort of goth or sci fi bronzer. Clipping the pink compact container shut, I rush back through the ship, only pausing to grab a bottle of water from the fridge.

When I burst into the open night air, the chill of it scrapes across my skin like fingers across a chalkboard and makes me suck air in through my teeth. "Shit." I wish I'd had time to grab a robe or something, but I promise my quaking body that I'll take care of it in just a minute. I need to handle the guys first if I have any hope of Colt letting me live long enough to take care of myself.

I turn to the right and find Avery lying on the ground, curled up in fetal position. A strange feeling tugs at my chest that might be worry.

My bare feet smack hard against the deck boards as I sprint in his direction. "Avery, Avery. I'm coming!" I slide to an ungraceful stop, slipping on a bit of wet decking, and crouch beside him. Putting my hand to his forehead, I can tell he's burning up.

"Okay. Okay. Here I am. Here we go." I talk to myself as I click open the compact and flip it over, pounding it several times against my hand to extract the black wafer inside. I shuffle forward until I'm right beside him, then drop my knees down as I reach for his face. "I need you to eat this, okay?" I split the wafer in half.

Avery simply groans in response.

I press the wafer against his lips and repeat my instructions. "Eat this. Eat the whole thing and you'll feel better."

He obligingly takes a small bite but immediately tries to spit out the black paste coating his tongue.

"No, no-no-no." I twist the lid off the water bottle and shove that in his face. "It's medicine. Swallow it down."

He gulps down the water and manages to down half the wafer, though there's a lot of coughing and hacking involved because activated charcoal tastes like what it is—ash.

Once it's down, I immediately feel a weight lift from my shoulders even though Avery's blond head just sinks right back down to the floorboards. His eyelashes flutter closed, and he resumes the exact same position he was in before but I know it's only a matter of time before he's up and about, and probably pissed at me.

I bite my lower lip in regret and lean forward to give him what might be my last kiss—depending on how he feels when he's no longer feverish. I press my lips gently against his forehead, a few of his wispy hairs brushing against me. Then I run a soothing hand over his head and stand back up.

Tyler's going to be the harder brother to navigate because I can still hear him yelling and when I make my way around to the back of the boat I find him struggling against Colt, who has him in a headlock.

As soon as the huge assassin spots me, he glares at me, and his look is so visceral that I feel like I'm drying out and shriveling like a shade plant set out in the hot sun. I have to fight against the urge to break eye contact and shiver.

"Tyler?" I ask softly, focusing on the other assassin as I approach. "I have—"

"Fuck you, Godzilla!" Tyler shrieks, eyes glaring out at the ocean—not aware of me or reality at all.

Shit.

I get a nervous, clenching feeling in my stomach as I move slowly closer to the hallucinating man. I try to keep my breathing slow and steady so that I'm as quiet as a mouse and don't set him off further, but between my anxiety and the cold, I'm not certain I'm doing the best job.

Clutching the second half of the black wafer like it's the cure to mankind's ills, I slide my feet forward until I'm right in front of Tyler's dark, snarling eyes.

"You bitch," Colt snaps as soon as he catches sight of me.

"At least he's hallucinating about pretend monsters instead of real ones," I offer, though I'm sure that's little consolation for Colt I'm sure when Tyler makes an attempt to kick out the big man's kneecap.

"I'm gonna pull out every one of your toenails." Colt's response to me is to be expected.

I nod and swallow hard because I know how he feels. If someone did to my sisters what I've done to these guys ... torturing them would be end game.

I'm going to have to hope that my information about the bounty is going to be enough to give me a chance to slip away. Otherwise...well, I don't even really want to think about it. But *The End* flashes through my mind in a white script on a black screen, just like in old movies.

A sad sort of longing hits because I was really having fun with these guys. Despite the fact that I'd nearly lost my chance with Yegor, the battle against them to see who could off him has been the thrill of a lifetime, a high fueled by adrenaline and lust and a sort of snickering glee that made me glitter inside.

Reality check, I guess.

Life can't be all flirty death threats. At some point the threats turn real.

"Tyler," I say softly, as I step closer.

Tyler takes a swipe at me, his hand a claw that rakes through the air right in front of my face, forcing me to jump back. I glance over at Colt, ignoring my startled heart's mad beating. "I need to get him to eat this," I hold up the black half circle. "Think you can hold him down a little better?"

The big man quickly wrestles Tyler to the ground and sits on him in a way that I'm certain would crush every single one of my ribs.

I don't have to pry open Tyler's mouth because he's constantly yelling something. Instead, I use my nails to scratch at the tablet, trickling powder in between his lips until he starts to cough. Then I slip my hand beneath his head, my fingers sliding through his silver-streaked hair to lift him up while I press the water bottle to his lips.

It's a slow, arduous process and by the time we're done I'm certain my lips are blue from cold. But thankfully, as we wind down, Tyler's eyelids start to grow heavy, and his shouts decrease to mutters. He's worn himself out.

I take a deep breath before turning to Colt and asking, "Do you think you could carry them both to a bedroom? Then I can look up where we need to go." And get changed, but I don't say that part.

"Don't fucking think you're in charge," Colt barks at me. "You fucking murderous bitch."

I stay quiet, though my inner voice wants to snark back that he's also a murderous bitch and we're in a competition to see who's the bigger, badder murderous bitch, which is why we're in this mess in the first place.

He rises to his feet and then scoops Tyler up like a baby, carrying the scarred man up the ramp and toward the rest of the ship.

"Go secure Babanin," Colt issues his own order.

I can barely move my fingers, but sure, I'll get right on that, I mentally shout. Aloud, I only have the energy to murmur, "Mmm," as I stumble to my sore, frozen feet and curse whoever invented heels.

I swear my toes are so frozen that I might not have toenails left for Colt to take off later. Whoever claims the Mediterranean is some tropical paradise is an idiot.

I make my shivering way back inside, where I hurry to the bedroom I'd picked out for myself and Avery. I strip and carefully throw my panties and shoes in the bathroom trash before hanging up Avery's suit jacket. Digging through a closet that was conveniently already full of clothes, I don a sweater and some leggings and a full-length gray fur coat.

I find some furry Ugg-style boots and quickly shove my feet into those when I hear the heavy trod of Colt's boots in the hall.

Darting out, I make my way over to the room I left Yegor in. This time, I find him—hands still tied, so he must not have found a way to cut his ropes—standing on his one good leg behind a chair, nudging it with his body as he hops along trying to scoot the chair underneath the open window. A trickle of blood is visible on the window and another trails down his chin, showing he opened the window with his mouth. The bastard is trying to escape again.

He's got a seriously slow learning curve.

Cold, exhausted, and already nervous for my upcoming conversation with a very pissed assassin, I'm fed up with this man's will to live.

If I didn't need him breathing, I'd seriously sit on his face right now and smother him to death.

As it is, I march over to Yegor, grab the chair and yank it away from him, causing him to fall forward and faceplant on the carpet with a thud.

"Knock it off," I tell him. "You're not making it out of here alive, but you're also not dying until we're good and ready to kill you. So sit patiently like a good little prisoner. Watch some TV if you want. I don't give a fuck. But cut the shit."

I reach over and slam the window shut so hard that the glass rattles in the pane.

Then I crouch over Yegor, who starts sobbing into the carpet.

"Next time I come in here, if I see you doing something this stupid, we're going to play Tooth Fairy and I'm going to collect some teeth. Got it?"

I sigh when he just keeps crying like an infant.

"Shoulda' thought it through before you started selling people like they were pet parrots, Yegsy," I tell him, before dragging the chair out into the hallway. I go back into the room and do a quick check to ensure that there's nothing in the room or bathroom he could get himself into trouble with. I take away all the hangers, any hair dryers or items he could try to electrocute himself with, even the toothbrushes because people get way too creative with those things. They all get carefully put away in a small hall closet I find full of linens.

Then I use the remote control to flip on the TV. Luckily, these richie rich people who own this yacht sprang for satellite and all the good shit. I quickly navigate over to a high-pitched, squeaky voiced Disney Junior show and turn up the volume before tossing the remote onto the top shelf in the closet.

I head outside and prop the chair up against the door. It won't stop Yegor from trying to leave the room, but it will definitely make enough noise for me to notice and come running.

Rather reluctantly, I leave the prisoner and his hissy fit behind and trek slowly down the hall.

It's time for me to go face much more terrible things.

Like the giant assassin who's standing in the middle of the living room, brown hair askew because he's thrown off his beanie, green eyes burning like acid, gun in his hand pointed right at my heart.

13

HEAD SHOT

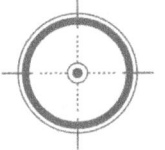

May 23
1:08 a.m.
Mediterranean Sea

Royal

I know I annoy people—that my personality and my OCD can make me uncomfortable to be around—but I don't know if I've ever been truly hated before.

But now, I know precisely what hate feels like. Fire.

I'm human bacon sizzling on a hot griddle.

I swear, there's a red ring of rage that hovers around Colt as I give him the navigation directions we need to take to sail to Casablanca, Morocco. It burns and generates an actual feeling of hot discomfort whenever he steps near me to look over my shoulder at the map on my phone. Of course, the fact that he purposely prods me with a loaded gun at the same time might also contribute to the fact that my pulse is currently a stammering, stuttering mess in my veins.

It's so uncomfortable that my stomach tries to self-destruct, to rip itself to bits just so I can stop experiencing this all-encompassing loathing.

"How long?" Colt punctuates his question with a stab from the muzzle of his gun.

"Um, well, four days if we sail right through, but we'll realistically need to sleep so maybe five days?" I lick my lips and though I'm staring at my screen I don't see a single image or word on it. My mind is shutting down defensively.

I can hear him breathe angrily.

I didn't realize that was a thing—breathing angrily. But it is.

"When will ... when will Tyler and—" Colt's gruff voice cuts off as if he can't even bring himself to keep talking.

My answer is a whisper that makes both our ears burn. "A few days."

"Fuck." He curses and pulls away from me, clearly thrilled with the idea that we're going to be spending some quality time together.

Shoving his gun into his pants, he suddenly bends and grabs an armchair, hurling it across the room until it crashes against the pool table. The back of the chair cracks and sags and I have never had more sympathy for an inanimate object than I do at this moment, because that chair could easily have been me.

Breathing hard, nostrils flaring, he marches off down the hall before barking at me. "Well, come on! We need to steer this thing."

I press my lips together as I silently point in the opposite direction—to where the wheelhouse is actually located.

Thank fuck the floor is metal underneath all this carpet, because I swear Colt's feet try to stomp holes right through it.

Meekly, I follow him.

This is going to be fun.

So much fun.

I go to the control room, which is a sleek padded tan leather room with an opulent curved control desk covered in glossy black glass with screens, buttons, and levers everywhere. A stereotypical pirate's wheel adds a bit of flare on the front of the desk, though it doesn't have to be used. Beyond the desk is a wall of windows providing a clear view in every direction. Another time, I'd appreciate the attention to detail, the pearl and anchor pattern in the navy carpet beneath our feet. But not today.

I lean over the tan leather captain's seat while Colt puts his hands on the back of a loveseat just behind my chair which allows guests to come ogle a captain's prowess. Ignoring the opulence, I pull open drawers until I find what I'm looking for.

I grab the anchor remote control and head outside with my brooding shadow tailing me. Depressing the button, I watch as the links of the anchor slowly rise from the water with a rhythmic clanking.

When the sharp anchor finally rises into view, I turn back around to head inside. Instead of going straight for the wheelhouse, I head for the galley.

"What the hell are you doing?" Colt barks when I open a cabinet.

"Coffee," I retort.

I hardly slept last night with my kidnapee and now it looks like I'm going to pull a second all-nighter. I needs the bean.

He grunts but doesn't protest as I look through the well-stocked cabinets for some caffeine. I find four boxes of herbal tea but no coffee beans, no instant coffee packets, no coffee pot. "What the motherfucking hell? These people are heathens!"

Distraught is an understatement.

How the hell am I supposed to survive five days without coffee?

I get the shakes just thinking about it.

I have to do the yoga-guru hands in front of my body moving up and down with my breathing thing to calm myself down.

"Okay, you can do this. You can do this. You have some emergency supplies..." I mumble to myself.

But can I? Can I do this? I can hardly *people* and now I'm supposed to be on a ship for the next five days with a man who wants to kill me at any moment and two other men who will wake up and definitely want to kill me and I'm going to die.

My stomach turns sour as my brain shouts out a hundred different ways they could kill me—all of them brutal and drawn out.

This is my fault.

My fault because I was too slow with my planning for Yegor. I should have been faster. I should have done better. I shouldn't have shot a dart at him from the rooftop. I should have just killed him then, even if it wouldn't look like a suicide.

No. It has to look like a suicide.

It has to.

I start to pick unconsciously at the back of my hand as I wander down the hall. Intrusive thought after thought barges into my head and starts knocking around my skull until I worry it's going to cave right in.

I have to kill Yegor. I need to or bad things are going to happen and I'm going to lose control. I'm going to lose control and hurt people. I've already hurt people. Because I'm losing control. I need to be in control or I'm going to hurt people. More people. I'm a killer and I hurt people.

Gruesome images splash through my mind. Some are real, from former jobs. Some aren't. Some are the wild fantasies that have plagued me for years.

Everything spirals.

The stress and anxiety suck me into a vortex and my mental worries start to shout at me.

My legs move without me consciously thinking. I wander out of the kitchen and back to my bedroom and the mess I made on the bedspread. I hardly notice Colt following me.

The piled jumble of things screams at me.

Chaos.

It's all utter chaos.

I have to fix it.

I'm nearly shaking when I grab the first item and pull open the top nightstand drawer with an audible thump. I give a sigh of relief when I find that it's clean and completely empty. I start to put the contents of my duffel bag away, carefully aligning each item until it's perfectly straight inside the drawer.

"Why the fuck are you unpacking?"

Shit. Two thin lines pull at my vocal cords and squeeze them nearly shut. But I can't stop my fingers from moving. I started. I have to finish. I have to fix this.

My hands keep picking things up and putting them in their place while my anxiety rattles around like a jar full of coins inside my head.

What do I say to Colt? I forgot he was here. He's seeing me like this. I don't want anyone to see me when I'm like this. Can I make him go away? Will it make him angrier if I make him go away? I can't tell him the truth. Should I lie? Will it make him angry if I lie?

"I'm looking for my instant coffee packets and my chocolate covered espresso beans," I finally manage to squeak, not glancing up because I don't want him to see the level of crazy sparking in my eyes right now. It's not a lie, but it's not the full truth either.

Only five more things.

"You organize when you get anxious?" he asks, seeing right through me.

Oh, God. How obvious is it? Can he see how I'm broken? How I'm not in control? How I have to do this even though I hate it? He can see I'm a murderer. Does he know how wildly unhinged I am?

"A little," I try to downplay it.

I expect him to call bullshit—I actually cringe, waiting for it. I expect him to call me a psycho or a neat freak or any of those other million things people say when they don't know.

He doesn't.

He simply watches me until I finish.

As soon as I finish, I have the urge to empty the drawer and start all over again.

But I don't. He's watching. I have to fight it.

My stomach coils and I feel sick, but I force myself to carefully slide the drawer shut and turn back to the few items left on the mattress. I gather up the box of chocolates I always bring with me for stakeouts and the three tiny little coffee pouches that I can simply add to hot water. Once I have those clutched to my chest, I turn around slowly to face the bedroom door.

My cheeks burn and I can't look him in the eyes, because he might not know it but I know it. He saw me start to unravel, saw the tip of the iceberg. I can't let him see more.

My gaze stays on his boots, which block the exit, though I can see him turn halfway, getting ready to leave.

"Feel better?" he asks.

"Yeah," I lie, because my chest is still wound up like a broken clock, the torque screwing me up inside without any true outlet. The compulsion to go back to the drawer whispers at me even though I try to fight it off.

He steps into the hall and I quickly follow, scurrying back to the kitchen, where I fill an electric kettle with water, plug it in, and flick on the switch.

Colt watches as I carefully take down two teacups and saucers—because of course there are no coffee mugs—get spoons and small plates and find the sugar.

"If you're worried I'm going to kill you, the answer is not yet."

His words smack me from out of the blue and I stop mid-step, head swiveling over to look at him in askance.

I wasn't worried about that—not at this moment—I've been too worried about him seeing me teetering on the brink of disaster. But now, I add my own death to the list of worries rolling through my brain and colliding like marbles.

"But, if Tyler or Avery—" he cuts himself off and swallows the words down as if they taste bad on his tongue. "Then I will."

I stare at him, unsure what he wants me to say. Okay, you can kill me, I agree to those terms?

He should kill me.

I turn back to the sugar bowl without responding. I use the spoon and scoop up a glittery pile before letting it slowly trickle back into the bowl. Again and again.

"So, I might kill you. Of course, we could be struck by lightning. The weather says there might be a storm in a few days. Or right now, while we're unmoored and just drifting to who-the-fuck-knows-where, we could be hit by a rogue wave. I'd be disappointed, but you could die that way too."

So many ways to die.

The uncertainty of all of them eats at me and I have to bring a hand to the side of my head to stop the clamor going on between my ears.

Refocus.

Refocus.

I try to find something to refocus on, the way the therapist Man got for me said to do. She always wanted me to fight the urges by centering my thoughts on something new. But it's so damn hard because I'm deep into it now, as if I've fallen down a well and am trying to figure out a way to climb the steep, slick sides.

"This yacht would tilt easily. It's so top heavy with the chopper right now, it wouldn't take much. Probably just a little wave and *bloop*," he adds, flopping a hand over to imitate what would happen to the ship, twisting the knife. "Would be such a shame if Yegor died by accident."

I inhale sharply, his words finally cutting through the haze.

Accidents.

There's nothing I hate more than an accident.

A loss of control.

I can't let there be an accident.

As if by magic, my brain shifts focus, and all I can picture now is the ship falling over like a child's toy. I can stop that. I can control that. Relief starts to fight against the bile-churning panic, enough to make other emotions, like my resentment of Colt and his very existence, appear. "Is this your way of telling me you want me to go steer the ship?" I snap.

Colt's quiet long enough that I turn around to look at him again. His mouth is pursed in a bow and lilting to one side almost as if he's smug about something.

Asshole.

I clench and unclench my fists, wanting to punch him in the stomach—but the kettle clicks off and he's right—I need to do something about the ship, something I can control—but I fucking hate that he's right simply because the suggestion came from him.

I finish our coffee in silence, mentally plotting out each next step I need to take, and we slog over to the controls again so that I can try to set our course. I take the captain's seat, expecting Colt to sit on the visitor's couch and let me work.

He doesn't. He stands right behind me, looming over me, like he's double checking my work because he doesn't trust me. I grit my teeth and wish I had dinosaur spikes on my back so I could just fling him off. I'm extra particular with my work at all times but his hovering is distracting me and literally making me so uncomfortably intimidated that my shoulders are nearly hunched around my ears from the tension.

"Can you back off, please?" I finally squeak with none of the actual annoyance or anger I feel. The words come out of my mouth like a soft, whispered request and I want to punch myself in the face for that.

"Only if you promise you're not going to press every button a third time after I point out that you put that dial in the wrong spot." His finger jabs at the radar screen and I want to shriek because he's right—I made a mistake.

The need to start from the beginning and fix everything until it's all perfect starts to ache like a knot in a muscle. It makes my body tense and my brain starts to whisper ... but a deep, dark smoldering shame forces me to tell those thoughts to shut up.

I stare out the front window of the ship instead, blinking, trying to make out the horizon in a sea full of shadows.

He knows.

He knows.

That comment proves it without a doubt.

He knows about the compulsions. The monsters inside my head. Nobody but Man and my sisters know that about me.

Not even the therapist I worked with because she's dead now.

I hate him for knowing.

I wish he'd disappear.

I wish I'd disappear.

Colt's voice cuts off my internal monologue. "We're out to kill Yegor for the money. But to be clear, you shot me—I thought you were aiming for Yegor and sucked. But that's not true, is it?"

I slowly realize he's waiting for an answer. I shake my head.

"Yeah, I've figured that out now. So, you shot me on purpose to stop me and fucked up our plans and fucked with my guys because..."

He stops, quite deliberately.

The sound of waves sloshing against the boat as we cut through the water is suddenly cut in half because the blood in my brain is smashing twice as hard.

Colt waits.

I don't breathe. I can't.

He wants me to finish the sentence.

He wants me to admit it.

His words are worse than manacles, worse than being locked up.

Horrified self-loathing rolls through me when I realize just what I've done and why. I hurt Tyler and Avery because I couldn't let go of this horrible, clawing need. Tyler made me feel like an electric light parade and Avery was so sweet ... and I hurt them. On purpose. Intentionally. This need to control and have things just so. This need to kill. I'm a terrible person. I've tried to justify my existence all these years by thinking I only cleared out the trash, the garbage humans without morals.

But I am one.

A garbage human.

He should shoot me.

"I'm waiting, Royal. You won't give up this mark because ... "

My voice is the scratch of a fingernail against silk, the softest sigh of the wind. It's barely sound at all. "Because I go crazy if I'm not in control. Because ... I'm ... not right."

A single hot tear rolls down my cheek and I lift my hand quickly to swipe it away, blinking the other eye until a matching tear rolls down the other side. Because even though I just admitted my chaos, my insanity, I'm still not able to rein it in. It still steers me just as surely as I'm steering this ship.

I expect him to push more. For him to make me admit I'm a monster.

He doesn't.

He knows I know.

Instead, we stand in the same spot in uncomfortable silence for a long time, so long that my limbs feel locked up.

That's when I hear a *clink*.

I turn my head to see two empty cups sitting on saucers.

Colt drank all the coffee and left me with none.

I don't even feel a flicker of fury, because I deserve worse.

14

HOLLOW POINT

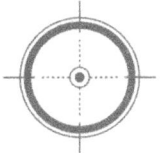

May 23
6:00 a.m.
Mediterranean Sea

Royal

Everyone hates themselves at least a little bit.

Me?

I loathe myself.

I loathe all the normal things—my cellulite, how one of my eyes appears slightly larger than the other, how I laugh. But I also abhor the broken scraps of my brain. Why do I have to have a faulty model? One that screams at me all these things that aren't true but feel true. A sullen, sodden sort of darkness settles over me and it's as if I'm walking through a mental rainstorm, trudging through the mud, cold wind whipping at me with a voice that whispers "awful, awful,

awful" and wracks me with a glacial, bone-chilling, life-stripping ache.

I shove down the sobs that start to expand in my chest, trapping them there, where they pulse inside of me.

Those two tears escaped but I don't deserve the release of a good cry. I don't deserve to feel better afterward because I'm absolutely furious with myself.

More than hating myself and my god-awful mental processes and this horrible condition that I thought was getting better but apparently isn't—I hate when someone doesn't get punished the way they deserve.

My entire life has been built around punishing assholes who hurt innocent people.

And now, I'm one of them.

Sure, Colt, Avery, and Tyler aren't pure little angels—but in the scheme of things, in the context of this whole job with Yegor, they're practically saints. Their halos are a little bit tarnished. Meanwhile, mine's a ring of fire.

It eats at me when Colt stays silent for hours on end.

Outside, the waves and the darkness are an endless expanse of sameness, so much so that I could almost imagine we're staying still. But the clock ticks and the hands move, and the screens show we're making progress.

And all that while, as we cut through the ocean, he sits in silent judgment.

The clock face said two, then three, then four, five, now six.

Six hours of misery.

I alternate between quadruple checking all our headings, adjusting every knob meticulously, staring out at the horizon dully and telling myself I shouldn't exist, and accidentally dozing in the captain's seat.

Each time I startle awake, I glance over to find him staid and stoic, just watching the waves or me.

He should be verbally whipping me.

He should have thrown me overboard and left me behind.

He left the room ten minutes ago and I thought, surely, he was going to get a weapon. That this was the end.

For fifteen heart wrenching minutes I mentally said goodbye to Man and my sisters.

For fifteen minutes I waited for death and didn't run from it.

Colt returns with empty hands and a quick, "They're still breathing," update before lapsing back into silence and taking a seat on the couch behind me.

I nearly piss myself in terrified relief/disappointment? I'm not even sure.

About half an hour later, he also adds, "Yegor was trying to drown himself in the tub."

I jerk upright at hearing that and grab onto the plush leather arm of my seat as I turn to look at him. "What?"

"I took care of it."

Took care of it? I want to ask Colt what he means. I wanted an explanation, but he didn't offer one.

I don't get to know.

He's showing me he's in control.

Strangely, that punishment feels right—to the logical side of my mind at least. He's smashing down on my compulsions, forcing me to live in the dreaded realm of uncertainty and questions. Making me wonder if he killed Yegor himself, even though it wouldn't make sense. He wants that money— or he seemed to want it pretty desperately before. But would he kill him out of pure spite?

I don't know Colt well enough to answer that question and it makes me stew, which is probably exactly what he wants.

I deserve this, I tell my writhing, spitting brain that's churning out all sorts of far-fetched ideas that inevitably end up with me locked in a padded cell, because that's what they always do. My heart rate accelerates and I stare at different dials on the control panel in front of me, not really seeing the green glow of the sonar, not truly aware of the digital map showing our ship as a red speck traveling along a dotted line. My nervous system—which should be wrung out and exhausted after all the chaos of late—goes into high alert for what feels like the millionth time. I find myself sweating and I have to shed the fur coat.

Then, in an effort not to pick at my hands as I try and picture one of any million of scenarios that could have taken place between Colt and Yegor, I end up stroking the arm of the jacket reflexively.

I must spend at least an hour this way, mutely panicked, half-a-second from leaping out of my seat and running through the ship so that I can go see what happened for myself.

The only thing that keeps my ass plastered to the seat is the fact that I am absolutely certain I deserve this internal torture.

Normally, I avoid uncertainty with meticulous planning, by keeping my distance, and working alone.

This time, I've broken all those rules—and at first, I thought it was fun. Thrilling, to be honest. I've never connected with men like me before—I've only ever had my sisters, but we're all so different and our bickering is so ingrained. Meeting the guys felt like a dream or kismet or some sort of alternate reality, one where I thought I was normal Royal. Happy Royal. A girl without a fritzy alarm system for a brain that blares and tells her the world's ending over the most inane shit like who commits a murder.

I'm not though. Not fun Royal. Not normal.

I'm just terrible, awful me.

So I allow myself to fester and the tense need for certainty to grow and claw its way up my throat. When it's strong enough that I can't quite stand it, I'll turn to him and open my mouth, ready to scream and beg for details. The look on his face punches right through my compulsion. He looks at me with lowered brows and a tense jaw, the loathing that I feel for myself reflected back to me on someone else's face as if it was a mirror.

God, that hurts.

It makes me shut my mouth and turn back to the front.

For once, I don't fight my obsessions. I let them roam through my chest even though they feel like buffalo trampling me underfoot. My eyes sting and my heart bludgeons my ribs.

But my limbic system can only generate panicked hormones for so long and eventually, the terror making all of my muscles clench recedes. The agonizing fear fades and a dull sort of tapping, then eventually to a slow drip ... like I'm a leaky faucet.

The pain and terror go away just like my therapist always claimed they would if I stood in the panic long enough.

Either Yegor's dead or he's not.

Even if he's alive, I doubt Colt will let me have my way and kill the man.

I'm not going to end up in control of this situation.

Now that Colt knows that it will drive me mad, he's going to make certain of it.

And I'm going to have to find a way to live through that.

THE SECOND TIME Colt leaves the room is near dawn. He's gone a good twenty minutes before he reappears with a single plate of sandwiches and two drinks.

He sets a plate down on the console, right in my peripheral line of vision. It's stacked high with four sandwiches made with French bread. I can smell the pesto he smeared on top of the meat, which smells like maybe ham. Or salami. I'm not sure because the two always smell the same to me even though my sisters laugh and say that's impossible because they're totally different items.

My mouth instantly waters at the sight because I didn't really get to eat much of that expensive catered dinner last night that's still rotting on the deck table as I speak.

But I know better than to ask for food. If Colt wants to make this an extended part of my torture, then I'm going to let him.

That's why, when he grabs a one sandwich from the pile and extends it toward me, I first stare blankly at it—not truly processing the idea that he might be offering it to me.

"Why?" The question darts out past my filter before I can catch it.

"You need to get us to where we're going. I need you conscious and functioning. Besides, you're so fucking sad I can't handle it anymore."

I take the sandwich, a little bit bewildered. What's going on? Didn't he just deliberately stonewall me for like a million years? Didn't he purposely sit there in silence in order to make me stew in my own horrible brew of barking absurdity?

I know I'm bananas but am I *bananas*?

I teeter uncertainly—wondering if I just spent the last six fucking hours torturing myself.

He points at the sandwich as if reminding me to eat.

No.

No.

He drank my coffee. He was mad. He was totally mad.

Was he that mad?

As angry as I made him out to be?

God, I don't even know anymore and it's impossible for my brain to tell me what's true or not.

I sniff a little as my throat gets tight as I stare at the sandwich and see it as much more than a sandwich. Suddenly, it's a peace offering. Or forgiveness. Or... I don't know but he said he couldn't stand seeing me sad. Oh, shit. He's about to trigger waterworks.

No way. No fucking way. He's already seen me vulnerable and cray-cray. There's no way he's going to see my ugly crying face too. So, to lighten the mood, I turn to him. Instead of offering him thanks, I self-deprecatingly say, "Well, sad girls give the best head because they don't care about breathing anymore."

He breaks.

Colt, the huge monster of a man with the serious stone-cold face and attitude, roars with laughter that's as loud and booming as a clap of thunder. He leans back in his chair as he laughs, mouth open wide, those yellow-green eyes scrunched up in mirth.

All of a sudden, his size and his presence don't feel like this intimidating thing. Other than the night we met, where we both were relatively keyed up, I haven't had the opportunity to see Colt as just Colt. Now, I feel like I'm getting a glimpse of the man behind the killer.

It's too bad it's after all this crap was drudged up between us, too bad I fucked up so big.

Feeling tender and tentative, but no longer on the verge of tears, I decide to continue this surprisingly pleasant distraction strike and draw it out as long as I can. "You like bad jokes?" I take a bite of my sandwich, and damn it's good. He's layered in tomato and cheese and sprouts. Perfection.

"I like blow job jokes, though I swear ... last chick I hooked up with must have been a vampire. She couldn't fucking keep her teeth covered."

Surprised by the overshare, I have to lift my hand to cover my mouth as I start to laugh and choke and then laugh again at the mental image of Colt cringing and hissing through his teeth during a blowjob. When I finish my food, I reply nonchalantly, "Guessing you didn't tip her very well then?"

He gives me a narrow-eyed glare as I hit an imaginary drum kit with my floppy sandwich and scat through my teeth. "Ba-dum Tsss!" When I don't get a chuckle in response, I twist my lips. "Come on, you have to admit, that was a sick burn."

"A sizzle at most." He raises a brow. "In the service, the guys would have piled on me 'til it felt like a semi on my back."

"Yeah?" I challenge. Living in a house with girls, we have snarky banter to a degree but it's nothing like what I've seen online between guys. My sisters can get touchy if you go too far. Curiosity makes me wonder.

Colt indulges me, green eyes sparkling as he leans forward and props his elbows on his knees as he elaborates. "Yeah.

Someone would have said, 'Dude you missed out on a free dick piercing.'"

Dammit. That's a good one. I should have thought of that. I'm not sure if I'm jealous or disappointed in myself right now.

"Then, my buddy Drew always liked to go too far. He'd have said something like, why stop at piercing? She could have circumcised you. Of course, if she did that there might be nothing left."

Wracked by laughter. Wracked.

I laugh until I snort, which only makes him laugh, which makes me laugh again. And God, if crying purges sadness, laughter eviscerates it. All that weight I've been carrying inside my stomach for hours lifts until I'm floating on a cloud.

When I finish with a sigh, I say, "I hate being tired because of all the thoughts...but I love being tired because everything's ten times as funny."

"Truer words were never spoken," he agrees.

"So, this vampire queen... I'm sure you managed to orgasm through the pain. Am I right?"

"It was a challenge, but I struggled through and persevered. I'm not a quitter."

Persevered. Shit. This man. I shake my head amusedly as I try out a Transylvanian accent. *You think Dickula's bad?* Scratch that. Nixing the accent. That's just plain old awful in an embarrassing way. "I see your vampire queen and raise you one guy who insisted he knew my anatomy better than I did. I kept trying to slide his finger up to hit my clit and he kept sliding right back down, insisting I'd orgasm better. Mansplaining the whole time. Complete strikeout."

Colt wrinkles his nose, which is an oddly endearing expression on a man that's so—not swashbuckling, but that's the only word that comes to my sleep-addled brain right now.

"We're pirates," I comment, tapping my nose dazedly. It's a non sequitur but those are to be expected with the current level of brain function going on in my brain. "We stole a boat."

"You just realized that? I ticked pirate off the bucket list the second I got out of the chopper." Colt grabs himself a sandwich and takes a bite.

"You have a bucket list?" I ask, curiously, my sleepy brain instantly switching gears because who doesn't want to know about other people's must-do-before-I-die wishes? I mean, maybe there's a thing or two on his list I could add to mine. "What's on it?"

"Twins."

It takes me a second to realize that Colt's cracked a joke because he executes perfect dry delivery. When I do though, I howl in laughter as I throw a dismissive wrist flop his way. "Typical! Typical male. Though, I have to tell you, been there done that. Italians named Lorenzo and Vincenzo."

Colt stops eating mid-bite and his eyes scan me and I lift an imperious brow, waiting for him to get judgey.

He surprises me when he just ruefully shakes his head. "Dammit. I resent the fact that you stole my dream."

"We can share dreams you know. Not like I've got exclusive access to the twin game."

"Worth it? No. Forget I asked that. My mother would kill me for asking that." He shakes his head before taking a bite and lapsing into a reminiscing sort of silence, as if he's picturing his mother right now.

He has a mother? And she'd still care what he's doing? I want to ask him about his family and find out more—like what it's like to have a mother.

Suddenly, since we've broken the ice, I want to ask a million things. Stupid, useless things like if he's ever had a pet and what his favorite month is. Most of all, I want to ask what the hell just happened these last few hours. Was he deliberately being mean to me the whole time or was it all in my head?

But ... I don't. I don't ask any of it. I don't want to prod or ruin the good mood we've got right now and I'm honestly a little scared of the answers and what they might mean. So, I turn in my seat after I finish my sandwich and start checking our heading again. I occupy my mind with dull tasks as Colt eats five more sandwiches before nudging the plate with the final one over toward me.

"Eat." It's a demand, but not a harsh one.

I reach out, feeling shy and vulnerable. "Thanks."

Taking the sandwich, he stands up and stretches, his arms so long that they nearly reach the ceiling. "I'm going to take a shower. Then we can trade. You can show me what to do."

I nod.

The rest of the day we spend practically separate.

He showers. I shower. He naps while I stay in the wheel-house, I nap while he takes the lead. But the massive anvil that felt like it was hovering just over my head in the darkness is gone and he even creates a little tap out handshake for us, where we swat palms as one of us tags in.

By the time the sun sets and I go to check on Avery and Tyler, who Colt put side by side in the master bedroom, I'm feeling a little more at peace with Colt, even if I'm still disappointed and angry at myself.

But really, what more can I expect?

When sunset hits, I go down and clean up the table, which has somehow managed to attract half a dozen flies even though we're miles out at sea. I get rid of the food and vigorously scrub everything down, tired, but not quite so wrung out as I was this morning. Physical exhaustion has nothing on emotional exhaustion.

Once I've tidied up the best I can, I force myself to march down the hall to the main bedroom. I press down the door handle gently and peer inside.

Tyler's arms are askew, one has fallen off the bed. His eyelashes are sooty black where they brush against his cheeks. I walk forward, nearly tiptoeing across the carpet to check on him. I carefully lift his hand and tuck it back in at his side.

The urge to brush his silver-streaked hair comes over me, but I don't indulge it. I simply look for a moment, watch the pulse thudding softly at his neck. Then I walk over and do the same to Avery.

My poor, sweet, former prisoner looks so young in his sleep. He and Tyler are a study in contrasts, his stepbrother embodies the dark and dangerous vibe while Avery could be a little speckled cherub with those freckles on his neck and arms.

"Please wake up soon," I whisper.

But neither of them responds, bats an eyelash, gives a sleepy moan. They're suspended in the space between life and death right now.

So am I.

15

SIDE BY SIDE

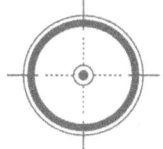

May 25
7:20 p.m.
Mediterranean Sea

Royal

For two days, Colt and I have worked side by side without killing each other—which is a miracle considering how we started. I'd call that not only a roaring success but like, spouse-level zen. Or what I imagine having a husband should be like anyway. Never really thought about it before.

I've learned a few things about him: he's far quieter than I would have initially pegged him. He loves to sit and stare at the coastline sliding by, especially when we get close enough to start seeing the ports dotting the edge of Morocco. He'll just watch the different boats and multicolored shipping containers stacked up like children's blocks.

I told him once, "You must be great at stakeouts."

He'd shrugged.

"Maybe that's why you and vamp girl didn't work out. Get it? Get it?" I'd elbowed him, goofy expression full force at my epic dad joke.

He'd glared down at me acting like he was unamused but totally fighting a smile. "Lame."

"Yeah, you are."

That exchange pretty much sums up a lot of our interactions.

In any case, I've discovered that I like staring at him a lot better than at the scenery, particularly when we do our daily workout, because neither of us can afford—or stand—to slack on fitness. The sight of him doing pushups in a tight t-shirt before ripping said t-shirt off to swipe at his forehead?

Hellooooo abs.

I might guiltily sneak off to the head once or twice and take care of my overheated lady lips once or twice. Guiltily because I really shouldn't be thinking naughty things about a guy when I know his interest in me is less than zero. We're talking subarctic, negative chance, he saw the worst and would definitely run in the opposite direction if he could.

Still though, a girl has needs.

Even though he's quiet, I do wheedle tidbits out of him here and there.

I credit my epic interrogation skills.

I'll say super sneaky stuff, like, "So—you come off all spoiled and shit. Are you a youngest child?"

Always pair the question with an insult because people feel the need to defend themselves.

Colt is the oldest of three brothers—which seems to fit his "mothering" of the other guys—the constant urge to check in on them or the way he chews the corner of his lip when he's worried. He also speaks bark—as in barking orders a lot. He doesn't appreciate when I tell him I don't speak dog, or when I yip at him like I'm a puppy and then pant or growl or run around with my tongue out whenever he slips into his army-mode or whatever it is. I think it's funny.

He tries to hold in his laughter but it's in there, I can tell.

In addition to hating onions, he hates broccoli, which I only found out after I make some epic Alfredo sauce and decided to make it healthy by cutting up a head of broccoli and sprinkling little bits in.

He refused to eat it.

"Seriously, you can't even taste it. It's hidden in there. Ninja-healthy," I told him, speaking with a mouth full of delicious food.

He'd just gone and made himself something else, so I've been eating my epic creation for the last three meals. His loss.

Today, we're outside on the upper deck of the yacht, quadruple checking that the helicopter is secure because we might have some bad weather tonight. The weather report seems like a load of nonsense because the sun is still shining happily along my back and warming it up. The breeze is muggy and warm, the air soupy today. All my doldrums from a few days ago have been sloughed off for the moment as I'm wearing a Valentino Barbiecore pink dress I found in the closet. Designer score! Bonus points for the fact that the impracticality and sequins made Colt roll his eyes earlier.

Though, I have noticed, said eyes do seem to appreciate how short the skirt on this outfit is ... just saying.

But of course, he's stuck here and I'm the only girl available to look at. I'm certain once we hit the shore, his looks will evaporate faster than acetone.

"Hand me that," Colt points at a thingamabob in a row of thingamabobs and I astonishingly pick the right one.

"Holy crap, it's like we're psychic. We should go on one of those couple competition shows. We'd kick ass." I note, as I try not to appreciate the way that his cargo pants fit when he's hunched over.

He just turns his head and grabs the thing from my hand as he shoots his brows sky-high and looks at me with an unnecessary amount of skepticism.

I backtrack because that was totally an unnecessarily awkward comment to make on my part. We aren't couple material. Like at all. "I don't mean like that! But like—seriously, how many TV couples could have done this without griping? And did you see I grabbed the right...I don't know what that's called. Thing?"

"Combination wrench. TV couples are paid to have drama. And there was only one wrench in that whole pile, it's not likely that you could have chosen wrong unless you were a total idiot."

I retaliate by sticking out my tongue and blowing a raspberry at him before I decide, "Just for that—you are going to be in charge of the wheel tonight. I'm gonna get drunk."

"Fuck that," Colt retorts, finishing up whatever he's doing and straightening. Holy shit, there's a little streak of black grease on his neck. That's totally making it into my next sexy-time fantasy about a mechanic because wow. Unaware that my attention has drifted to the way his neck is flexing and his biceps are bunching as he puts his tools away, he continues, "We've been sailing and eating healthy ass yuppie food for two days." It's true. Whoever we stole this boat from is annoyingly healthy. We haven't found any kind of sugary treats anywhere. And we've already split all of my remaining caffeine because it turns out that Colt is just as addicted as I am. We downed that stuff like we were starving. The next few days are going to be painful.

Might as well make sure tonight's fun.

"And I've had to deal with Babanin's shenanigans trying to escape."

Last night, the Russian had opened his door, run down the hall, and tried to book it for the deck, where he'd no doubt have thrown himself overboard.

Luckily, we'd been playing pool and Colt had easily smacked the man in the gut with his pool stick. Unfortunately, that had snapped the stick and the fact that the assassin had dragged the gangster onto the table and punched him in the face had totally ruined the game—displacing all the balls.

A game I was winning.

Part of me wonders if Colt threw Yegor on the table so he wouldn't have to lose.

Suspicious.

Still, though, he took care of locking Yegor back up, duct taping him and throwing him in the tub in case he pissed himself.

I'd thought about offering up my original plan for the gangster but I'd swallowed down the desire because even though I'm doing better, the guilt over what happened with Tyler and Avery, how I took things too far and let them stay poisoned too long, still has a hold on me.

Colt's in charge.

Mostly.

"True. Ok. Fine. Let's get drunk together," I concede.

We grab a bunch of bottles from the liquor cabinet, not bothering with glasses—because what a waste. Then, I decide that the swim deck the ideal location to get drunk because it's nice and flat and bonus—if we need to puke, we can just lean over the rail.

When I tell Colt about my brilliance, he just laughs.

I tap my noggin. "That's called genius. Might be hard for you to recognize but...there it is."

"It's definitely...one of a kind."

We trot down the ramp one by one like we're in a parade before we settle on the deck on our butts, three bottles around each of us. It's like a picnic for drunkenness. A drinknic. A liquornic. Liqnic. Yes, that's it. We're having a liqnic.

"What'd you get?" I query as I lift my first bottle, which looks like it has frickin' diamonds actually put on top of the bottle itself. God, what a marketing ploy for rich people. Show off how wealthy you are by buying diamond-encrusted bottles you're going to throw away. Of course, the diamonds can't be real. They're just for showing off. Right? Nobody'd be stupid enough to put real diamonds on a bottle. "Limoncello supreme. That sounds yummy."

"Got vodkas. Don't really care what kind." Colt shrugs a massive shoulder as he stares out at the water and the lowering sun.

He picks up a tall, deep blue bottle and I twist the lid off mine before holding it out. The necks clink in a small toast and I say, "To murder, mayhem, and motherfucking money."

"Damn. I'll drink to that." He takes a big swallow, actually more of a chug. Dang. He's serious about getting drunk.

I'd better keep up.

Like this is a competition, I take a huge swig of the limon-cello. Ohhh! Delicious. "This is like drinking lemon candy! You gotta try it."

I push my bottle toward Colt, but he shakes his head and reaches up to scratch at his dark brown hair. "Don't like lemons."

"Gah! You don't like anything good!"

By the time the sun starts to set, I'm bussin'—feeling so damn good. A little swimmy and floaty. A lot giggly. I hold up the nearly empty limoncello bottle to the bright orange sky, which is the offensive orange of a post-it note right now, all eighties and highlightery. It's not nearly as pretty as the soft yellow of the liquor sloshing in my bottle and in my belly. "Yellow is better than orange!" I declare.

"Careful. Those are fighting words." Drunk Colt warns.

Drunk Colt is much more talkative than Sober Colt. I like Drunk Colt.

"I could take you." My lips feel heavy and smooshy on my face. I put down the bottle to press at them with my index finger. When did they get so poofy like pizza dough?

He makes a dismissive *kkkkk* noise. "You couldn't take two steps right now, so don't run your mouth."

Rude.

And arrogant.

And for some reason those things are both hot and infuriating right now.

"Fuck off. I can take steps. All the steps." I stand up and sway, arms a little noodly.

Colt starts to laugh but I shush him with a stern finger and a "Shush! That's the boat. Not me."

"It is not the boat."

"It's the heels." I totter over to the railing and lean against it as I try to shed the heels I'm wearing, but the clasp must be broken. It doesn't work. "Fucking fuck," I mutter under my breath. My head feels really heavy for my neck, like my brain gained two pounds.

Meanwhile, Colt's turned his attention to the sky. He reclines back on his elbows and stares up at the clouds lolling above us. "I think this is a gorgeous sunset."

"The light's too thick here," I tell him as I try to wriggle my finger underneath the little gold tab of the clasp.

"Thick? How can light be thick?"

I stop what I'm doing and put my foot down because 1) the shoe's not cooperating and 2) he needs a lesson about light and I happen to be an expert on this subject. Probably because of my big brain.

"Look. You been around right?"

"Yeah, I've been around." He gets a weird smile on his face like I'm funny or something. Which I'm not. We're having a scientifically educational discussion here.

"K. Well, you ever noticed that like in California, the light is all goldy. But on the east coast it's more pastel. And in the southwest it's like *boom*."

"Boom. The light is like boom?" He bites down on his lower lip and his yellow-green eyes start to sparkle with an amusement I don't appreciate.

He's totally missing the point here. "Yes. It's like in your face. Like harsh. White. Boom." I do a mic drop gesture to emphasize my point.

He starts to laugh. The sound dances through the air and gives me a wind-chime vibe, as if he laughs with a chorus of notes instead of one long continuous band of sound like most people. Maybe there are bells hanging in his lungs that jangle.

"You have such a good laugh." I didn't mean to say that. I shouldn't have said that because it makes Colt's chuckle cut off, the epic sound just dissolving to nothingness.

We stare at each other for a long moment—the man with the green eyes and me. The look grows strangely intense, as if the clouds are moving, and the other boats near the shore are sailing, and the birds are flying but we're tucked into a secret pocket where time doesn't exist.

I'm the first to blink. The first to look away and rub at my chest, trying to expel the funny feeling there. Almost as if I ran a mile and can't catch my breath.

I stare out at the water and spot a few fins breaking the surface in the distance.

"HOLY SHIT! DOLPHINS!" I squeal because dolphins were my dream animal as a little girl. I forced Man to buy me all the dolphin posters, had a dolphin stuffed animal. Dolphin folders and notebooks for all the lock picking and combat techniques we had to take notes on.

I teeter over to Colt and shove my foot up on his thigh. "Hurry. Help me get these off!"

He does not understand the urgency. I am forced to lean forward and take his face in my hands, squishing his cheeks slightly when I overestimate the amount of force I need to apply. "I have got to swim with them."

"You're too dr—" He puts his big huge hands on top of mine. His skin is warm as he gently pulls my hands back so he can speak normally.

"You're too drunk to swim."

Fuck him!

"You're not the boss of me. So just take off my shoes."

"No. You're not the boss of me either."

Oh, he's getting sassy. I do not like that stubborn look on his face, the expression that tempts me to dig my heel into his inner thigh. But, most likely, he'd throw me off and then I'd hurt something and lose out on my shot at swimming with dolphins. So I reluctantly remove my leg and plop down next to him, digging with fumbling fingers at the stupid shoe and grumbling all the while about men with a superiority complex.

When I get the shoe off, my head pops up to check the status of the dolphins. I relieved that it looks like they're a little bit closer.

That gives me the determination necessary to fight the clasp on the second shoe, which is a total bitch. "If you weren't a Jimmy Choo, it'd be the ocean for you," I tell her as I fling her off.

I stick my tongue out at Colt who just shakes his head and takes another swig of vodka. See? I'm not drunk, he's drunk.

I wriggle out of my clothes and he's instantly all, "Whoa! Whoa! Whoa!"

"I'm not swimming in Valentino. So shut it. You've seen panties before." I have neither the time nor the energy to stick my tongue out at him the way he deserves as I make my way over to the edge of the swim platform. My dolphins are close.

I tug up the straps of my bra, adjusting them like I would swimsuit straps. Then, I take the plunge.

I forgot to take a good breath! Water fills my lungs and salt-water stabs at my eyes. I end up surfacing, not the way I want to, which is all Sports Illustrated swimsuit edition glamorous and sexy. Unless they have a centerfold model who's spluttering and choking, I think I kinda miss the mark.

Dammit.

I know Colt might never *like me* like me, but do I have to always look like an idiot in front of him?

Maybe he wasn't watching.

I turn to look at him and he's totally watching.

Double dammit.

But when he stands and starts running toward me, a dark look on his face, jaw clenched but teeth visible in a snarl, I get primal shivers. Not the kinky kind. The full-blooded, about to die, fearful kind.

I turn my head and see...not an adorable bottle-nosed dolphin frolicking in the water next to me.

No. The shadow under the water becomes a grey beast with gills, beady black eyes, a pointed nose, and a mouth that opens...

HOLY SHIT.

A SHARK.

A full body tremor wracks my skeleton painfully as panic crashes through my system with all the unstoppable force of a landslide.

The jaw distends. And distends. And distends until I'm staring at a gaping black hole. Fuck, this thing is like the snake of sharks, a mouth big enough to suck in my entire lower body in a single gulp. White bones edge the interior of its mouth like a cage.

Terror. Muscle-locking horrified disbelief pins me in place.

Of all the ways I've ever imagined I was going to die, I never imagined this.

Something gets trapped in my hair and I'm yanked upward as a burning twinge shoots down my skull. Then I find my upper arm squished, compressed, bruising on contact as something closes over it and my head is released. I shriek in pain as I'm pulled up, up, up and then backward, right out of the water, gasping and flopping like a fish.

I tumble onto Colt's lap at the edge of the swim deck, feet still beneath the waves. My back smacks against him and my mind hasn't caught up with my reality quite yet. I'm still under the water inside my head—still seeing that black maw slowly swimming toward me. My heart's a screaming steam engine and my thoughts all chug, *get away get away get away*. His brick wall of a chest is in my way so I scramble to the side, slipping across the wet deck as I yank my feet from the water and then frantically crawl, trying to get as far from the edge as possible. Colt moves with me the entire time, his arm wrapping around my waist when I finally stand. He's the only thing keeping my shaking body upright as a jagged sob erupts from my lips.

"Gahahahaha," the cry comes out with the sounds associated with laughter but the wailing tone of grief. Colt draws me closer to him and I claw at his back, trying to climb him, desperately needing to feel safe. I end up burying my nose in his neck and just breathing him in.

It's a long, hard minute before my nervous system releases me from my panic and I'm able to pull away. Able to finally gulp down a deep, searing breath so that my burning lungs can flap weakly and begin expanding once more. Once I swallow enough times to clear the knot in my ragged throat, I ask, "What the fuck was that thing?"

"A little shark." Colt's tone is way too mirthy for this situation.

"You think it's funny I almost got eaten by a shark?" I smack him on the back, right where I know I shot him because I see the bandage there every day during our workouts.

He grunts but his amusement doesn't let up. "Well, I didn't realize it until after, but I think that it's a *basking shark* ... so I don't think you almost got eaten."

I pull back to look at him, because while this encounter sobered me the hell up, he's clearly still operating in drunkland.

"Excuse me?"

"I'm pretty sure basking sharks are vegetarian. They eat plankton ... if I remember right."

"I was attacked by a *vegetarian shark*?" I try to piece together what Colt is saying but my body is still undergoing the painful aftermath of shock. My limbs are heavy and tired and still tangled with his. I'm suspicious and offended but also as dependent as a baby on him right now.

Staring down at me solemnly, reaching out to tuck a wild strand of red hair behind my ear—because the butthead is so strong he only needs one hand to hold me up—Colt replies, "Yup. You must have smelled like broccoli. Guess that'll teach you. Don't eat disgusting vegetables."

My eyes narrow and I suddenly hate his big square-jawed face. "I wish I'd shot you through the heart."

"Then nobody would have been here to save you from the little shark kiss."

Smug bastard.

I should climb out of his arms right now and smack him.

I should...but I don't.

I simply stay where I am, soaking up his heat, staring up at unshaven jaw and his green eyes, which are growing darker each second as the sun slides down beneath the horizon— because I realize that ... other than Man—who's my father and doesn't count—no guy has ever made the effort to save me before.

No other guy has ever played the hero on my behalf.

And even though this might have been a faux rescue mission, it was still a rescue.

Colt saved me.

I stare at him, awed bewilderment swirling through my chest...because I don't quite understand why. Goosebumps flare along my spine and my pulse starts to swirl inside my veins like a babbling, chuckling, giddy little stream. And even though my pulse is racing, I still somehow manage to feel breathless.

Of course, the dark voice of practicality whispers in my ear then, breaking the moment with her toxicity. She says, "He wants his money."

She's right.

He only yanked me out so that we can clear up this whole Yegor mess and collect the bounty. That's it.

Reality clicking firmly back into place, shutting down whatever foolish fantasy was starting to build in my head, I break eye contact and wriggle out of his arms. I try not to notice how his muscles stiffen beneath me, or the chill that pervades my skin once I leave his arms as I somehow manage to stand on my own two feet. "Night. I'm going to bed."

I stumble up the ramp, arms wrapped tightly around my torso to contain the sinking feeling of disappointment that builds with every step I take away from him.

16

BULLET PROOF

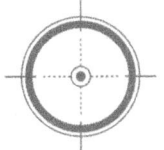

May 26
9:45 p.m.
Mediterranean Sea

Royal

You know what's more annoying than the baby shark song? When someone sings it at you as a reminder of the fact that you were attacked by a vegetarian shark.

I've been hearing "do do do" all afternoon. Thank fuck getting drunk is on the agenda again right now (because that's all there is to do on a boat at sea) or I'd be super annoyed. Day three of confinement didn't go as smoothly as the past two.

Colt was gruff and grumpy this morning, and at first, I thought he had a hangover, because I had a blaring headache myself and had to bust into some of my home-made remedies in my blush palette. But he avoided eye contact and his silence was accompanied by a tight expression and a bit of a grimace. He didn't complain about being hungover, which I feel is a universal thing to do. And he didn't try to cook himself up anything greasy to soak up the alcohol.

Also, yesterday, we'd done nearly everything side by side. This morning, though, when I was in the kitchen, he bypassed it, muttering something about checking the wind. Then, when I was in the wheelhouse, he went out on the deck. When I took a break to join him on the deck, he went into the wheelhouse, leaving me alone.

For a little while, I'd wondered if I'd done something wrong.

But around noon he finally grumbled, "You said they'd wake up in a few days."

And it all clicked. He was upset about Avery and Tyler, which made complete sense—far more sense than any of the wistful little things I was thinking. That he wanted me to thank him. To kiss him last night. Ridiculous things.

Swallowing and nodding, happy to at least finally understand where we stood, I'd stated, "I'm sorry. I seriously thought they would. But I heard Avery sleep talking when I checked on them earlier. So, I think they're close. I hope." I offered up my official diagnosis as a non-doctor.

Honestly, with Google these days, I'm probably about as good as a real doctor anyway.

Colt had nodded and lapsed back into silence after my answer. But it wasn't quite as stony as before. And the afternoon got progressively better, especially after I accused him of constantly going outside and chumming the water to entice more sharks to traumatize me.

That's when he started humming that obnoxious children's song.

At first, it made me smile because it meant we were back to being semi-friends again. Now, though, after three straight hours of it? I interrupt his latest humming session with, "I'm going to untie Yegor and let him loose in your bedroom while you sleep if you don't stop it." It's a super effective and not-at-all slurrily pronounced threat made from where I recline on a deck lounge chair beside Colt, bourbon bottle in hand.

The dark probably doesn't help make my extremely menacing expression very effective either, but we both decided that leaving the deck lights on was way too harsh for our current vibe.

Tonight, I'm wearing another outfit I pilfered from the lady who owns this yacht. A loose beachy dress with side slits that are a little risqué and make me think, *Go her. Way to own it at her age.* Of course, she isn't here to own it, so I try to do the emerald-green dress justice myself. It's the perfect get drunk attire, in my opinion. Easy to walk in. Hopefully easy to get off when I break the seal later and pee.

Colt only has one outfit. I swear, the man is a hunky cartoon character come to life. He wears black t-shirts and cargo shorts like no other type of clothing even exists. Of course, he wears them well. The way his t-shirts hug those pecs and biceps... Lord forbid he ever find a suit because I don't think my ovaries would survive the experience.

The huge, boringly-dressed man beside me chuckles at my ultimatum, making that expansive sound I love so much and causing a smile to climb up my cheeks when he says, "You let him loose in my room, then I'll be forced to come sleep in yours."

Whoa. Damn. That sounded flirty.

I glance at the bottle of bourbon I'm nursing and then over at Colt before looking back at the liquor. "Did I hear him right?" I ask the bottle.

It does not provide clarification.

An awkward silence descends because I want to think of something funny to say back. Something snarky. But I glitch.

Nothing comes to mind. Me, who's always got a million words running through her head at any moment.

I've been able to pull off all these ridiculous things for the first time during this assignment. But now ... now ... I'm at a loss.

Apparently, my brain is not fond of bourbon because I struggle with what to say and instead of making me clever ... I feel sad that I'm not. My chest feels soft, almost like it's on the verge of caving in, which is ridiculous. But my swimming, empty head can't find the words to tell my body to stop already with the emo shit.

No. Instead, I feel weariness and weakness invade my limbs. My eyes strain in the darkness and my stomach falls like a feather shed by a bird, spinning and swirling before it lies useless on the ground.

Why is Colt flirting with me? He shouldn't be. Not when I nearly killed him and his friends and don't deserve to be flirted with.

That series of thoughts then lends itself to jaded self-mockery over the fact that I'm deluded thinking this is flirting, certain that it's just my brain playing tricks on me just like it always does.

I drag my fingers up and down over the smooth neck of the bottle, staring at the dusky liquid inside. I want to blame the liquor for my problems ... but I don't think I can. Not all, anyway. Most of them are self-made right now.

If he is flirting, it's only flirting to pass the time, I tell myself as my mood plummets, like a cold front has swept in, taking my mental temperature from a balmy seventy down to a frost-bitten, depression-ridden sub-freezing.

Morose and on the verge of weepy, I look from the decanter back across the water and stare at the dark waves, blinking. A dull sort of ache fills me, pulsing with each breath I drag into my lungs.

Colt starts to apologize, "I'm sorry—"

"I think I might cry. You hate crying right? I hate crying. You seem like the kind of guy who hates crying." My tongue, which felt thick and heavy just seconds ago, is suddenly laden with words, none of them the kind I actually want to say. But confessions spill out of me like water spilling over the edge of a dam that's beyond its capacity, that's been trying to contain too much inside.

I didn't even realize that I'd reached my limit, that I've been holding onto so much sadness, but apparently I have. The words just flow. "I'd love you in my bedroom. I don't think *you'd* love you in my bedroom. I'm not a good person. Damn ... this liquor is strong. Here you take it. Fuck bourbon." I'm horrified by the babble emerging from my lips as I hold out the bottle and he reaches for it, his warm fingers brushing mine and making me feel baffled and bewitched.

My eyes automatically trail over his fingers gliding over mine and lift to look at Colt, who's pressing his lips together and giving me puppy dog eyes as if I'm something cute—as if drunk unhinged me is as adorable as I found Drunk Colt to be yesterday.

"Newsflash, I'm not cute so stop looking at me like that." I scold him, releasing the bottle, and reclining back in my seat against the rough, waterproof fabric before putting an arm across my eyes as if to shield myself. From what, the starlight? Him? Myself? The world? Who the hell knows?

I'm only loosely in control of myself at the moment, like a novice puppeteer trying to make a marionette dance. I'm just tangling everything up and making a grand ole mess. Especially because the next words out of my mouth are, "I'm not cute. I'm an utter train-wreck."

Like a gentleman, Colt tries to argue. "None of us are here because we're whole. We've all got damage."

"You might be a little dented here," I move the hand shielding my eyes to tap my chest with my pointer finger, which nearly makes me scratch myself because I jab a little harder than intended. "But I've got it up here." I raise my finger to tap the top of my skull. "I was twelve the first time I tried to kill myself. Pills." Self-conscious unease spreads across my cheeks and heats the back of my neck.

I don't know why I just said that.

Why did I tell him that?

The only people who know that are my family and my old therapist.

God.

Now I really am going to cry.

I just ruined the whole evening.

I need to apologize and go to my room and lock myself away until this idiotic melancholy runs its course.

But I can't find the will to move.

I sit in stillness, trying to find solace in the gentle shushing sounds of the waves, but all that seems to happen is I find myself sobbing silently. Salty tears stream down my face and they're warm. I don't know if they're warm because I'm burning up with heated humiliation or if it's just the humid night air. Either way, when I smudge them off my cheeks, my palms stay damp. I sniff and tell myself to say goodnight.

But the raw need to tell someone my truths and to be seen overpowers common sense. For some unknown reason, I have this compulsive, hungry urge to tell Colt everything, as if this confession will be healing instead of humiliating.

"Second time, I got closer." I hold out my wrist and show him a scar. It's faded quite a bit now. I'm not even sure he can see it all that well in the shadows.

He sets down the bottle on the deck with a low clunk and his big, thick hand reaches for mine. His rough palm closes over my wrist before sliding down and threading our fingers together.

Colt holds my hand.

He. Holds. My. Hand.

The gesture spurs me to finish, or perhaps I'm so wound up at this point that I can't stop the profession, no matter how agonizing it is and how wretched the aftermath might be. "The man who raised me, Man—he won't ever let us call him dad or even know his real name—got pissed the third time when he found me in his office with a rope trying to tie it to his chandelier."

"Fuck," Colt finally utters a word.

"He redecorated after that," I continue, "Because of that." I end up needing to take a breath and my lungs quake, the air going uneasily in and out and making each breath an audibly shaky sound just short of a sob. "Why do you think I picked suicide as my assassination type of choice?" I try to laugh as I say the line but there's no humor in the sound. "I'm pretty much an expert at this point."

There's a long pause where Colt turns my words over in his head and I stare out at the waves, wondering why I just confessed all of this to him. Wondering why he's still holding my hand and he hasn't run away.

"I've tried," he confesses, and his words shoot right through me, the revelation a thunderbolt appearing in a blue sky. My head turns, and I stare at him through the film of my tears as his big fingers close and press against the back of my hand before opening, gently caressing the sides of each of my digits, before closing once more and pressing our palms tightly together—as if touching me grounds him. His voice holds the same sort of stern and gruff tone I heard from him on day one, and I realize he's probably not told very many people. Just like I haven't. I mean, who would?

Fuck bourbon.

Seriously.

I absolutely hate that we're here, sharing this moment. But right now, I wouldn't leave for all the world because Colt just confided in me.

He shouldn't have.

I shouldn't have.

But we have.

Colt speaks again, continuing his prior thought despite the gaping silence between his words. "More recently, in fact. It's why I'm here. Tyler ... he knew. Bribed me to come on this job." His eyes squint out at the horizon, where the sun is gone but the rays still linger weakly at the edge of the water, and I see his neck bob as he swallows hard, reining it all in, trying to remain the tough, stoic guy he wants to be.

I give him his time, respecting his stillness and his confession the way he respected mine, even though I'm brimming with questions because I never—not in a million years— would have known.

He seems so calm and confident in everything he does. Knowing that he's raw and wounded inside the way I am, knowing he hurts, creates a tender fissure in my own chest.

At the same time, right next to that fault line, a snarling rage appears—almost beast-like—a rage that says whatever makes him hurt this badly should be attacked and ripped to pieces. I feel ... defensive on his behalf, a sensation I've only ever gotten on behalf of my sisters before.

The new revelation startles me.

It's a sort of connection I've never had, and I absolutely, one-hundred-percent feel incapable of processing it. It's too damn much. It's too overwhelming, with implications that all lead ... to places I'm not able to understand or compre-hend. So, I shove it aside and lock it away in a tiny little box to examine later. Or maybe never.

"You still try?" He finally breaks the silence.

I shake my head, then realize he's still looking away and can't see me. "No." It comes out as a breathy whisper.

"Why not?" The question is blunt and someone else might be offended by his tone, but I know why he's asking. For a long time, I couldn't imagine my answer ever being no.

I watch the horizon steadily, and I might be mistaken—it's awfully dark out here—but I think I spot a whale breaching the surface in the distance ... emerging from the compressing darkness he lives in day in and day out so that he can take a breath. One long breath before he plunges back down again.

I sort through my thoughts and finally settle on, "After that last attempt, Man sat me down and said we needed to have a talk about selfishness. He said all the world's problems stem from people who are selfish, and our job is to take out as many of them as possible."

"Our?"

"Our family. I'm a Belladonna. Ever heard of them?" I glance over to see a surprised expression on his face, which makes me smile. "Yeah. You have."

"Guys dug that up, but we didn't think they were real. Thought it was a cover story that made the rounds. Misinformation." His fingers are playing gently with mine again, moving around, testing the size difference between our hands by folding his index fingers down gently on top of mine. His hands have to be at least a third bigger.

This time when I laugh, it's from pure amusement. "Of course, men would think that."

"Hey now. Everyone we contacted thought that. Belladonnas have quite the rep."

"Because we're good at what we do."

"Killing."

I tsk. "It's more specific than that. Killing *bad people*."

"Sometimes, when you try to kill bad people, good people get killed too." He's gruff and curt but I can hear the painful truth underlining and bolding those words.

"You lost someone." I don't say it as a question because it isn't one. His pain might as well be screaming it on his behalf.

He releases my hand then and grabs the bourbon, taking a long pull before he turns slightly, shielding himself from me, facing the shadows and whatever demons he's got lurking there.

I think our conversation might be at an end.

I might have ruined it.

Typical.

I am excellent at ending lives and conversations.

I'm a conversation killer.

Get it? Get it?

Fucking hell, where was that wit a few minutes ago? Why did I trudge to Depressionville and back?

A whole-ass mental monologue starts up inside my head during the span of silence that it takes for Colt to collect himself. When he does speak, I'm so caught off guard that I have to repeat his words inside my head before they finally sink in.

"Drew was my best friend. Good guy. Better than me. Knew him since grade school. We enlisted together."

Immediately, mental pictures of two young guys with their arms around each other's shoulders, smiling for the camera as they wear their combat gear, start flickering behind my eyes. I wait for Colt to continue the story that I'm certain has a tragic ending.

Meanwhile, the waves swell and fall, swell and fall. The breeze brushes against my skin with a featherlight touch.

Why is it that tragedy shapes who we are more so than comedy?

I'd much rather have a personality cobbled together by dick jokes than mental illness and self-loathing ... but I don't. Deep down, on the inside, despair has a leash around my neck.

And it seems like it has one around Colt's.

"Drew got shot. I carried him up a mountain in Afghanistan ... We had to climb to get to our LZ—doesn't matter. He died in my arms." Colt's voice is thick, laden with the heaviness of a painful truth.

His ache fills the air around us and settles deep into my skin, a phantom bruise.

Reaching out, I gently put my hand on his back, careful to touch lightly. I don't make eye contact because I'm pretty sure he wouldn't want that right now. Vulnerability is a volatile creature that can quickly turn vicious and Colt sounds like he's just barely holding on.

I keep that point of connection as I stand up from my chair and then deliberately set my hands on his shoulders so that I can begin kneading the huge tense muscles there.

"He left a wife and kids behind." Colt inhales sharply before blowing out a breath and forcing his muscles to relax under my touch. "That's why I'm here. She can't make the mortgage."

His drive for the money suddenly makes so much more sense, and the reason behind it makes him appear like a knight in a fairy story, or maybe more like a seventh son of a seventh son. Someone downtrodden who still chooses selflessness despite their own pain. God. I swallow so I don't start crying for him.

No crying.

Stupid thoughts, where are you?

Come and save the day.

Please.

Unlike earlier, this time, my brain does serve something up. It's not great, but it's better than nothing.

"You could have been a bag boy at the grocery store to help with the mortgage."

His chuckle is rough, but I'm glad to have pulled at least one of those out of him. "Don't think I'd be very good at that."

"At putting your hands all over my apples when you checked me out? I would have liked to see that."

"I'm more of a peach guy, myself."

I giggle and then, with a tenderness that erupts suddenly and spontaneously out of all these tiny little moments together, I lean down and plant a kiss in his soft brown hair. "I think what you're doing for them is wonderful. He'd be proud."

"Would he?" That question sucks the air out of our light-hearted moment and makes our conversation plummet back into the dark realities of our lives.

"It might be an uncomfortable truth, but deep down, I'm guessing you're like me. I like killing assholes. I stole one of my sister's assignments before all my attempts at...you know. Killed my first mark at twelve. Hated myself for liking it. Not just liking it but craving it. Thought of myself as a monster. And with all those good people around, why does the world need one more monster?"

My question floats through the air, out across the waves toward the horizon, but it won't stop there. The question will keep going, traveling around the globe and circling back to me right when I least want to deal with it.

It always does.

"Why are you still here?" His voice is just a croak.

"I need another shot in order to handle this continuous level of honesty." I tell him as I reach around behind myself and swayingly bend to pluck the bourbon from the deck boards. After taking a long swig and swallowing through the burn, I hand it over to Colt, who does the same.

Instead of staying behind him, I climb over the seat of his lounge chair and perch beside him as I try to find the right words to answer his question. "I don't think I believe any religious mumbo jumbo ... but if I did ... if I do have a soul— what better way to use it? Someone has to take these fuckers out. Someone has to get blood on their hands. And what better use of my tainted "soul"? Air quotes on that last word please. Other people get to stay free and innocent when I'm already broken. They'll get their happy lives, happy eternities in the afterlife, all because I give mine up."

"But you said you enjoyed it. So, are you really giving up your happiness?"

"Yeah, well ... hmm. Good point. I suck at philosophy. I'm way better at blow jobs."

The mood instantly lightens as his laugh shoots across the waves with all the force of cannon fire. The sound rings through the dark night and brightens it, bringing a soft expression to my own face. I love making this man laugh.

He turns to grin down at me, his face painted with shadows, one side so dark it almost looks like he's wearing an eye patch, and for a second I can picture Colt as a pirate. He would have been gloriously dark and tempting. I'd definitely have been "all aboard" that ship.

Oh dear. There goes my runaway horny brain again.

Well, at least I'm back to that. It's better than when my sad side comes out.

All systems are back to wackily, partially operational it seems.

"I would like to make a suggestion."

"Yes?" Colt's voice still contains warm amusement.

"I suggest no more bourbon. Like ever again. That shit is sadness truth serum." I say as I point an accusing finger at the bottle still in his hands before standing. A thrill runs up my spine at the slow way his gaze follows me up and heats my skin. "But, if you decide you'd rather have an orgasm than think about crap anymore tonight, my door is gonna be open. I fucking love orgasms." That last statement is punctuated by a fist to the thigh, because it has to be. "Can you imagine the first person who learns to bottle them like soda? Damn. Zillionaire."

My thought is cut off when Colt abruptly stands, dropping the bottle so that it bounces against the deck. His eyes burn intensely as he grabs hold of me, wrapping his hands around my waist.

Then his lips descend on mine for a life-altering kiss.

17

DEAD EYE

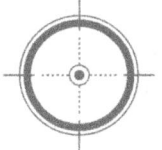

May 26
10:30 p.m.
Mediterranean Sea

Colt

I've obsessed over thoughts of kissing this woman for the past two days. So when I finally get the chance, I'm not gentle. I'm rough, uncontained. Our confessions unleashed something harsh inside of me—something feral that feels the need to claim her.

I press my lips roughly against hers as I feed her my tongue and she responds with all the enthusiasm I hoped she would. Our mouths fight one another for dominance. I want to devour her, for her to surrender her body the way she just surrendered all her secrets.

Cinching my hands around her tiny waist, I lift her up until she wraps those long legs around my waist, legs that have been driving me mad. I can't help but glide my palm over the underside of her thighs, finally taking the opportunity to feel them, even if it is through fabric. God, yes.

I can't wait to run my hands over every inch of her silky-smooth skin.

Royal kisses me with a ferocity I've never had from a partner before. Other women have been passive, receptive, but Royal matches my wildness step for step. Her teeth nip and bite, her hands come up to grip my face, as if our connection is the only reason she's not flying apart into a million pieces right now.

I have to have her. Need to feel her, fill her, make her mine.

I make my way across the deck, breaking our kiss only long enough to open the sliding door when Yegor Babanin—bane of my existence—tries to dart past. His greasy unwashed hair flops onto his forehead in thick chunks, his eyes wild, a little manic ribbon of sound erupting from his lips as he bolts by us.

Motherfucker!

Fury instantly blazes through my system as I lower Royal to the ground and turn toward the piece of shit who's chosen the most inconvenient time to escape. That stubborn asshole somehow wriggled his way out of the bathroom and got rid of enough duct tape to dart through the cabin of the yacht.

"Get naked," I order her because I'll be damned if I'm going to let a little thing like a prison escapee ruin my chance at hot sex.

"But—"

"No arguing," I yell over my shoulder as I stomp, all the force and fury of hell guiding me, toward the asshole who's trying to climb without hands up the side rail of the ship to jump. I reach him with a few quick strides, latching onto the back of his shirt and hauling him down. My pulse, which was thundering in excitement just a moment ago, is now full of nothing but rage and I'm sorely tempted to punch Babanin until my fingers are coated in his blood.

I don't, solely because Royal's waiting for me.

"You're a lucky bastard right now," I whisper in his ear as I drag him backwards by his shirt, ignoring the thunderous kicks he's pummeling against the deck boards, the way he's wriggling like a snake trying to get free. "I don't have the time or interest to punish you right now the way you deserve." Babanin's shirt rips and I snarl at him as he starts to fall, my hands reaching out to latch onto his hair instead, one finger hooking inside his ear in a way that must be uncomfortable because he whimpers.

I don't give a shit. I stamp through the living room and drag his sorry ass behind me, gritting my teeth, cutting the corners deliberately so his fucking shoulders will slam into them as I carry him back to the room that's a more elegant prison than a piece of shit like him deserves.

"You goddamned motherfucker," I curse under my breath at the inconvenience, at the way he's brought out my bloodlust and the savage side of myself that aches for violence. My heart is raging, the vein in my forehead throbbing, and my lungs feel likely to burst. I try to breathe deep and slow so that I'm not a raging lunatic after I deposit this asshole back where he belongs.

I throw him into his room with a little more force than necessary, sending him flying into the dresser with a thump. He groans but lays still while I glance around, trying to figure out what he used to free himself. I'm about to step into the bathroom to continue my search when Royal appears in the doorway, completely nude.

Fuck.

Oh fuck.

With that red hair drifting down across her shoulders she looks like a siren. My siren. The sight of her perky breasts with pale pink nipples pointed and ready for my mouth. The flare of her hips ... her pussy ... I'm very much in danger of short-circuiting and going full cave man here. The need to claim every inch of her pale skin. To wrap that hair around my wrist. To bruise those lips with my kiss. To feel the hot, wet heat of her.

I have to swallow repeatedly because my throat's gone dry.

There's movement on the ground and I suddenly remember Babanin's still here.

Like hell if I'm going to let him see her like this. She's mine.

I stomp over to the doorway to block his view, realizing just how much I tower over Royal. Her personality is so big and bright that it can be easy to forget how small she is. And while she might not need or want my protection, the primeval part of my brain doesn't care. She's fucking getting it. I place myself between the two of them, grabbing onto the edge of the door and closing it halfway in order to help shield her.

"Wait in your room." I move to shut the door on her, though it's the last thing I actually want to do. I want to grab her and throw her over my shoulder, smack her ass and watch it jiggle under my touch, feel her breasts press against my back as I carry her. Ugh.

I try to suppress those thoughts because they're just torture —I'm going to have to wait.

"Wait!" She holds out a thin, delicate hand, turning her fist palm up to reveal a little vial. "Force him to drink this. It'll knock him out for a few hours."

Thank you, God.

I don't want to deal with this headache, this bastard, right now. I swipe the vial from her hand and turn back into the room before calling over my shoulder again. "Bedroom."

I make quick work of dealing with Babanin and then washing my hands of him—literally, because he's fucking disgusting.

As I shut his door and wedge a chair in front of it to block him in, I try to regulate the angry ache in my chest, the wild beating of my heart. I don't want to take this adrenaline out on Royal. It's not fair to her. She deserves better than a barbaric brute, especially now that I know just how utterly delicate she is.

I feel like I'm doing a decent job clearing my head until I hear a whistle in the hall, which sends me whirling around.

There she is, my fellow assassin, standing thirty feet from me. She's naked as the day she was born and dangling a row of six silver foil packaged condoms from one hand, staring brashly over at me. "Think you can use all these up?"

A rush of blood goes right to my dick and I'm instantly hard as a rock. A cocky grin perks up one side of my mouth as I answer her challenge. "Oh, I know it. But I thought I told you to get on the bed," I state as I prowl toward her, eyes roaming over the delicious length of her legs.

"Technically, you said in the bedroom. Not on the bed."

I flex and release my hands, trying to shake out some of the tension that's still coiled in my gut. "And you aren't there because?" I ask, as I get close and she starts to slowly back up, this bright, intense expression in her hazel gaze that I want to memorize.

"Well, I suck at following rules." She licks her lips, tongue darting out and wetting them temptingly. I can't help but instantly imagine what her tongue will feel like against the underside of my cock.

I reach for Royal, but to my surprise, she backs up a few more steps. "Actually, I was thinking ... beds are boring. I'd rather you chase me."

With that, she dashes off, ass flexing deliciously as she scampers down the hall. My cock twitches in my shorts and I try to force the limited amount of blood left in my brain to process her words.

Oh, she wants to play.

Instantly, all the adrenaline that I've been trying to quash comes racing right back up to the surface. My muscles tense and coil, but this time in excitement.

When Royal releases a giggle as she reaches the corner, her breasts bouncing as she has to grab the wall to help her round it, I'm off. That giggle is like a starter pistol and the sound triggers me to bolt after her. I don't run at top speed as I round the corner because I quickly realize that if I do, this little chase will end far too quickly. No, I let her make it to the sunken living room, where she leaps over the back of a custom leather couch and spins to face me.

Her neck and face are prettily flushed red, and I love the effect her breathing has on her chest, drawing my eyes with each inhale. God, she's beautiful, even as she dances on her tip toes and waggles her shoulders to mock me.

"Run, run, run, as fast as you can, you can't catch me—"

I barrel forward, leaping the couch like it's a track hurdle. Royal squeals and turns, but my hands wrap around her waist before she gets two steps. I yank her back against me, pressing my hardness into her, so she can feel what she's done.

"Think you can run from this? Think again."

She gives a delighted little gasp as I roam my fingers up her taut belly to grab her small breasts and knead them in my hands. God. So good. The feel of her in my hands. My brain goes haywire, and I start to grind against her as I drop my lips toward the junction between her neck and shoulder. I bite down, turning her breathy gasp into a vocal one, until she's reaching up and grabbing at my hair. But instead of trying to pull me off, she simply groans my name.

"Colt."

God.

Yes.

I want to hear my name on her lips like that every day.

I release my mouth, drop her breast and spin her around to face me. I don't even have to force a harsh tone, because I'm only holding onto control by a thin string and it's liable to snap at any moment, when I tell her, "You ran from me and now you have to pay the price."

"Price?"

"Suck my cock."

Her eyes light up and she reaches forward with both hands, despite the fact that one holds the promise of the number of times I'm going to fuck her. I'm going to take her so hard and rough that she won't be able to walk tomorrow. Maybe for two days. I'll have to carry her in my arms wherever she wants to go.

Royal unzips my shorts and I help her get them and the rest of my clothes off. Then she drops to her knees in front of me, glancing up as her hand comes to grab the base of my cock. I stare at the way her eyes get heavy-lidded, the way her eyelashes contrast her skin, the way her lips part and her warm breath ghosts over my tip as she leans forward. When her tongue darts out and she licks the head, my knees lock out. Heat builds at the base of my spine as a web of delicious sensations spreads across my dick with every movement Royal makes.

I stare down at her, the round peach of her ass as she perches on her knees, the protrusion of those nipples I can't wait to get my mouth on. That gorgeous face and those cheeks that start to hollow out when she takes me in more fully, until the tip of my cock bumps the roof of her mouth.

So good.

I would have been content with that, but Royal pushes further. She sinks onto me, tightening her lips and swallowing so that I feel her throat pulse around me. My balls boil and gold flecks invade the corners of my vision. She adds suction and I swear it feels like she's about to pull my very soul from my body.

I bring a hand up to cup her cheek as she draws me higher and higher until I don't think there's any blood left in my toes. Until I'm light-headed in addition to drunk. Until I'm pretty certain this is what it feels like to be a god who's worshipped wholeheartedly.

My balls start to draw up and I quickly tap her cheek, pulling away, hissing as her tight mouth opens and that delicious edge I was teetering on disappears.

"Fuck. Me."

"I plan on it," the sarcastic minx replies with a cheeky grin.

I laugh as I grab her wrist and yank her to her feet before glancing between the couch and the wall. I push her toward the wall because I want to hear her nails scraping and scrabbling against it, hear her ass thumping when I fuck her. The couch can come later.

I kiss her mouth, hungrily, as I reach between her thighs to see how wet she is for me. "You're soaked," I groan, with an impatient moan, because that knowledge makes my dick twitch. But there's no way I'm fucking Royal until she's begging for it. After yesterday, when I was certain she'd friend-zoned me, I want to blow her mind to bits so that this woman can't ever think of me without getting damp panties.

I press her up against the wall and pin her with my hips for a moment as I try to steal her breath. I reach for her nipples and tweak them as I move my lips from her mouth down to the pulse in her neck, which flutters wildly as my tongue lashes at it. Pressing kisses against her collarbone, I let my hands move to cup her breasts, to trace the shape of her, trying to feel every square inch of her delectable body beneath my palms. I glide repeatedly up and down over her hips, the front of her legs, her inner thighs. But by the time I reach her pussy, she's cursing up a storm.

"You'd better fucking touch me, Colt or I swear I'm going to shoot you worse next time, you motherfucker! I'll rip your damn head off!" Those fingernails I wanted to hear scramble against the wall as she tries to pivot her hips to get me to touch her where she wants it most.

I smile against her naval as I plant a kiss there, moving my hands away and leaving her frustrated until she stills.

"You're a dead man."

I let my tongue out, using it to weave a pattern down her lower stomach while my hands come back to caress her thighs as if she was whispering sweet nothings instead of death threats.

When my tongue finally laps at her slit, she gasps and her hands immediately fly to my hair. Her hips pump against me and I suck her clit into my mouth. She whimpers as her release overtakes her and her body jerks wildly. I use my shoulders to pin her hips against the wall and continue suction until she's yanking on my hair, gasping "Stop! Stop! Fuck."

When I pull back, she slumps forward, as if her limbs are too heavy to hold up. That's how I know she's ready.

I stand up and rip a condom from the pack she's carrying, tearing open the foil along the serrated edge, then rolling the rubber onto my dick. Protection ensured, I lift Royal, wrapping her arms around my neck because she's too dazed to do it herself. I love the way her eyes blink up at me as I sheathe myself inside of her.

She's so tight and hot that I have to pause halfway in, leaning my forehead against hers just to catch my breath.

Fuck.

"You gonna fuck me or you gonna get off on daydreaming about it?" she challenges.

That does it. I grab her arms and pin them to the wall with one of my own

She wants to be mouthy, she's going to get it rough. I pull back until just the tip of my dick remains inside of her. And then I slam home. Fuck. God. Yes. I start to piston in and out of her hard and fast, the sensation as intense as a rough wave, one with the power to drag you under. My mind and body jump into euphoria, swimming through this alternate bliss as I reach underneath her body with my free hand. My finger dips right into her ass, no warning. That makes her yelp and wriggle against me in ways that make my mind detonate.

"You want to get sassy, you get a finger in your ass. Keep it up and I'll replace it with my dick."

I thrust harder and faster and the boat feels like it's working with me, the waves rocking in opposition, letting me hit deeper, letting me breach this soft pussy in ways I've never done before. I pump my finger in and out of Royal's ass as I work her pussy, eventually freeing a hand and grunting, "Touch that clit."

She doesn't argue.

No, the red-headed vixen in my arms moans and throws her head back the second her fingers pinch her clit. I can feel her start to spasm around me, to tighten, and so I speed up my thrusts until—BAM.

Hyper-focused pleasure washes over me. My ass and balls contract and my hips move on autopilot as I cease to see, to hear. I only feel the surge of energy flowing through me, out of me, this epic, amazing sort of release that's not just physical. Something bursts inside of me, something that makes me lean forward and snap my teeth around Royal's lower lip, something that makes me bite and mark her.

When my dick stops pulsing, I slowly lower Royal to the ground, but I don't slide out of her, because for some reason ... I feel this need to hold her. Keep her close. A voice inside me whispers that whatever I just gave her ... it was a lot more than a good dicking and a little cum.

My throat tightens as I gently pull back, arms still at her waist, eyes carefully darting between each of hers to see if this was as intense for her.

As her dazed glow recedes, Royal's eyes blink up at mine. She swallows and I think I catch a glimpse of vulnerability in her expression, but it's gone before I can be sure.

She pushes aside one of my arms and steps away before looking coyly over her shoulder at me. "Anytime, I mean, *anytime* you want to have primal angry sex, I volunteer as tribute." She winks and then crooks her head in the direction of the bedrooms. "Round two in the shower?"

"Sure." I say, my throat tight. "Be right there." I watch her walk away, but this time, I'm not staring at her ass.

This time I'm wondering if it's possible to fall in love with someone you should technically fucking hate.

And I'm wondering if it's possible to make them love you back.

.

18

SWEATING BULLETS

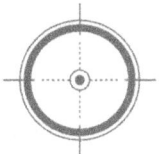

May 27
9:25 a.m.
Mediterranean Sea

Royal

Sometimes, after sex—when I'm sore in all the right ways—I can feel almost a shadow of a bruise, a slightly pained memory from a man's touch. I think of them as naughty post-it notes. Bright little pains with tiny sayings written on them: remember this hickey, that pile-driver was intense, you took a chance on ass fucking—go you. This morning, every little motion I make brings up a memory from my night with Colt. Damn, but that man can put out.

He also has this slightly strange, but kind of cute addiction to after-snuggles. And he insisted we sleep in the same bed all night. I mean, I did that with Avery but we didn't really have much choice then—we were in a one bedroom hotel room. Now, though? I kind of would have guessed Colt would want his own space. But he'd pulled me tight against him, spooning me and holding my hand while we slept, and I swear ... I've never slept more peacefully.

How strange is that?

Colt is huge and his chest was hairy pressed up against my back all night long. He produces enough heat that he could probably power a nuclear reactor ... and yet, having his body curved behind mine was a strange sort of wonderful. Especially after everything I drunkenly confessed—all those things that make me feel broken and unlovable and unworthy. He still held me like I was precious.

That man's delusional.

Now, as I go about showering while Colt cooks us breakfast, I stand beneath the steamy water, hot spray pounding against my neck, blinking at the tiles as I wonder what exactly is happening between us.

I don't know what it is, but I know it's something fragile.

Something I could easily break.

Something as delicate as glass or as tenuous as a spider web.

I don't want to shatter it ... but at the same time, I'm not sure what *it* is, so I don't know how to protect it. I bring my hands up to my hair to rinse out the conditioner I'd put in and as I scrub my fingers through my locks, I mutter, "I wish men were as easy to handle as a fucking Glock." I sigh in disappointment at the fact that even though they both love to shoot rounds into people, and even though their trigger mechanism is relatively easy to understand ... the inner workings of a dude are not quite so clear.

What does Colt want?

That question pops open a can of worms that I immediately slam shut because worms are fucking gross.

Then, another notion hits me.

I could be projecting.

Isn't that what always happens? Women catch feelings from sex and guys get annoyed? And heaven forbid you try to talk about feelings because you might as well ask a guy if he wants a prostate exam.

Maybe that's what's going on.

Maybe handholding is just hand-holding and that's that.

I press my lips together as I turn the knob to cut off the water and then carefully wring out my sopping hair. *You know what? I'm not going to worry about it. I have too much other shit to deal with right now.*

We've made good time so we should hit Casablanca later today, which means I need to figure out a route, clothing, supplies ... I bring a hand to my forehead, feeling over-whelmed. I've looked at it a little bit, but compared to what I usually do, I only feel about five percent prepared. Why did I leave this stuff until the last minute? I never leave things until the last minute. I'm typically planning and re-planning, and then over-planning, until I've got five back up options memorized.

Not today, Satan.

I've never really understood that saying.

I mean, why *not today*? Why isn't the saying, *not ever*? Do people mean not today but maybe tomorrow? Does that saying even really fit right now?

Fuck. I got mentally sidetracked.

I'd better hurry and finish up because I need at least two back up plans in case things get wonky with Fadoul today. The guy who set the bounty is known as a bit of a hothead, so if we piss him off, we'll need to be ready for him. He's a shoot first and ask questions later kind of guy. Normally, I approve of that. Today? Not so much.

Other people's lives are on the line this time, I mentally scold myself for my failure to obsessively scheme as I dry off, toss my wet hair up into a bun on top of my head. Then I don a pale blue, long-sleeved maxi dress embroidered with navy and white flowers so that I look conservative enough for the city we're about to land in. I pick a blue scarf to match the outfit and tie it around my waist for now, though I'll use it over my hair later.

I sigh, wishing I'd brought another dye kit with me since red hair stands out. I suppose I could always grab a wig if I'm desperate but with a scarf and some sunglasses, maybe I'll fly under the radar.

I'm mentally debating all my options as I walk down the bedroom hallway in the direction of the kitchen, a huge smile on my face as I smell sausage and eggs. "Sex makes me so hungry. I could eat a—"

I round the corner and stop dead. My throat dries out and my heart forgets how to do whatever it is it does.

Every part of me just shudders to a halt.

Tyler Monroe's awake.

Other than the tiny sips of water I've forcefully encouraged him and Avery to take over the past few days, he hasn't opened his eyes. But now, he's upright, leaning against the kitchen counter, his hair dark and slicked back against his skull as if he just had a shower too. Though he hasn't shaved, it looks like he's cleaned up the beard that grew while he was passed out and two gray streaks run down either side of his chin. He's wearing a white button-down shirt and charcoal-gray pants with boat shoes. Everything looks like it fits him perfectly, so Colt must have had a go bag for him in the chopper or something. He looks so damn good but at the same time, the sight of him is a punch to the gut.

I'm on edge as my eyes travel across his jagged scar and meet his dark gaze.

A flash of prickling fear runs through me.

"You fucking bitch! Poison? Motherfucking poison? Couldn't even shoot us?" Each word is punctuated by a step as he pushes off the counter and comes toward me. His limp is even more pronounced than normal after having slept for four days straight but it doesn't make him feel any less dangerous. Even the slightly gaunt look to his cheeks makes him all the more menacing. Vicious, murderous energy emanates from him and makes the air thick, makes it hard to breathe as he draws near.

Somehow, I manage to fake nonchalance. Something about Tyler's energy compels my hackles to rise and my nipples to tighten even though my spine is practically liquid from fear. Tyler brings out the cornered kitten in me and I can't help but hiss and swipe ... and enjoy the fact as I do. "It was three on one. I had to even the odds somehow."

I blink and *boom*.

Tyler's there. His fingers are around my neck, squeezing and lifting. He pulls me up, until I'm suspended on tiptoe, his hand pressed tight against my airway, compressing it. Oxygen becomes rare and precious as I gasp underneath his touch.

I hate it and love it.

"Guess instead of a win, you've got a mulligan," I wheeze, because if he's going to kill me like I deserve, then I at least want to get in one parting shot.

Tyler's mouth twitches on one side, almost as if he's battling a smile. His fingers tighten for a millisecond.

Colt ends up speaking up behind him. My huge man scratches at his black t-shirt as he says, "Hey, man. I know you're pissed, but ... "

Is he standing up for me?

Tyler's head does a slow, dangerous swivel to look at the other member of Triple X, who's standing in the kitchen with a spatula in one hand, looking like he belongs on some cooking/stripping competition show. (Why don't they have one of those yet? Fuck. I need oxygen. I'm getting loopy.)

My hands fly up to try to pry Tyler's fingers away, those strong digits as hard as steel bars, but my scrabbling just makes him whip his head back to me. And if I thought he was angry before, now he appears absolutely livid.

"You slept with both of them?" he snarls. Apparently, Colt questioning him is a dead giveaway. I would have thought the fact that I rounded the corner talking about sex would have been the giveaway but ....

"Jealous?" My question is hardly more than a whisper.

Tyler literally shows me his teeth as he grits them together. His fingers tighten, cutting my air off completely. For a second, I feel certain he wants nothing more than to snap my neck, but something passes through his eyes, a phantom emotion. A flicker of a feeling I can't identify.

He releases me. I fall from my tiptoes to my heels, gasping for air, throat aching with each breath as though oxygen molecules were filled with tiny razor blades.

The assassin spins around and stomps back to Colt, stealing the pan of scrambled eggs from him and a fork from one of the two place settings on the counter. He shovels wobbly bites of egg into his mouth with a force that I didn't know was possible.

If a human being could steam, curls of heated water would be rising from his shoulders right now.

When Colt starts to speak, Tyler jabs the fork at him threateningly and the big assassin shuts his mouth.

Apparently, Tyler Monroe is hangry. As I rub my sore neck, I wonder if he's a little sex hangry too ....

Maybe.

Ugh, or maybe I'm just into too much wishful thinking this morning. Maybe it's all just fury and I want it to be something else. I need to dial the hormones down a notch.

Planning brain, where are you?

Carefully circuiting around Tyler, giving him a wide berth in case he decides to lash out with that frying pan in his hands, I give Colt a small smile and I get a soft one in return, one that makes my chest feel sunshiney and bright.

No.

No hormones.

Sit back down.

We aren't in happy mode.

Work mode.

Work mode, activate.

I open my mouth to say something to Colt. I'm not exactly sure what, but something along the lines of, "Guess I'll be eating toast," when Avery walks in, using a towel to dry off his hair. He's got on khaki pants but no socks or shoes and more importantly, no shirt.

Any words building on my tongue evaporate when I see Avery because a dump truck loaded with guilt pours a metric ton of horrible feelings onto my head at the sight of him. Every freckle on his chest screams out that I'm a traitor and I don't deserve to look at them. My shoulders suddenly feel the heavy weight of disgrace. I blink rapidly, eyes flashing from him to Tyler, to Colt—whose lips have thinned and who is standing in silent expectation or judgment, I'm not sure which.

Panic fills me.

Pure, unadulterated panic as potent as helium swells inside my chest until I might explode. I'm not sure I'm grounded on earth any longer, I might be floating away. Someone could probably stick a needle in me and I'd just pop—fear bursting out of every pore of my body.

I didn't just fail to plan for our meeting later today. I've deliberately avoided thinking too much about this moment right here.

About facing these men after I hurt them.

I close my eyes and try to find a tiny sliver of calm somewhere inside. Just a tiny little scrap in the wreckage of my mind. I don't find one.

I breathe in. And out. My fingers flex and my nails dig into the skin of my palms.

And then, without opening my eyes, because there's no possible way I can face the reality or consequences of what I've done, especially to Avery who didn't deserve it ... I whisper, "I'm sorry. But I'll make it up to you. I'll get you this bounty and then ... I don't know. But I'll find a way."

"WHAT THE HELL!" Tyler's offended yell slams into me as I hear the clank of his fork hitting the pan. His voice is so loud, I'm pretty sure everyone back in Marseille can hear him. "Avery gets a fucking apology?"

My eyes pop open because his ire makes no sense. "Avery was just trying to help me—"

"Fucking sleep with my teammates and then fucking apolog —" The pan does go flying, just as I predicted, scrambled eggs falling like gelatinous yellow rain drops until the pan smashes into a wall, denting it before tumbling ungracefully to the floor.

What the hell?

Is Tyler throwing a fit?

Red lines my vision. God. Everything about him just winds me up. He wants an apology? He doesn't deserve an apology. He gave me an orgasm as he tried to one-up me. The bastard. Every step of the way the man has been pushing me, challenging me, trying to beat me at this game. And is it hot? Hell yes. But am I going to apologize to him for fucking winning?

Hell—and his balls— will have to freeze over first.

"Don't have such hot teammates if you don't want me to fuck them!" I manage a hoarse shout, though my throat feels raw. "Seriously. There are plenty of ugly assassins out there. Pick some of them. Don't blame me for your poor life choices."

"MY—" Tyler's hands fly to his head and I'm actually slightly amused, but also a smidge concerned he's about to pull out his gorgeous silver-streaked hair by the roots as he angrily hyperventilates.

"Tyler." Avery moves farther into the room, giving me a totally scolding, *stand down* look. "Don't get all riled up."

"Yeah, you need your strength. We're about to go see the bounty poster. Then we'll have a Russian and a thief to kill, so save your energy. I need to go plan." I'm proud of how calmly I speak, despite the fact that Tyler looks like he wants to tackle me and try out some of the krav maga moves that my cyber stalking showed he studied.

Fuck, Royal.

You need to calm down yourself.

What I need to do is get out of here. The amount of awkward swirling through the air right now is enough to make a girl choke. I'm unable to make eye contact with either Avery or Colt because I don't really want to see what they think of me in this moment. Instead, I reach into the pantry and grab a random container to serve as my breakfast. "I have to go check our heading and make some plans."

I scamper off, walking away as quickly as I can without making it look as though I'm about to run.

I end up checking on Yegor because I hear him messing around in his room and I'm surprised to find him crouching in the bathroom, drawer open beside him rolling out a lipstick I must have missed in my purge. That makes me stop short. Why the hell does he want lipstick?

When he bites down on the colored wax, making his teeth turn an odd shade of orangey-red, I realize we might have forgotten an important part of prisoner keeping. Feeding him.

Oops.

I sigh. Looks like I'll be sharing a bit of my breakfast. "That shit's toxic, you know. It'll kill ya." I chuckle at my own ironic cleverness as I look at the box in my hand. Cream of wheat. Of course it is. Yuck.

I walk over to the sink and run some hot water before plugging it up and pouring in some of the dry cereal flakes. "There you go, Yegsy. Breakfast of champions."

The Russian doesn't even have the energy to snarl at me. He simply clumsily maneuvers to his feet and shoves his face into it, like a little puppy dog.

Leaving him behind to enjoy the fancy feast I just made him; I go to the control room and get to work.

I try really hard not to glance at the door every five minutes, not to notice that no one comes to see me for hours, not to dwell on the fact that Colt and I have spent days in one another's company and suddenly—everything I'm used to doing alone feels lonely.

19

GUNS BLAZING

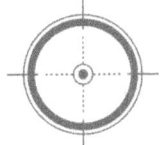

May 27

10:43 p.m.

Casablanca, Morocco

Royal

Casablanca is supposed to be one of the most romantic cities in the world but in my opinion, all that hype is wrong. The city is loud and ugly, just like the looks Tyler keeps giving me.

Jerk.

The long lines of art deco stone buildings that make up the metropolis on either side of us are lit up by streetlights that cast golden glows up the sides of the white walls. Some of them are decorated with patterned tiles wrapping around the middle of the buildings like colorful belts.

This place could be pretty ... if I had someone to appreciate it with, which I clearly don't.

My jaw clenches as the man in front of me in the suit—always a damn suit—glances over his shoulder to glare at me as if he's expecting me to throw a knife at his back at any moment.

"If you don't trust me, then let me walk in front, idiot," I mutter under my breath.

"What's that?" Avery, who's on my right side acting as my escort (since this town isn't necessarily always that safe for women or tourists at night), asks.

"Nothing." I don't bother looking over at him. He's dressed to draw more attention than Tyler or Colt, wearing a flower print shirt and khakis so that he and I look like a tourist couple. The goal is that hopefully outsiders see Tyler, Colt, and Yegor in front of us and think of them as one group and Avery and me as a separate, unrelated couple. Of course, Avery's ruining the couple vibe by being a nervous nelly, refusing to even hold my hand, and constantly glancing around nervously—though that does fit the tourist bit to a T.

It also hurts my feelings that he won't touch me ... but what else should I expect?

I mean you can't kidnap and poison a guy and then just assume he'll forgive you.

If he did just forgive you, he'd have a screw loose.

But if I hate Tyler's hostile scowls, I hate Avery's disappointed glances even more. It's like someone took a cheese grater to my heart and just started rubbing, peeling it into painful little red ribbons.

Maybe I should join Yegor at the end of the night.

Fuck.

Fuck.

Fuck my life.

I blow out a breath and crack my neck from side to side, trying to shake this melancholy. The guys might not like me very much right now, but they do need me. And I want them to get that money. It doesn't repair what I've done at all, but I can at least help them get what they came for.

I want one good thing to come from this debacle.

I glance up at the stars and wish that something else would have come from it. But I don't know why stars would grant my wishes anyway, so it's fitting when I can't find one to wish on. The sky is dark overhead, stars washed out by light pollution, and the road on our left side is basically a raceway because drivers here zig and zag as they zip along, using the shoulder like it's a lane, hurrying to their destinations without a care for traffic rules. The driving part of this town is kinda great. It makes each step you take outside an adventure, a little bit of a risk. One car rushes by my side, wheels squealing as it jumps the curb for a split second before veering back onto the street.

Nothing like a near death experience to make my blood fly nearly as fast as that dude's tail lights.

I almost chuckle, the burst of adrenaline just what I needed to jumpstart my mood and help me flick off my sadness and move into the zone. I'm focused Royal. Professional killer Royal. I'm not teenage-heartbreak, toxic, sappy Royal. I'm a badass.

The air smells like smog and play-dough, the latter because there's a bag of uncooked couscous scattered across the road that must have spilled off the back of someone's motorbike earlier.

While I love the food here and most of the people speak French, the entire vibe of the city is ruined by one pouting assassin and another sulking mobster who refuses to walk on his leash like a good boy.

We abandoned the ship two hours ago, a couple of cameras and another little bomb from my sister planted onboard. The first are to ensure there are no surprises in case we still need La Sirene or the helicopter for a getaway. But the bomb is there in case we don't—in order to erase any DNA left behind. It's set to go off when I trigger it but not before … one of the backup plans I determined earlier today.

Since we came ashore with Yeggsy, we've been making our way to the rendezvous point that I coordinated with Fadoul.

Colt has had to fight with the mobster every step of the way. Apparently, the Russian doesn't have a big interest in us providing proof of life just to be able to kill him. Honestly, I would have thought after the past few days, he'd be relieved to be nearly done. Doesn't death seem more peaceful than constant anxiety?

But he keeps ducking and bobbing in Colt's hold, as if he's going to get away. I think maybe that lipstick he ate has already poisoned his brain, because he must be forgetting about the cuffs connecting them.

Duh-dumb dumb.

Oh … is that what that sing-song sound is?

I never realized it literally says dumb dumb.

We walk two more blocks and curve around a tall pile of trash bags stacked near the street. Yegor tries again, ducking his head and sprinting to the right as if he's strong enough to drag Colt along behind him. He gets all of two steps before Colt's grip is locked onto his arm and Yegor slams onto his ass on the sidewalk.

Maybe it's my nerves about the upcoming meeting and how Yegor's unexpected little movements might set off Fadoul's jumpy trigger finger. Or perhaps I'm punchy because of the cold shoulder Tyler's been giving me all day, which resurfaces again when his eyes lift from the gangster on the ground to stare accusingly at me. As if it's my fault Yegor's still alive. But the need to defend myself swells in my chest. I want to yell at him that I only saved Yegor to save that bounty for them ... It might not have been true at the time. I originally wanted it all for myself. But it is now, and that's what counts.

Tyler lights up this ferocious side of me that just wants to lash out. Since I'm feeling belligerent and can't exactly mouth off to Tyler at the moment, I lean down toward Yegor who's still sprawled on the sidewalk and looks like he has no intention of rising. Tucking back the scarf that's tied over my hair as my face dips down, I hiss at him, "You belong in that pile, you piece of excrement."

The Russian man simply says, "A man must make a living."

"Selling that entire fucking family? Really? You had to do that to make a living?" I shove roughly at his back, figuring it won't much matter to Colt since the Russian's seated. "Stand up, you coward. Walk to the death you earned."

"Royal, don't break character," Avery says nervously, glancing around. But there aren't many people out on the sidewalk, and we aren't to the old cathedral yet, where we're going to show proof of life to Fadoul.

"No one's watching. And if they were, what do they care? I'm some tourist checking on an idiot who tripped on the sidewalk," I justify myself as I stand back up, fuming at the fact that Yegor refuses to acknowledge my question.

I actually find myself hoping that Fadoul is a little wild and unhinged tonight, mostly because that's how I'm feeling. And I wouldn't mind letting off a little steam by getting into a hand-to-hand combat situation.

Colt has to pull the prisoner upright, and the huge assassin turns to me with an upset expression. Great. He's mad at me too. Tyler. Avery. Colt. They all fucking hate me. Brilliant. Best night ever. I wish I could burn this entire city to the ground just so I would never have to see its name on a map ever again.

"Sorry if that jerked you around," I apologize. "Wasn't thinking. Just pissed."

Colt shakes his head, his green eyes narrowing. "What family?"

"What?" I'm lost.

"What family did he sell?"

My lips twist a little as I confess a fact I'm not proud of. "While I was doing my research and getting ready for this hit, he sold a family of four to a factory owner in China. I tried to figure out where he sent them ... but I had to choose. Time was of the essence. It was them ... or him."

Spontaneous tears erupt in my eyes and I have to scrunch my nose, sniff, and look off to the side at the cars dodging one another to take my mind off the intense guilt that hits me.

Goddammit. I can't keep the emotions in check tonight.

Colt doesn't respond, but when he turns, he yanks Yegor up roughly and starts walking at twice the pace he was before.

We reach our destination, Casablanca Cathedral, after ten more minutes of walking, solely because we circumnavigate the entire thing before deeming it fit to go inside. We walk around, and Tyler pretends to snap photos with his phone as I zoom in on rooftops to check for snipers. Meanwhile, I have to keep pretending to drop things in order to look underneath the cars parked around the place to see if they're rigged to blow. Once, I actually do lose my phone underneath a car and have to get on my knees to dig a little to retrieve it. When I emerge, I find all three assassins staring at my ass.

I swipe my hand across it, wondering if something got on my dress. "What?"

Their eyes all instantly drift back to their tasks, and I realize, with a mix of ego-boosting congratulations and horror, that they were checking me out.

"No distractions," I scold them. "Not the time for sexy thoughts."

I say that even though I'm having trouble resisting myself, particularly when Tyler's wearing his serious grumpy face and that damned prosthetic again. I just want to rip it off him and fuck in public against one of the cars—though that would definitely be a bad idea in this uber conservative place.

This is why there's a saying: don't mix business with pleasure. The pleasure side always interferes with business.

Too late.

Saw that warning sign and drove right past it and now I'm off-roading with these motherfuckers. Tonight's gonna be a bumpy ride. Unfortunately, not a bumping uglies one.

Avery uses an app on his phone to check for drones nearby. We're trying to be prepared for anything we can think of because I trust Fadoul as far as I could throw the heavyset bastard.

Once Avery looks up and those baby blues blink as he gives us the all-clear sign, I say, "Alright. Let's move. Tyler, you go in first. We're early, so you should have time to set up in sniper—"

"No." Tyler's answer rings out around the road, which is empty right now.

"What?" I turn, a bit miffed, because I ran through all these plans with them on the yacht and he didn't say a word against them.

"Ave, you stay out here and hot wire a getaway car. Colt, I'm taking point. But be ready to end this fucker and act as my backup at any moment. I need you, I'll call."

Colt nods.

Tyler turns toward me. I'm not just irked or irritated. I'm fuming, boiling, seething right now. That pompous jerk is trying to pull the rug right out from under me, after I spent hours figuring out every last detail of this meetup—all with the intention of keeping his ass alive.

Tyler turns toward me. "You can leave now. We don't need you anymore."

He might as well have dumped a bucket of ice water over my head. His words don't just shock me, they send painful prickles digging deep into my skin over my entire body. My vision ripples for a second as the implications of his words roll through me. He doesn't want me here. He wants me gone.

God, that cracks open the abandonment wound inside, the one that's never fully healed but just constantly oozing sadness.

If one of the other men had said it, it would have broken me. I would have taken my gun, right here, right now and been done.

But it's Tyler.

So, instead of reaching for the gun strapped to my inner thigh, I convert all my sorrow to anger. And the exchange rate for those two emotions is really good. One to two. Highly recommend. You can be well-off in Sadland or fucking mobster-rich in Furyville.

A flaming inferno starts to spin inside my head as I cross the space between Tyler and me. Grabbing his lapels, I lever up to my tiptoes, before hissing, "Oh no, honey. You don't get to win that easy." Then I shove him backward and storm off toward the cathedral steps, leaving them behind.

"Why'd you have to—" Colt starts to say.

But Tyler cuts him off. "Fuck! Come on."

Footsteps hurry to catch up to me and I can't help the dark, satisfied grin that spreads across my face.

Tyler wants to pretend he's in charge?

Game on.

20

SHOT DOWN

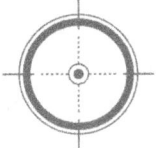

May 27
11:30 p.m.
Casablanca, Morocco

Royal

*W*hat a beautiful location for my terrible mood, I think as I stomp up the steps. The cathedral is another Art Deco era beauty—white stone with narrow, delicate stained-glass windows on either side. Arches galore. Topped by matching minarets on either side of the front doors, the place could easily be mistaken for a palace, particularly with the way the moonlight and streetlights are casting romantic glows on it.

Never used as a cathedral, since Catholicism doesn't really predominate in this Muslim country, it's actually more of a cultural center here. Supposedly, there's an art exhibition set up inside right now, though the building is officially closed for the night. Some kind of abstract sculptures or something. It's a big open space inside though, no pews, which means there aren't a million hiding places. It's also got thick walls, with the exception of the stained glass, so if we end up in a shootout, it will take a bit for people outside to notice. Slower police response. More getaway time.

I'm pretty proud of myself for thinking through all those tidbits and also whipping up a sexy standoff location that's worthy of a movie set ... but there's no one to pat my back or share my pride right now.

A month ago, it wouldn't have mattered.

I wouldn't have wanted or needed that. Shit, even two weeks ago. But now...

Tyler's fucked up plan B and C by changing things up on me.

I glance back at Avery, who hasn't followed me, but stayed behind to obey Tyler. Part of me thinks he deserves to be tied up and spanked for this poor life choice, but when I see his expression, my anger softens. He's running his tongue nervously over his teeth as he glances around, his blond hair glinting under the streetlights.

Fuck.

I don't like leaving him outside alone. Of the three of us, he's got the least experience in dealing with this shit, so I understand what Tyler's doing keeping Avery out of the line of fire. But at the same time, I'd feel safer if he was behind me and I knew I could physically protect him.

Out here ... he's on his own if Fadoul has some creep try to sneak up on us.

I want to promise him that nothing will happen to him, that I won't let it, but if I do, then I'll probably end up dialing up all kinds of emotions that I can't afford to have blaring in my ears right now. Anger's the only one I can really deal with.

I zip my lips and throw away the key, a physical gesture which makes Colt furrow his brow and glance at me curiously as he drags a reluctant Yegor up to stand beside me. I turn away to stare up at the giant doors instead of bothering to explain my quirks.

Squaring my shoulders, I take a deep breath and stride forward, hoping that if I act confident then I'll trick my brain into thinking I am. "Alright. Let's do this thing."

I go before Tyler makes it all the way up the stairs, his limp causing him to be a little slower than Colt. I don't want the head of Triple X to think that he's still in charge as we walk in this place. And I don't want Fadoul to think that either.

I set this meeting up.

I'm running it.

I wish we had a badass soundtrack. I wish my hair was uncovered and blowing in the wind—that wish is granted suddenly, when the wind picks up right as I reach the door handles. I immediately regret calling on the universe because the breeze carries a rancid scent and I'm sure there's a dead animal in an alleyway somewhere nearby. It makes me hurry to tug on the doors a little faster than is cool. But gagging isn't cool either, so...

I yank hard and am horrified/humiliated/offended to find that the metal front door is too heavy for me to open.

"Stupid fucking metaphysical-loving bastards," I curse at the cathedral's builders under my breath. "Showoffs."

"Ladies first," Tyler snarks, coming up beside me and pulling open the door with an ease that makes me want to smack him across the face as he gestures with his hand to usher me in, like he's being a gentleman.

"Gladly. I'll be sure to dodge the first bullet so that it hits you," I tell him.

"Right. You're faster than a bullet."

"Faster than you, limpy," I chirp.

His narrowed gaze does make me feel a little bit better as I saunter past, that is, until I feel him looming behind me as I walk down the center aisle. His body heat falls over me like a shadow and damn...do I love the dark. I'm so tempted to lean back into him right now...but I have to stay focused.

Or try.

I scurry a few extra steps ahead so that I can breathe normally again and then drink in our surroundings.

The cathedral is massive, as cathedrals are—with all the normal columns and archy stuff that is supposed to look fancy. I've always thought all those columns just looks like mistakes. Like, *Uh-oh, we forgot to measure the ceiling right. Better throw a post in there, Jim. Now, toss one on the other side to make it look like it's on purpose.*

Why else would there need to be columns every four feet?

Though the floor area is dark and full of oddly shaped, semi-phallic shadows from all the geometric sculptures around the place, there are some small lights on up in the arches and near the back of the cathedral where the altar would have been. They showcase the patterns in the stained glass, and on the ceiling, but I don't take more than a second to look at them, because I realize I miscalculated.

An hour early for this meeting wasn't enough.

We aren't the first to have arrived.

Fuck.

Scattered throughout the cathedral, I count at least three men in suits, arms crossed in front of them in the fig-leaf pose that seems to be universal for armed guards everywhere.

Why do they stand like that?

Are they expecting a kick to the jewels at any moment?

Trying to pass off my irritated nervousness that nothing is going to plan right now, I give a little ditzy finger wave to each man in order to ensure that Colt and Tyler see them— though I assume they do because they weren't born yesterday.

The click of my heels fills the cathedral and echoes ominously as I make my way down the middle aisle. "Fadoul. If I'd known we were having a party, I would have brought food," I call out with an ease I don't feel.

I have to force my jaw to unclench and paste on a fake smile as I get closer to the back of the church, because standing on the altar like he's a gift from God himself, is Fadoul.

He wears a suit and his beard, though long, has been trimmed and oiled. His dark hair is combed smoothly to one side. His eyes glitter with all the beady depth of a snake's eyes. He's got a slightly larger nose than normal, but what really is striking about his face are his oversized nostrils. They flare open with each breath, and I can't help but feel like I'm approaching a dragon. I note the gun carried openly at his hip. I've got no doubt there's another perched in a holster right above his ass. Maybe even one at his ankle too. He's probably wearing body armor. Meanwhile, I'm not. In order to pull off the whole, non-threatening, just-here-to-talk vibe, I've gone without.

Premonition trickles up my spine and I worry I've made a foolish choice.

That's all I seem able to make lately. Foolish life choices.

Fadoul spreads his arms wide as if he's welcoming a long-lost friend. "Royal. As-salamu-alaykum. So good we can finally meet. And you have brought ... your brothers?" It's a prodding question, because he's trying to find out what the guys mean to me.

I give him a respectful dip of the head as I say, "This is my harem."

I grin when his expression tightens slightly, as if he's both off-put and confused by my statement. Part of me wishes I could see the guys' reactions, but that's not in the cards right now.

Rather than letting my little shock bomb statement rattle around too long in Fadoul's skull, I move onto business as I stride closer to the altar, stopping beside a strange stone sculpture that looks like it's made of a series of giant-sized children's toy blocks. There's a little plaque in Darija to explain the art installation, but I have no clue what it says,

maybe *No Climbing*. If I were here under other circum-
stances, it would be hard to keep me off of it.

But, right now, I only appreciate the way it helps block the
sight lines of Fadoul's goon on the right.

My heart's beating rapidly and my skin is prickling with
awareness, my spine is a live wire as I come to stand right in
front of the older man. The fact that Tyler's right behind
me is a comfort for once, instead of an irritation. The man
might want to personally one-up me, but in this moment,
we're on the same team.

Money can unite people in the strangest ways.

I swing my arm wide, gesturing back toward Colt, who's
standing in the middle of the center aisle like my very own
statue, dressed all in black and holding a squirming Yegor
by the neck. "As you can see, we've brought in Yegor
Babanin ... " When I turn back to Fadoul, I can hear Colt
dragging him forward so the Moroccan can get a better
look.

Yegor's pleas fill up the cathedral for a moment when he
spots someone outside our little group. Someone he hopes
might be a savior. "Please. Sir. They are madmen. They—"

"Save your breath," Tyler barks. "He's the one who put a
price on your head." He sounds horribly grumpy, and I
wonder if it chafes his ass that I'm in charge right now.

I hope so.

I smile pleasantly at Fadoul as he eyes Yegor up and down
with distaste. "Why did you bring him to me?"

As Yegor gets closer, he obviously recognizes Fadoul. "You prick!" A slew of Russian curse words accompany the explanation as Yegor lambasts the man who tried to off him. Colt ends up picking Yegor up and clamping a hand over his mouth to shut him up.

I turn and glare at the prisoner. "Do that again, and I'll have one of the boys spank you."

The threat of humiliation in front of his worst enemy does the trick, at least temporarily. Yegor quiets.

Men and their egos.

You can bet a spanking wouldn't scare me.

Depending on who was giving it, I might even like it.

I deliberately avoid Tyler's gaze because I'm thinking about just who I might like to spank me.

Mission, Royal. Hello? Did you forget about that?

Shut up, brain.

I turn back to Fadoul with a smug expression that hopefully hides the chaotic inner workings of my head. I put a hand to my heart. "Clearly, you and Yeggsy go way back. I'm loving that I get to be part of this little reunion between you two. Heartwarming. Totally."

"I wanted him dead. I don't want him alive."

BAM.

A shot rings out through the cathedral and immediately, I hear every one of Fadoul's men racking their weapons.

"There you go. Dead." Tyler's voice is calm as I hear Colt click open the handcuffs and let Yegor's body fall to the floor. It lands with a double thump.

My OCD twitches because this is not at all how I wanted to off the mobster, but I have to shake it off. Shake it off.

Be Taylor Swift, I tell myself and my hands automatically come to my hips to do the little hip swivel she does in the music videos, though I'm able to stop myself before I actually do them.

I want Fadoul to take me seriously after all. So, instead, I channel Taylor's darker stuff as I strut forward.

"So. Yegor's dead. And you know we killed him. Now, the important question is ... clearly, whoever told you they took him out before was a liar." I give Fadoul a flat look, one that screams I mean business. "Who has our money?"

Fadoul's expression changes. He swallows a little too hard. His limbs stiffen up just the tiniest bit. Perhaps not enough for someone else to notice. But for me and my OCD...I'm always obsessing over little details. The clincher is when he glances up and to the right, trying to pass off the look like he's thinking. That's the look of a man who's about to make something up.

In a flash, I realize what's happened.

I don't really know how I know.

I just know.

"BASTARD!" I leap at Fadoul, tackling him to the ground.

At the same time, gunfire erupts behind me. The purr of an assault rifle pushing out a continuous stream of bullets fills the air. The stone columns erupt with tiny puffs of dust and I hear the yell of the assassins behind me. His henchmen clearly have been paid enough to be loyal to Fadoul, even when someone gets the drop on him.

Fuck. The guys!

Fear foams inside my veins, rabid and frantic. I shouldn't have done that! I shouldn't have leapt on Fadoul! *Dammit, Royal!*

A sick, churning sort of agony crashes over me but I don't have time to look around to check on them, not when Fadoul's hand is heading toward my face.

They're not novices. *They'll be okay. They have to be okay.*

Instead of the cool, calm, methodical bitch I normally transform into on a job, this time, I feel like I'm a snapping piranha. I don't run down the checklist Man made me to disable a dude once you get him to the ground. I just fucking punch the daylights out of his face and try to ignore the fact that his own fists are smashing into my sides, my gut.

"You kept that fucking money for yourself. Didn't you? Didn't you!?" *That's Colt's money, motherfucker.*

I dig my knees into the Moroccan man's ribs and wrap my hands around Fadoul's neck. His hands scratch and grab at me, but I'm a woman possessed as I lean forward over him. I can't see my own expression, but every part of my face feels like it's on fire. Fury burns right through my skin like acid as I hiss, "You posted that bounty and set up all these little assassins and figured that with them all competing against each other, you'd just claim that someone else took the bounty, that the cash was digital, that it was gone, untrace-able... You planned to send us on a snipe hunt. Didn't you?"

God. Punching isn't enough. I need to hurt this man. Colt and Avery risked their necks for that bounty ... and it was all a fucking set up.

A trick.

I grab onto the Moroccan's collar and roll us so that I'm on the bottom—my scarf falling from my hair in the process and the red strands fanning out across the floor. Fadoul's expression morphs to brutal savagery when he thinks he's gotten the upper hand physically once he's on top.

What a typical, disappointing male.

Fadoul. Fadoul. Fadoul.

I could cluck my tongue at him.

On the other hand, I appreciate him being the typical, disappointing male because it allows me to employ my sick-ass combat moves, which I've had to practice daily since the age of seven.

Man always promised I'd end up using them one day.

I always blew a raspberry at him, thinking it was all talk.

Today's the day I have to swallow all that raspberry spit.

I leverage our momentum and the fact that the asshole starts to push himself up to slide my hand between us. The second my fingers are around his gun, I shift my hips to roll us again. He fights, using his bodyweight to press against me —but that's exactly what I expect him to do. He thrusts that pelvis forward trying to pin me down. But that gives me the gap I need at his waist and I swivel his weapon up and pull the trigger—shooting him through the gut, right above his dick. I might even give him a second asshole.

"Ouch. That must hurt," I say, with a scrunch of the nose. "Gut wounds are supposed to be a painful way to die."

He gasps and falls forward.

"Here, let me help you," I cheerfully offer as I slide to the side, keeping hold of his first weapon with my right hand as I use my left to roll him off me. He smacks onto the floor with a sound that clearly indicates he does have another weapon at his back, so I scramble against the ground, knocking my knee so hard it sings in pain as I hurry to stand beside the nearest sculpture, which happens to be a giant peacock feather.

I train my weapon on Fadoul, struggling to hold it steady.

Inside, my heart is thumping. Behind me, gunfire is erupting and cursing is occurring in two separate languages simultaneously creating a cacophony of sound. Outside, somewhere, I hear the rev of an engine.

I hear my own voice, which feels strangely disconnected from my body as I say, "Here's what's going to happen. You're going to call your goons off." I stop after the first instruction, because I'm not certain Fadoul has the ability to process more than one thing at a time right now.

To be fair, a gunshot wound is a little distracting.

I mean, it didn't do much to Colt, but we aren't all Hulks.

Fadoul's definitely not.

"Royal!" Colt's voice echoes across the cathedral in warning. Immediately, I drop to the ground, rolling. A bullet ricochets off the thick stained-glass window just behind me and lodges deep in the marble floor.

Fuck.

That just made this all more real.

Fright starts to dart through me, and I try to ride the edge of it as if I can mold it from dread into adrenaline. Instead of trying to stand and risking being shot at again, I shoot Fadoul in the foot from where I lie. Relishing his pained cry when the bullet shatters the delicate bones and his body naturally curls in to protect itself, I repeat my words in a low, hostile tone. "Call. Them. Off."

Fadoul gives a pained whine as he pants, "Look. It's not what you think. I needed the job done. But the money ... "

I shoot his other foot. "I don't want excuses." Colt earned that money fair and square. And Fadoul's barely better than Yegor. He deals in expensive secrets. Lucrative evils.

The Moroccan squeals like a piglet.

"This little piggy won't get to go home if he doesn't start talking," I say.

I'm not sure he gets the reference.

Behind us, there are scuffling sounds. A loud thud that makes my heart jump in my chest, leapfrog over my throat, and pulse right inside my lips. I long to turn around, to check on Avery and Tyler, but if I do, I'm deader than a doornail. Fadoul will grab that second gun from behind his back and it will be lights out for me. I can see his hand sliding in that direction even now.

I want to call out. To ask. I open my mouth, almost making a sound. But what if I distract one of them? It's my fault we're here in the first place. This was my stupid fucking idea.

Ruined by Tyler.

But still.

So the guys are in their own firefight behind me, while I lie prone on the ground, nervous sweat sprouting up all along my spine, keeping a weapon trained on the man who was just supposed to give us a goddamned fucking name.

What the hell is it with criminal men, huh?

Why can't they just—for once—keep to their word?

Why does it need to be all betrayal this and blood money that?

Fuckers.

They need to read some fucking mafia romance. Learn a thing or two about honor. Probably orgasms too, if I'm honest.

Fadoul yells out a phrase I don't understand and the gunfire ceases.

Finally, after I've basically crippled him, the idiot shows some sense.

Still, though, I keep my gun cocked and ready, heart in my throat as he reaches a shaking hand into his pocket and pulls out his phone. Tapping a few times on the screen, he then says, "It's done. You let me go, you get the money."

"Nah. You give me the money, then we let you go."

We stare at one another, locked in a battle of wills, while the scent of his blood starts to foul up the air. I realize that the front of my dress is wet, as are my hands—not from sweat but from that first shot to his gut.

I'm a mess. An itch starts up underneath my skull, threatening to expand, but I tell it to shut the fuck up. I can't deal with that just yet.

"You want to wait and bleed out? Then I'll just take your phone and hack your accounts. I won't just take what we're owed. I'll take everything." I threaten.

With a grimace that conveys loathing and spite, he taps at his phone a few more times before his head collapses back onto the ground limply. "It's done."

"Slide it over. Prove it."

He tosses it weakly, and it slides over the stone floor, but doesn't even make it halfway to me.

I'll have to move to get it.

I keep a hard grip on the scream of fear and frustration that's trying to slip through my throat.

"We've got you covered," Colt calls out.

"There's one on your left," Tyler calls out. His voice sounds farther away than I expect it to be which makes me wonder if he's moved. They are both trying to help me. But their help is—overwhelming, distracting, unnecessary. Not unwanted but I don't fucking know how to *team*.

Don't they get that I've been doing jobs alone since I was in braces?

So, when I turn my head and spot Tyler slowly gliding closer to the steps, backing away from the block statue that's been serving as his cover, I grouse at him. "I fucking got this!" I don't need him to hold my hand.

"No. You don't. One more foot and this motherfucker has a straight shot at you." Tyler's rage is in full force, meaning it's basically casting a forcefield of doom-like shadows all around him. He draws closer, his suit splattered with blood in a way that has no right to make my nipples tighten.

He herds me over to the left side of the altar, so coverage is provided by a statue shaped like a giant Ouija board planchette.

If I asked it whether we'll survive the night, I wonder if it would point to yes.

"I'll dive behind Fadoul," I announce with a shrug that's far more casual than the nerves tiptoe-dancing on my back feel right now. I glance in the direction of the shadows that Tyler indicated held a shooter, but whichever goon of Fadoul's is lurking there is doing a good job of hunkering down and hiding.

Damn me for leaving my night vision contacts in my makeup case, but I thought orange eyes might draw too much attention on the streets.

"We could just set off the bombs we planted around the edge of the building." Tyler's no-nonsense tone is a sharp contrast to his face, because his expression is shouting all sorts of angry things at me. His expression says I'd better listen or I'm going to be tied up and whipped later ... possibly not in a sexy way.

Maybe.

But possibly not.

I'm disinclined to think it would be the fun way, which makes me resent his suggestion all the more.

Why does he have to go and be reasonable at a time like this? Yes, we could blow up the building. But ...

I hear a door squeak open and one of the goons flees into the night.

Dammit all. That fucking coward. One of Fadoul's men just bailed.

"Where's your sense of adventure?" I challenge, biting down on a smile because now I see Tyler's plan. Cut down the numbers of the other bastards. Let them think we're about to end them. He convinced one to leave.

I'm pretty sure I'm good to go now. My foot slides across the smooth marble floor toward Fadoul, who's getting a pretty little red pond going around himself.

"Don't be stupid. It's just cash." Tyler's words slap me.

Blistering rage blinds me and tastes sour on the back of my tongue. How dare he call me stupid? Tonight is about money—for Colt's friend. But also redemption. My redemption. "To you."

We square off against one another and I stare into his dark eyes. The stained-glass windows cast demonic red glints on his irises and I swear I'm fucked in the head because that only makes him look more attractive in this moment. I honestly don't know if Tyler's about to draw his gun on me or sweep me into a kiss.

Our attraction and animosity build up until my clit is pulsing with just as much force as my heart. God, maybe we should blow up a few of these walls just so I can fuck Tyler right now and get it out of our systems.

That's when I see a shadow move behind him.

Without thinking, without breathing, just on the basest of instincts—the bone-deep need I have for him—I dive toward Tyler and shove him down just as the sound of a gunshot pierces the air.

I've hardly registered the noise of the blast before I feel my skin ripple and flesh tear, before pain bites at my hip and devours my stomach.

21

PARTING SHOT

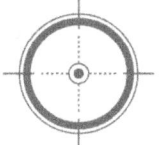

May 28
12:01 a.m.
Casablanca, Morocco

Tyler

I'm so pissed I could punch through a wall right now, and my dick's so hard I think I could use it to jackhammer through one.

I toss off a shot of covering fire in the direction of the bastard who just shot at us and then turn around and nail Fadoul right through his skull as he brings up a tiny snub nose gun. I don't even watch him fall to the ground as I dive to my knees, ignoring the pain that shoots up my thigh. I kneel next to Royal, who's gritting her teeth and panting—trusting Colt to take out the motherfucker who just shot her.

I hear a blast, and I assume that's my teammate doing his job.

Meanwhile, I have to deal with this gorgeous, utterly infuriating, injured assassin.

Fucking Royal.

"Why the hell would you do that?" I growl at her, my tone harsher than I intended as I reach for her wound.

She weakly bats me away. "It's nothing."

Fuck that.

I shove her hand aside and push up her skirt—modesty be damned. Her muscular legs and soft skin make my throat dry out. The sight of her panties makes my breath catch. But the bullet wound to her flank, just above her delicate hip bone, makes the very air around me vibrate with a turbulent force, as if I'm capable of starting my own fucking thunderstorm. Rage, disbelief, and pain collide within me, the different temperatures of the varying emotions swirling into dark clouds.

Part of me wants to move her. Part of me is utterly terrified of what I'll see if I turn her over to check the exit wound.

Diving in front of me was a fool's errand—I'm half dead inside anyway. A bullet would only finish the job started long ago.

She ... she's got so much life in her. So much spark and fire. She kindles the same in everyone around her. Even me.

I glance up at her eyes, which are rimmed in pained tears right now, but still gloriously beautiful.

I shake my head as I swallow hard on the sudden lump in my throat because that's not going to help anyone. And what I feel doesn't matter. The fact that she makes me feel anything at all after such a long and endless numbness doesn't matter. This little vixen hates me, does things to spite me every chance she gets, which nullifies the fact that she'd have the power to resurrect my heart if she wanted to.

A massive crash echoes through the room and the wall behind us, made entirely of stained glass, shatters, tiny shards raining down and bouncing across the floor. I move my body to shield Royal from the fallout as I'm pelted with sharp little rainbow flecks. The car screeches to a halt and I hear Avery yelling, "Calvary's arrived!"

Fucking idiot.

Colt must have signaled him.

But he's got surprisingly good timing because I need to get Royal out of here.

Colt's still in a corner of the room near the front door, leaning around a sculpture that's shaped like a melting popsicle as he exchanges fire with the last goon. At this point, after the entire fire fight, their singular shots sound like child's play. I turn my attention back to the girl beneath me, whose cheeks are growing pale and colorless.

"Help me up," Royal orders, still trying to boss me around even when her blood is sliding down her side in dangerous little rivulets.

"No. Stay still. I'll find something to wrap you up and then we'll drive you to a doctor."

"No fucking doctor's going to help a foreigner who got shot without a shit ton of questions," she spits.

Always fucking arguing.

"They will if I put a gun to their head."

"I'm fine. It's a through and through. I've had one before. Just like breaking a nail," she jokes. Always with the little quips.

She's been shot before? My fist clenches automatically because I immediately have the irrational desire to travel to the past and destroy the entire family tree of the last motherfucker who took a shot at her. I might still do that to Fadoul's relatives.

Right now, I'm feeling frantic, wanting to shove my hand against her wound even though my skin is probably swimming in germs. Something inside me demands that I make her okay. Make her better. Fix this. My head is more of a cluster fuck than when my own leg got shredded and I had to run on it to escape, permanently ruining the muscle.

Royal tries to push up on her own, so I'm reluctantly forced to help her to her feet because I can't stand the idea of her falling on her face. Her hands are disturbingly ice cold and soft where they clamp onto mine, and her dress is soaked in blood. Is the wound worse than she's admitting?

I know not all of the blood on the dress is her own, but the sight does make a nervous sweat break out on my lower back because my mind can process that reality—but my body? My muscles are tensed and tuned up and ready to go bash in skulls at the sight of her injury. I have a furious need to do damage.

Royal shoves one palm against her side to try to staunch the bleeding, but her face remains drawn and determined.

"Let's get you over to the car," I say, keeping my gun out and raised while my other arm circles around her carefully, unsure where to touch since the injury is at her waist. I settle on her shoulder.

"Stop telling me what to do. I can still kick your ass, even with a bullet wound." She limps next to me, leaning into me, wrapping a small hand around my waist. Even though her touch is reluctant, out of need rather than want, it makes my charred insides glow orange.

And her sass. The constant verbal smacks coming from her lips, the fight in her. If she wasn't hurt, I'd shove her up against the nearest column and kiss her until she saw stars. Then I'd finger her until she wailed so loud the echoes bounced off the walls of this place for days. Instead of doing either of those things, I simply say, "Don't get mouthy, woman," as I pull her further into my side and help her hobble over to the vehicle that Avery crashed through the glass.

"We have to hurry. Cops will be on their way, what with Avery's grand entrance and all." She doesn't acknowledge my last line, eyes darting around, and I know immediately what she's looking for.

"I'll grab Fadoul's phone," I tell her.

She nods. "Will you bring it to me? It'll distract me while we drive." Her request is soft and her eyelids are starting to look heavy. Fuck. It's as if I can see the fight and the life draining right out of her, which makes a vein inside my forehead throb frantically.

"Sure." I say, as I settle her into the backseat of the rundown little car that Avery hot wired.

He turns in the driver's seat so he can peer back at us. "Oh, shit."

"I'm fine. Just a flesh wound." Royal's tone is light but far too breathy for my liking.

I exchange a hard look with Avery.

"Give me your shirt," I order.

He doesn't hesitate. He whips it off immediately, exposing the bullet proof vest I forced him to wear even though Colt and I went without for negotiation's sake. I grab the material and a knife from my belt and cut a makeshift bandage, wrapping it around her tiny form. Each hiss of pain she gives is like an electrical spark inside my own body, as if I can feel the ache myself. In contrast, the relief when I see her claim about the through and through is correct nearly melts my kneecaps.

"Colt!" I yell as I tie the bandage off in a quick knot. "Finish the fuck up."

"Fine." His voice echoes off the stone walls around us as I scramble backwards off the bench seat of the car and run to the altar to grab that fucking phone.

I hear a final shot and a thump. Just in time, because the wail of distant sirens starts to reach my ears. "You dead, Colt?"

"Not yet." His tone is smug, which makes me think he doesn't realize how badly Royal's hurt yet. I don't tell him, because yesterday he'd seemed so damned protective of her, even after all she'd done. I can't afford for him to lose focus.

"Fire this place up," I call to him, yanking a small flask out of my pocket. I unscrew the lid and pour the contents all over Fadoul. In my interior suit pocket is a pack of matches. I reach in and rip one off, striking it to light it. I watch the tiny flame flicker for a moment before tossing it on top of the Moroccan.

A satisfying blue blaze erupts across his chest and my only regret is that he isn't alive to feel it.

Pissant.

Another fire starts up in the corner Colt just cleared, the scent of smoke starting to fill the space like incense as I hurry to the car. I stop short when I find Colt has squished himself into the back seat, Royal's head pillowed on his lap, his hand stroking her red hair as he whispers softly to her.

Something angry claws at my ribs and scrapes them raw.

What the fuck?

My mind immediately conjures up an image of me doing all that shit with Royal. I should be the one to comfort her. She took the bullet for me.

But I don't have time for jealousy right now. We have to get out of here. I shut down my emotions just as I shut the car door I'd left open and circle the vehicle, getting in on the passenger's side.

"Hope you've planned a route out of here," I tell Avery.

"Take Date Palm Drive," Royal croaks weakly from the back.

"No backseat driving," I order. "Your job is to shut up and feel better."

"You shutting up would make me feel better," she sasses, but her words are followed by a stifled moan of pain as Avery stomps on the gas and we jerk forward. I don't follow our route, don't see what's going on outside the windows. I'm hardly aware of our surroundings, trusting Avery to get us to the safe house the three of us predetermined earlier in the day. All of my attention is focused on the shallow breaths of the woman in the backseat. The tiny gasps. My heart seems to jump each time she makes a sound, absurdly worried it's going to be her last because she doesn't keep arguing. Doesn't ask for Fadoul's phone. At some point, she just slips into a haze of pain.

I don't think I've ever been this scared and it's infuriating because it's goddamned irrational. The shot was a through and through and she's going to fucking live. I'll make goddamned sure of it. And yet, I clench my gun in one hand and my knee in the other as we weave through the city, fingers ratcheting down so tightly they ache. I can't stop my heart hammering or bile rising in my throat. Because there's a logical disconnect. A leap I just can't get over.

It doesn't make sense why she'd jump in front of me. I can read that loathing in her eyes, that burning rage that lights her up whenever she glances at me. I'd misread it as attraction when we first met. It is attraction on my part ... but then she fucking tried to kill me and Avery. I understand her attempted murder far more than I understand what happened tonight. Or even earlier today after we woke up. Why the fuck would she sass me but apologize for almost killing my brother?

The woman's a fucking infuriating mystery.

She avoided the three of us, even when the rage and challenge pulsing between us was so intense I'd nearly come just from locking gazes. Something about her stirs up this deep, darkness inside of me and I want to smother her in it, just put my hand on her neck and nearly choke the life from her while I fuck her raw. I thought I was a bad man before meeting her, but since I have, my fantasies have gotten a whole lot darker than I ever believed they could. That sassy little princess thinks she can go toe-to-toe with me. Always thinks she's going to gain the upper hand.

She tried to sashay into this church like she owned it and I'd wanted to paddle her ass. That delicious, sweet curve of an ass.

Goddammit.

The sight of her pale and bleeding somehow strips away what I thought was a carnal connection. This fear for her is so much more intense than that.

And I don't understand it at all.

It's a relief in more than one way when we arrive at the safe house and hurry inside the orange, flat-roofed home that Avery booked on Air BNB. I'm no longer captive to the inside of my own fucked up head for once. I don't have to keep examining why Royal did what she did or what I feel or what she feels. There's too much to do. Secure the perimeter. Get her settled in and hold her down as we pour a whole bottle of vodka over that wound. Steal her phone and set off the charge to blow the boats. Check Fadoul's phone to see the money hovering mid-transfer, just waiting for me to type an account number and hit enter, which I do.

Action I'm good at.

But after all of that?

When the only thing left to do is watch her restlessly sleep, tossing and turning on the mattress set upon the floor? When I go to check on her, I find Avery and Colt already in the room, hovering at the foot of her bed, talking to one another in low voices.

Nope. I'm done.

I can't handle that shit.

Whatever calm, reasonable shit they're saying doesn't work for me.

I want to throttle Royal for jumping in front of me when a bullet would have just finished the job she started.

I end up stomping up the stairs, ignoring the screaming ache in my leg and standing on the roof. I scan around the building we're hunkered down in, though I've done it twice already and no one's out and about. Then I reach into the tattered remains of my suit jacket and pull out a cigar. I light it and inhale the smoke, blowing soft rings up toward the dark sky.

After a few minutes, Colt appears on the roof beside me. His brown hair is bedraggled and there's a streak of dirt or dried blood on his cheek. I can't tell and don't really care. I'm sure I look worse.

"Thought I'd find you up here," he states.

I acknowledge him with a nod, but don't speak, because what is there to say? Thanks for having my back in the shootout but I wanted to sock you in the face for taking my seat in the car? I take another puff, letting my lungs turn as black as my heart.

"She's complicated, man," he says.

I want to put this cigar out in his eyeball. Instead, I just tighten my grip on it.

"Imagine, her whole life, this is what she's been trained for. It's her everything. Now, she's trying to reconcile that with the fact that she ... well, you know ... " He trails off as if I'm supposed to know what he's saying.

I don't fucking know what he's saying.

"Look. When it comes right down to it, there aren't many people in the world who'd take a bullet for someone else. And she did that," he snaps his fingers, "instantly. Without thought. Without regret. For you. Just think about that. It's all I'm saying."

My stomach muscles tighten and then do something strange, something that hasn't ever happened to me in over a decade. They grow light. Almost fluttery.

That's when Avery bursts through the door and onto the roof, eyes wild and panicked. "I just had to take a shit. Fuck!" He runs his hands through his hair, eyes darting between us.

"What?" Colt asks, reaching immediately for his weapon.

Avery swallows hard before whispering, "She's gone."

22

BOMBSHELL

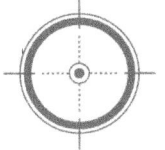

June 25
9:02 a.m.
Rose Hill, Kansas

Avery

I wake up panting, hard as a rock, because Royal invaded my dreams again. Last night, I relived our morning in Marseille, cuddling in bed and alternating between lazy kisses and slow lovemaking. That day still feels like an illusion to me, a fantasy—the kind of thing a guy like me would never really get—so I suppose it's appropriate that I keep on recalling it in my sleep.

Turning over in bed, I gaze out at the wheat field of the farm just outside Wichita we bought with some of that reward money from the Babanin job—the leftovers after Colt paid off his friend's mortgage. The gold light of morning hits the young growth in a way that normally would bring a peaceful smile to my face. But not today. Not on days I dream about her.

On days like this, it's hard to hide the fact that something's missing inside my chest. That I'm incomplete. The memories of her and what could have been, what should have been, glimmer in my head like sunlight across a lake. Everything else pales in comparison to the deep, thudding longing that aches as painfully as a physical wound.

It's been nearly a month since the red-headed beauty disappeared in Morocco and we haven't seen hide nor hair of hers since. We nearly tore apart that fucking city looking too.

I've never seen Tyler so unhinged. He was a fucking psychopath. Wouldn't sleep. Wouldn't eat. Would rage at the slightest thing.

He's a little better now, but distant.

We all are.

We'll work the field during the day because it's something to do until we take on another job. But we'll all lapse into silence, staring out across the rows of wheat, thoughts drifting to her.

Each of the guys has a certain expression he gets when he thinks about her. Colt's eyes grow sad. Almost puppyish. Tyler's jaw always grows stiff and hard like he just swallowed a rock. I'm sure I have a look too, I just haven't bothered to figure out what it is. Because why does it matter? If she left us all behind ... she clearly doesn't want us.

We're all pining in one way or another over a ghost.

And she is a *fucking ghost* because even with all the hacking I do, the little bribes I pay, I can't get me more information on her. It's almost as if there's someone out there watching the dark web, monitoring it for mentions of the Belladonnas, and carefully planting unhelpful, useless garbage for me to find.

Best assassins of all time.

Exclusive.

Elusive.

Expensive.

Fuck that shit.

Where the hell is she?

We've gone around and around debating every detail about her. I swear, Royal's accent sounds American, so I think she's from the States. Both Colt and Tyler think I'm naïve. They say that anyone can pull off an American accent. But I spent hours in her company. I made her orgasm more times than I'll ever tell them, and I don't think a woman—even if she's an amazing actress—can fake her words during a climax. Especially when said words are, "You are a motherfucking God!"

She's definitely American.

The red hair helps. That's rare. It means she's most likely of Irish descent. I've flipped through Irish mob families to see if she might be part of one of those, but no dice.

I just have to keep searching.

I shove off my comforter and sit up in bed, stretching my arms above my head and circling my neck, trying to decide what lead I want to follow today.

Tyler would say I'm stupid to keep trying. I've stopped telling him.

Sometimes, Colt and I will talk in the barn a little about her while we feed the horses, but then he'll grow quiet, almost like it hurts him too much to talk about her. Makes him too sad. Something.

I still don't know what query I'm going to put out there after I'm showered and dressed and my teeth are brushed. I pad into the kitchen mulling the options over and wondering if my black-market weapons contacts might know anything. I mean, Royal did have quite an arsenal in her go bag. I doubt those suckers are registered.

I ponder the right way to word my request as I start the coffee maker, grabbing a filter and some ground beans down from the shelf. Once that's brewing, I move to the round kitchen table and open my laptop, which lives there, before navigating to the dark web. I type and erase my question a few times and the coffee finishes before I do. Standing up and walking over to jumpstart my brain, I nearly run into Colt as he comes into the kitchen, scratching his bare belly, wearing nothing but basketball shorts.

"Thank fuck. There's caffeine," he mutters, going to the cabinet and grabbing a cup, cutting in line.

I let him, because after the Babanin job, he's developed a strange, almost worshipful stance about coffee. He's even taking to carrying a few instant packs in his pocket even when we're just going out in the field for the day.

I'm pouring my own cup of coffee when an alert beeps on my computer.

That's odd.

I finish pouring, add a little milk, and stroll over to see what's going on.

Instead of an application update notice, there's a strange pop up on my screen that almost looks like a virus. Like I got hacked. The box has a strange background. Little green aliens wearing bow ties. What the fuck?

Even stranger is the message on it.

There's just an address. And it's not too far from here. Just down in Texas. It's actually in a little town I've been to several times before when I worked the Iron Pipeline, determining routes for smuggling weapons around the country.

"What the hell is that?" Colt squints down at the screen.

"Not sure. It just showed up," I respond, chewing my lower lip and setting down my coffee mug to lean over the table. I type in a few codes and try to trace the message's origins, but there's nothing.

Whoever sent this to me is a pro.

"Could be a set up," he muses as he nurses his coffee, staring at the screen with narrowed eyes.

"Could be," I agree, though there's a strange sort of excitement lining my stomach that tells me it isn't. A jumpy, hoppy sort of irrational feeling that resembles hope on steroids. "But ... that screen. Who would send a background like that?"

It's kooky. It's silly. Completely unprofessional.

Colt bends to look at the screen closer and I swear his expression goes from hard to soft in under a minute, from suspicious to utterly and completely hopeful. "Royal," he breathes.

He turns to look at me and the light in his green eyes is as manic as the emotion bubbling inside my own chest. "We have to go," I say.

He nods immediately.

Thank fuck we're on the same page. I let out a deep, relieved breath. Now, the hard part is going to be convincing Tyler.

"THIS IS the stupidest fucking thing we've ever done," Tyler repeats for the eightieth time as he racks his weapon and tosses on a tactical helmet.

We're parked in a field, three miles out from the deserted house that matches the address that showed up on my screen two days ago. The sun has gone down behind us and the only living things in the vicinity are a flock of pale birds twittering as they fly overhead. Though the sky is clear where we're at, the clouds streak nearly to the flat Texas plains in the distance, where a rainstorm is obviously taking place.

I slide on night vision goggles, not bothering to look over at my stepbrother.

Unlike him, I'm not worried. I'm so fucking excited I could run the entire length of this field because I honest-to-God think that Royal's inside that building waiting for us. The hurts she's given me, from poisoning and then leaving us, can't outweigh this sheer joy cascading through my chest at the thought that I'll get to see her again. There's a literal rush of euphoria in my system right now that's so intense I have to fight against a rising smile.

"Those people you worked for are untrustworthy shits," Tyler adds. "This could totally be them tying up loose ends."

We've had this argument literally every hour since I got that message. I'm sick of it. He's wrong and I'm going to prove it. "Well, let's be the ones to tie up loose ends then." I say that just to shut him up, because all the gear we have on is his ridiculous, paranoid requirement and it's completely unnecessary.

Colt grunts beside me as he hefts a heavy machine gun up onto his shoulder.

The assholes I used to work for before Tyler extracted me were not low-key, easy-going dudes so we're bringing in heavy firepower.

The march across the field to the little house on the prairie seems endless, especially since Tyler makes us stop a ridiculous number of times. I swear, every fucking cricket has him jumping out of his skin.

When we finally reach the windows and use our infrared vision to peer inside, I'm startled by what we see.

I'm sure it's a mistake.

It has to be.

The goggles must be malfunctioning because there's a slightly warm human shape outlined in fuzzy oranges and reds. But its feet aren't resting on the floor. It's floating.

"What the fuck?" I whisper.

"Shut up," Tyler hisses as he circles the entire building. When he returns, he says, "Looks like it's just the one corpse."

Corpse?

Chills creep over my arms and my back turns into a steel rod, frozen in place.

"Let's move in," Colt replies and the two of them head for the door, leaving me behind, still reeling.

Corpse?

I have horrible visions of Royal staring blankly. Of her red hair plastered flatly against the sides of her cooling cheeks. I rip off my infrared goggles and peer through the darkened window. With my normal eyes, I can clearly see that some-one's hanging from the ceiling.

Fuck. Fuck. Fuck.

My stomach cramps up in panic. Ties itself in knots.

But then a light flicks on inside—probably one of the guys. And instead of the horrible vision I'm expecting to find, I see a dead surly old man with a bowl cut, a thin black mustache and his trademark plaid shirt. My former boss. George.

I have to lean against the side of the building when my heart restarts. My entire body goes limp with relief, muscles just giving out. Fucking hell.

What the hell is going on?

Who'd bring me here to see this?

Curiosity drags my shaky legs forward until I navigate to the room George hangs in. I come to stand beside Colt and Tyler who are frozen, staring—not at the corpse, but at a bottle of Crown Royal set on the floor just in front of it. Taped to the neck of the bottle is a note that reads: *Avery, I'm sorry.*

My heartbeat speeds up before my mind registers why.

Her.

The note's from her.

Royal killed George for me.

"But why?"

Tyler's the first to move, the first to investigate the scene. He finds a stack of paperwork on the table behind George. It doesn't take him ten seconds of flicking through it before he mutters, "This bastard. He kept a file on you. And was planning to clean house."

My eyes dart back up to the body, looking at George's unseeing eyes for the first time. But instead of seeing him ... I see Royal's gift to me.

She protected me.

She killed for me.

Holy fuck.

23

SPILLING BLOOD

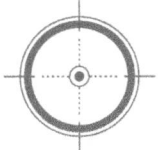

Colt

I'm two seconds away from throwing every fucking tool in our barn.

Goddammit! Where the hell is Royal?

Thoughts churn angrily in my head as I muck out stalls in the heat of the day. Probably a poor decision but the hot weather and the hard work match my sullen fucking mood right now. I dig the shovel deep into a pile of hay and shit, stewing, temper just as foul as the smell.

After that stunt Royal pulled for Avery, the drive to find that woman and make her ours has been top of mind every fucking day. Avery and I are up before dawn talking tactics as we take care of the animals, thinking through options as we plow the fields, and working on executing said plans each night after we eat dinner.

I've tried to be patient. I've tried. But I'm reaching the end of my rope.

I need to find that woman and put my arms around her.

I need to tell her all the things I didn't before.

Like how I love her fucking sense of humor. How I think every day about her goddamned vegetarian shark ... so much so that it's the background on my phone because I don't have a fucking picture of her.

What was I thinking?

The most beautiful woman in the world was at my side for days and I didn't even take a picture.

God.

I just want her back. I'd give up coffee. I'd give up anything.

The ache for her is like a black hole expanding inside my body. It's consuming me, the pressure building, until it's swallowed almost everything else.

I know it's the same for Avery. We both share this drive to see her, to find her, to win her back.

For Tyler, though, it's different.

He's grown quieter since the discovery down in Texas.

Angrier.

It doesn't seem to matter the number of times I tell him Royal got shot for him, and that's her fucking apology tour for his sake—I think he's jealous.

What? Like I'm not?

Who wouldn't want a dead man as a gift? In our line of work, that's like the holy grail of gifts.

But Avery clearly needed that gift. That's what I tell myself anyway, whenever the longing gets to be too much and morphs into an angry sort of resentment. He was in trouble. In danger and didn't know it. He needed it. Sometimes, though, logic can't talk down the green monster.

Fuck.

I toss aside the shovel I'm using to muck out the stalls because there's just no concentrating when my brain is like this. I need to go in, eat some lunch, maybe take a midday shower to cool off and reset. Then I'll come back out and try again.

Maybe tomorrow will be the day we find her.

It better fucking be or I'm going to blow a gasket.

I've just stomped out of the barn into the blinding blaze of August sunlight when I spot Avery sprinting toward me from the house, waving his arms back and forth in the air like a lunatic.

"Colt! Holy shit! Colt!" He yells my name on repeat as he runs, stumbling a little in a pothole in the grass.

"What?" I ask, just as Tyler drives up on the riding lawn mower, looking as sullen as usual. He cuts the engine and we both stare at the youngest member of Triple X, wondering what the hell has gotten him so worked up.

"Come. Inside." Avery pants as he points back toward the house. "You got a package."

"From her?" I ask, heart immediately hammering because I can't see any other reason he'd sprint to me.

He nods.

Silent, excited expectation fills the air as he turns around. Tyler leaps off the mower and all three of us book it through the grass. I bat aside a yellow butterfly that gets in my path when I lengthen my stride because I can't get inside fast enough.

Dizzy sparks are shooting off inside my head and an elated thrill bursts like fireworks behind my eyes.

Fuck.

She sent a package.

Avery said she sent *me* a package.

What is it?

My head becomes a confused snarl of intertwined thoughts. Not a single one of them is clear enough to give me a clue about what might be waiting for me. All I know is I'm about to have an aneurysm because my heart feels like it's swelling painfully inside my chest and I'm sure it's going to burst.

I reach the screen door first and yank it open, not bothering to hold it for the other two. When I step inside, it takes a minute for my eyes to adjust to the dim interior but once they do, I spot a package sitting on the table. A box.

I approach it cautiously, suddenly nervous about what it might be.

The guys crowd behind me when I finally reach the table and stare down at the parcel. It's immediately obvious why

Avery realized it's from her. The box is decorated in little green aliens wearing bow ties. Instead of a return address, there's simply a crown.

Royal.

My name and our address are printed clearly on the front of the box in black sharpie.

She knows where we live.

Why hasn't she come to see us?

A tiny dart of hurt pierces me though I try to dismiss it. Who knows what kind of jobs she has to take? What if she's always on a job? Always away ...

My hands reach for the box, greedily. I have to know what she sent.

"Wait. What if it's a trap?" Tyler asks, tone low and gruff.

Avery and I both turn to look at him. I imagine our annoyed expressions are eerily similar.

"It's not a fucking trap," Avery tells his brother before looking at me and nodding encouragingly. "Open it."

I peel off the tape and slowly unwrap the package. Inside the bubble wrap is a box of Crown Royal.

Seeing the purple box is a letdown.

I don't exactly know what I was hoping for ... but it wasn't a bottle of liquor.

Is this her equivalent of a "thinking of you" card?

Is that why she left one in front of that corpse for Avery?

I pull the box across the table and go to yank off the sticker that keeps it closed, because even if it isn't the present I wanted, I'm going to drink this whole fucking thing.

That's when I notice that the plastic sticker is loose, like it's been reattached.

Odd.

When I pull up the bottle, there's not just liquor in it. There are little flecks of things floating inside of it. Little scraps that look like dirt or sticks.

She sent me dirty liquor?

Avery leans forward next to me, nose practically touching the bottle as we examine it together. "Is that a finger?" he asks.

I quickly lift the liquor closer to the ceiling light. And there on the bottom, next to several fragments that look like bits of skull, there is indeed a charred finger.

A strange, wrong sort of giddiness fills my chest at the fact that this isn't just some alcohol.

But ... what is it?

Avery grabs the box, and quickly pulls out a few sheets of paper.

Printed on them is a news article about a bomb that went off in the mountains of Afghanistan, killing a group of militant rebels who've been hiding out there for years. They suspect either an accident or a rogue person inside the group used a suicide bomb.

I'm punched in the mouth, kicked in the gut, stabbed right through the heart.

I have to sit down.

Avery yanks out a seat for me, as if he knows, and my knees basically give out as I cradle that bottle to me like it's a fucking baby.

"Get out," I mutter.

Their footsteps fade and the door thumps shut behind them. When I know I'm alone, I read the article again and again until my eyes grow too hot to hold back the tears.

They slide down my cheeks silently. Tears for Drew and the justice I couldn't give him. For everything that happened to him and the other guys in our unit.

And tears of gratitude for Royal.

The woman I fucking love.

24

SHOOTING FOR GOLD

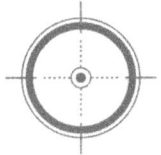

August 18
9:45 a.m.
Rose Hill, Kansas

Tyler

What can you do when someone's dug in their heels and is determined to cling to their delusions?

My brother slams his fist into the kitchen table, making it shake and his shot glass falls over. He's worked up with the kind of furor I never see from him. "I'm fucking telling you, that's her plan!"

He's drunk.

So is Colt, who's carrying around that bottle of floating body parts like it's an infant. He's had it tucked against his side all night, even when he went to the bathroom. Right now, it could be set down on the table, since we're sitting at it. But no. The bottle's in his fucking lap, which says a little something about his mental state at the moment—and my ability to trust his judgment.

"Sounds right," he agrees with Avery by giving a series of at least eight nods, which is six nods too many.

"She is *not* going after the motherfuckers who took me!" I argue for what feels like the millionth time, dark rage clinging to my ribs with all the heaviness of tar.

I sigh as I stare at the wallpaper we've always intended to rip down and replace but haven't. The lilac stripes surround lines of purple flowers and all I can think whenever I look at the ugly-ass thing is that whoever owned this place before us had shit for taste.

Just like Royal.

She's handing out fucking murders like they're apology roses or some shit and they're going soft in the head over it.

What the fuck does she see in these idiots?

I mean, they're not terrible, but still.

Colt's practically a mime most days. And Avery? He's fucking naive. This whole rant is case in point.

Royal's not foolish enough to go after those Isis bastards who took my squad.

They aren't like George, who was a fucking peon in the weapons' trade and an idiot to boot. And they aren't like those fucking cave-dwellers who got lucky when Colt's division passed by. The assholes who kidnapped me were brutal fucking operators.

Precise.

Planned.

It took weeks for us to figure out an escape and in that time, they carved us up like we were turkey dinners.

Royal knows better than to pit herself against something like that.

Those are shit odds.

I swallow as my gaze moves to the wooden floorboards, thinking. Gut twisting uncomfortably. Because that woman was foolish enough to take us head on. Almost won, too.

My stomach sinks as if I've just caught a monstrous fish and he's dragging me to the edge of the boat and I'm in danger of falling overboard. Worry starts to percolate through my stomach and fear sluices through my veins.

Dark images flicker behind my eyes.

Some are memories.

But some replace Royal in that dank dungeon I was kept in. Some force me to picture her chained like a dog to a wall, hair grimy, ribs showing because they won't fucking feed her. Fingernails gone.

Fuck. I can't!

If there's even a chance that she would do something like that...

A brick drops inside my stomach as suddenly, I'm certain she would. She will. She might even be there right now.

"Goddammit. We've got to stop her." I shove up from my seat to stand.

"That's what I've been saying," Avery slurs.

"Go get some goddamned coffee and sober up," I declare as I stride through the house, going toward the cellar we've converted to a weapons room. "Then find us the fastest flight possible." Adrenaline pumping, pulse pounding like a bass beat inside my skull, I can't believe my next words because they're the antithesis of everything I've lived for the past decade. Everything I've done has been to end these assholes' lives, to wipe them out like smudges. Now?

I'm going to have to protect my worst fucking enemies.

I'm going to have to go back to the one place on earth I swore I'd never visit again, the place that stains my soul and devours my heart. All so that Royal doesn't get mixed up with them. So they can't find or hunt or hurt her.

God, this woman.

When I find her ... her punishment is going to be unlike anything the world has ever seen.

FOUR DAYS LATER, we're wearing turbans and walking through a small town in Nowheresville, Iraq, where the air is shimmering because the afternoon heat is so intense. Tiny flecks of golden sand blow through the air with each little whip of the wind and coats every available inch of skin. For me, that's only a narrow strip visible from my eyes to my forehead.

We've been to two towns already, searching without finding her or the group who took me.

My patience was thin already but at this point, it's practically transparent.

"We've got to stop her." That's become my mantra, my motivation, the reasoning behind every bribe I slip to anyone out here who might talk.

And talk they do, because the group who took me doesn't engender a lot of loyalty. Their cruelty didn't just hit my squad but extends, to this day, to almost everyone outside their circle.

They're a canker.

But I hate the fact that their whereabouts are given up so easily, so eagerly, because it means that Royal could have gotten that information too.

When I ask about a red-haired woman though, no one has seen one.

Of course, as we walk away from our last informant, a little boy who was begging in the market of this village, Avery points out, "She's not dumb. She dyed her hair while I was with her and I'm pretty sure she's got the disguise part of the job down pat. I mean, she really likes to dress the part. I told you about how she made me help her rob the museum, right? Because she wanted to dress Babanin up like a pirate and then drown him. All because she said that walking the plank was like a forced suicide."

Underneath the fabric shielding my face, I grimace. Avery talks too fucking much.

At least Colt keeps his mouth shut.

"Shut up. We don't want everyone knowing we're Americans," I say, in a low, hushed tone as we weave around a few stalls.

That's when I spot an anomaly.

A woman in a typical black hijab strides quickly through the market. But as she rounds a corner, I catch a glimpse of what looks like a painted purple sneaker.

I blink.

Then I burst into a run, heart pounding, dismay and disbelief layered with excitement inside my throat until I'm practically choking. My wounded leg twinges and strains when I have to make a quick turn, but I ignore it. Just like I ignore the guys behind me, the press of the small crowd, the scents of spices filling the air.

Nothing else exists.

God, it has to be her.

It better be her.

I don't want it to be her because that means she's close to them.

But at the same time, I can already anticipate the stab of disappointment if it turns out to be anyone else.

Royal.

My eyes lock onto the back of the black veil she's wearing as I prowl through the market stalls, stalking her.

My eyes drop to her ass, and a dark perverted sense of delight shoots up my spine when I realize she has the exact same walk I first watched in Marseille. The same delicious curve to her ass.

I bite my lips as my eyes start to scan our surroundings, looking for an opportunity.

One appears up ahead. Two narrow stucco buildings part and a narrow alley stretches between them, a crisp dark shadow falling across the walls where the sun can't reach.

Perfect.

Nerves crackling, every sense alight with expectation, I shuffle quickly around people so that I'm right behind her as we near the mouth of the passage.

I reach forward and my fingers close around her arm, yanking her backward to me. "Hello, Royal," I breathe near her ear, before I shove that woman sideways into the darkness.

Not a person in the crowd notices or speaks up. Of course, she doesn't put up a fuss either. Like the brazen little brat she is, she says, "Tyler Monroe. You came a little sooner than I expected. Of course, I'm guessing all the girls say that to you."

Fucking minx.

I shove her through a doorway, gun coming out, startling a pair of women who are cleaning pots inside.

I don't bother dealing with them or their terrified retreat. I let Colt take care of it, tossing money their way and speaking in Farsi to tell them the house is ours for the night —find other accommodations.

I can't focus on anything other than Royal right now. On the fact that she's here, in my grip. That we've found her. After months of searching, we've finally found her. And we were right, the fucking woman was here where she shouldn't be, dipping her toes in danger that's far too deep for the likes of her.

I shove her roughly against the wall, pinning her in place with my hips as I rip off my turban and then yank the veil from her face.

The cascade of red hair is brighter than I remember. The ashen color of her eyelashes seems darker. The warm spark in her hazel gaze seems intensified. But the smirk on her lips is like tinder to a flame. She sets me off. A blaze of white-hot emotion engulfs my stomach until I'm burning from the inside out.

I smash my lips into hers and devour her. Nipping. Licking. Kissing. Grabbing any bit of her that I can reach. Her hips. Her waist. Her neck. My hands can't seem to settle on a single spot because nothing is quite enough. The kiss doesn't soothe me. Touching her doesn't calm me the way I thought it would once I knew she was safe. It only makes me more frantic, makes the feelings inside of me start to untangle and unfold until they're more massive than I can contain. Inside I'm combusting. I'm exploding, bursting and collapsing before erupting all over again with the sort of emotional force I didn't even know was possible.

When the other guys step closer, I go feral, pulling back only long enough to drag her away, toward an interior arched doorway. I growl at them, "You've had your turns. This one's mine."

Avery puts a hand on Colt's shoulder to hold the bigger man back. My brother gives me a nod.

I scoop Royal up and toss her over my shoulder, smacking her ass as I grumble, "You are in so much fucking trouble."

Her response is typical, cheeky, irresistibly her. "Yeah? Well, I like trouble."

25

BULLSEYE

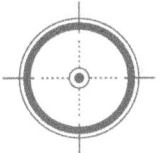

August 22
3:45 p.m.
Outskirts of Kirkuk, Iraq

Royal

I've always loved seeing Tyler irate but right now, he's livid on an entirely different level, so frantically mad that the air around him seems to pulse. And I want to live in this energy field forever. I want to feel this powerful swirl of ferocious, aggressive passion filling up my lungs and pervading my bloodstream.

Tyler sets me down but doesn't undress me. No. That would be too tame for him—for us and the way we operate when we're together.

He grabs a knife from his belt and literally cuts the clothes from my body, pressing the blade against my breastbone and slowly gliding right down. Instead of backing away, I simply spread my legs so he can cut right down between them, panting as the knife glides over my most sensitive spot. The blade pricks me once, but I hardly feel it, as desperate as I am to have his body on mine. I kick off my shoes and shed my underthings, licking my lips in anticipation.

For months, I've thought of nothing but these men and how I could redeem myself. How I could re-earn their trust after I broke it. I thought about it as I healed from that fucking gunshot and had nothing better to do all day than mope and research. Mope and plan. Mope and let my OCD over plan and re-plan and triple plan.

There may have been spreadsheets.

I'd never admit it, but there may have been.

Based on Tyler's reaction as he tosses aside the knife, on his reaction as he steps forward between my thighs... as he wraps his fingers around my neck... Based on the way his face descends to my throat and his tongue darts out to lick my pulse...I think I might have chosen right.

The sweep of his tongue alone nearly sends me to paradise. My body aches and pulses for him and I'm wet, ready for anything and everything he wants to give me.

Of course, I don't tell him that. It wouldn't be fitting.

No.

I have to prod this man, poke the bear, awake the beast.

Everyone knows beast dick is better than human dick.

And I've been waiting so fucking long—long enough to fully destroy two vibrators. I want beast dick today.

"You interrupted your present," I scold him to the best of my ability. But my words are breathy because he's got a delicious grip on my neck that's putting just the right amount of pressure on my throat.

"Don't you even fucking joke about messing with those assholes," he growls, pulling back and straightening up so that he can glare imperiously down at me.

God. I missed that glare. That scar that almost glistens, which is a softer white shade than the rest of his skin. Those deep-set dark eyes that feel like they drill right through me.

"Please, old man. I know what I'm doing," I tease, running my fingers through his hair, which looks like it might have even more silver streaks threading through it. Is that possible?

He punishes me with a kiss, his tongue lashing mine as he presses my naked body against his fully dressed one. As if his mouth could ever punish me in a way I didn't like.

Between furious rounds of kisses, he manages to say, "You. Will. Never. Pull. Something. Like. This. Again."

A golden little thread of delight ties itself into a pretty bow at the fact that he said the word "again" like he's going to be around to stop me.

God, I hope that's what he fucking means.

If not, he's going to be really annoyed when I just show up at their farm to ogle them.

Honestly, I'm surprised they haven't noticed the bug drone cameras I've been flying around their place for weeks. Colt almost batted one out of the sky recently, so I'd thought I was busted.

I open my mouth to argue with him, but his hands find my nipples and tweak. Anything I was about to say flies right out the window and migrates south. South to the equator. Where it's hot and damp.

Fuck.

As he plays with my nipples, I glide my hands down over his muscular arms, over his narrow waist. I want to drag my hands over his length through his pants, but he presses closer to me, his firmness hard against my belly, and there's no space left for me.

I nip his bottom lip because I know he did that on purpose, to keep control.

He retaliates by smacking my ass.

But the joke's on him because I fucking like it.

I toss my leg up, trying to climb him so I shift that hard length from my belly down to where I actually want it. He clutches my thighs in each of his hands as I wrap my legs around him and grind shamelessly against him. "God, I've wanted you from the second I saw you following me in France," I confess.

He carries me over to the mattress in the corner of the room and dumps me down on top of a brightly colored bedspread. His eyes roam hungrily over my naked body before settling on the scar just above my hip, the scar I try never to look at because it reminds me of how my hips are uneven now.

He leans down over me, kissing a line down my chest, across my belly, right to that scar. He laves the healed spot with his tongue before planting a circle of tiny kisses around it. Then he nuzzles it with his nose.

The worshipful attention fills my head with swirling stars.

But I can't handle sweet from Tyler.

Not yet.

Not this first time. I'm already on the cusp of being overwhelmed and consumed by him. If he adds sweetness into the potent mix of hot combativeness between us, I think I might literally explode. Pop just like one of those birthday poppers. Shoot confetti all over the room. This beloved shit has got to stop or I'm going to be spouting out the L word first.

I'm not an L word first girl.

Not an L word ever girl.

Unless it's Loser. That L word I can say.

I reach for his hair, latching on and twisting it roughly. "I've always heard guys can't find the clit, but damn, you're way off, honey. Let me help you out." Then I shove his head down between my legs. I clamp my thighs around the sides of his face and admire how good he looks in that position.

Instead of arguing, Tyler destroys my pussy. His tongue waggles like it's been possessed by a demon.

If it has, I'm happy to draw pentagrams and make sacrifices to keep that sucker around, because damn.

Hell.

Fucking.

Damnation.

He strokes my seam, uses his tongue to prod me open, then fucks me roughly with it while his nose nuzzles my clit. The combination of sensations sends me bucking against his face, grabbing his hair and riding him as pleasure dances all the way up my spine. The orgasm shimmies and shakes and does all the dance-y moves before it leaps into my skull and completely defies gravity.

Pleasure.

I float through clouds of pink puffy pleasure.

When I finally unclamp my thighs, Tyler surges up over me with a gasp. My wetness is still shining on his lips when he dives down to kiss me, that hand of his coming back to my throat and holding me down as he makes me taste myself.

He pulls back with a raspy order. "You're never fucking leaving my sight again. Ever. You hear me?"

I scrunch up my lips to one side and say, "Yeah. We're going to have to negotiate that. I'm not leaving the door open when I go to the bathroom. That's fucking weird."

He shakes his head, but I catch the smirk before he smothers it. "That sassy mouth. God, you deserve to be spanked."

"Oh, yes please. While you fuck me raw, doggie style. Actually, can you play with one of my nipples at the same time?" Questions and requests erupt from me like water from a fountain.

Tyler throws his head back and groans. Then he glares down at me. "If you want me to do all that shit, you'd better get me naked."

I have never sucked so much at undressing a human being.

Eagerness does not make the fingers more nimble.

I get his shirt stuck on his head, he's forced to help me with his belt, and fuck those motherfucking boots, they're impossible to get the hell off!

But finally, Tyler is naked in all his glory.

And damn.

"I'm gonna need you to pose for some naughty pictures for me later," I tell him, as my gaze roams down his pecs and over washboard abs. He has just enough of a dusting of chest hair to be manly without it being overwhelming. And I've never been drawn to a man's nipples before, but hello new fetish.

I start to kiss every inch of skin I can reach, starting at the junction between his shoulder and neck and working my way down. I drag my tongue across one of his nipples and am gratified to hear a gasp.

That's when Tyler's hand comes to the back of my neck, and he forces me to freeze. "Next time, you're going to suck my cock until your jaw aches. I'm going to fuck those lips raw. But right now, get on your hands and knees and take it like a good girl."

Shit.

Shit.

Shit.

That little phrase he tacked on at the end, he must know what it does to me. I must have some kind of tell. Like maybe it's the fact that my eyelashes flutter shut when he says it, or the fact that I bite my lip. Or maybe the moan I make.

My kneecaps turn to puddles and I'm scarcely able to scramble across to the other side of the bed and get in position for him. His hands come to my back and his palm traces slowly over my spine before he lifts it.

Smack.

He hits my ass with enough force to push me forward an inch or two and a delicious sting spreads across my backside.

Then I feel his body lean down over mine and he guides his hardness up to drag along my seam. "You want this dick?" he asks, tapping gently at my clit.

"If you don't give me that dick, I'm going to call the other guys in here so they can give me theirs," I threaten—because this is how Tyler and I flirt.

I get another delicious spanking in response before Tyler's hand wraps in my hair and he plunges straight into me without any further warning.

Fuck.

So full. So thick.

He starts to slam into me hard and quick and my breasts bounce in time to his thrusts. The leftover warmth from his smacks makes my ass cheeks extra sensitive to each thrust

and adds a layer to the sensations. I curve one hand underneath myself, moving my fingers toward my clit but Tyler's
hand comes down and smacks mine away. "You'll orgasm
when I let you orgasm."

Oh God.

Why is him being bossy so fucking hot?

Why?

Just that rude fucking dominance makes me clench and
draws me so much closer to the edge—I can almost taste it.
"Tyler," I growl in warning.

"Beg," he responds.

"The only thing I'm going to beg for is forgiveness," I say, the
truth accidentally spilling from my lips instead of a snarky
quip.

Tyler doesn't even slow his thrusts down. My confession
doesn't seem to phase him at all. "Too bad. The only begging
I want is for orgasms. You can't get forgiveness when you
didn't do a damn thing wrong."

His hand reaches down and circles my clit as he fucks me,
giving me a gentle sort of stimulation that keeps me just on
the brink. Just in that hazy space where I'm not quite
capable of rational thought. Where I'd do anything, say
anything, in order to be able to come. I'm so deep into my
emotions and into these sensations that I feel drunk. Tears
line my eyes as I say, "I did too. I poisoned you."

Leaning down over me so that his chest is cradling me from
above, Tyler braces himself on one hand as he thrusts even
harder, hitting a spot deep inside that tingles. "I would have

done the same. Besides, you took a bullet for me already, baby. And guess what that did? It marked you as mine. Permanently." He pinches my clit as he groans, his dick twitching inside of me as his own orgasm hits. I spiral out into unfocused, dazed bliss as he continues tugging. Rapture rolls through me but it's accompanied by such an intense sense of relief that I start to cry. For months, I've been carrying the weight of their well-deserved hatred and disdain inside my head. To find it lifted, to find out it might not have existed at all, but even more than all of that—to hear him claim me and want to keep me?

It's as if everything I've ever wanted has coalesced into a single moment. A single sensation. An orgasm so intense that it feels like it's ripping apart my very soul.

Tyler holds me close and helps me down onto the mattress, caressing me with a gentleness that's a little out of character for him. When I roll over and nestle into his chest, he simply holds me and caresses me until the tears abate.

Once I finally have control of myself, I glance up at him ruefully. "Sorry."

"Did I break your pussy?" he asks.

I burst into laughter, which I'm sure looks and sounds awkward with my raw throat and tear-stained face. "You wish. It was ... you just said all the right things."

He gives a thoughtful nod before furrowing his brow and eyeing me. "Don't expect that to be a thing."

I roll my eyes. "Trust me, I won't." I jab at his stomach play-fully and he tries to dodge, smiling.

"Good. Just don't want to raise the bar too high."

"Considering I buried the bar for you near the earth's core, I doubt that will be a problem." I stick my tongue out at him.

"Yeah, yours isn't high either. I figured you were too short to reach very far so—"

"Excuse me, short jokes? Really? Aren't those *beneath you?*"

He stares solemnly at me before shaking his head. "I'm going to go get Avery in here. I can't deal with you when you're like this."

"Emotional?"

"Punny. Ugh." He makes a gagging sound.

God, he's being silly and it's so damn adorable. It reveals a whole new facet of his personality and I love that I'm the one who gets to see it.

His silly expression shutters however, and he slides over a bit on the bed, chewing his lip. "Actually, the guys are probably standing just outside the door—"

"WAIT!" I hold out a hand and catch him by the arm because he can't leave just yet. "Stay right there."

I grab his shirt and use it to clean myself up before I stand and scour the floor for the remnants of the hijab I was wearing. I dig around the inside until I find one of the hidden pockets I'd sewn in. I extract a phone before scurrying back up onto the bed to sit beside Tyler.

I tap on an app on the home screen—a little alien wearing a bowtie. The app opens up to a series of camera feeds. "Here," I hold the phone out toward Tyler. "Pick one."

His brow furrows as he takes the phone and taps one of the tiny images to make it bigger.

An older man's face appears on the screen, his grizzled beard and dark eyes sliding up and down in the field of view.

"What am I looking at?"

"My bug collection," I tell him. "My sister built all these little bugs. Some have cameras on them. Others have fun little surprises. Now, see that little red button right there? Press that."

Tyler taps the button and the man's head on screen explodes, a fountain of red and a spray of little chunky bits flying in all directions.

I clap excitedly. "Surprise! It's a bug bomb!"

Tyler cocks his head as he studies the screen.

"Pick another," I urge. "Hurry. Before they start to realize what's going on."

"What ... is this?" he asks as he taps another square.

"Well, I told you your present wasn't quite finished. But you know what? This way's even better. You get to watch it live. And do it yourself."

Gravity shifts and all the air leaves the room as Tyler realizes what I'm saying. He stills, staring at the screen. Then he jams his finger hard against one red spot. He pulls up another picture. Another red spot. Head after head explodes on screen until all ten of the men who held his squad are dead.

He stares at the phone, as if he's not quite certain what just happened.

With epic timing, a voice calls out, "Um ... hey, we just wanted to check in ... " Avery hesitantly appears in the doorway.

I give him a friendly finger wave but Tyler throws the phone at him. "Get the fuck out. Until morning at least. She's mine tonight."

Ohhh man.

He shouldn't have done that.

Tyler getting angry at his stepbrother was so hot that now I'm going to be tempted to start fights just so he can caveman out on me.

Avery scurries off just as the founding member of Triple X turns toward me. His eyes smolder like he's pissed at me.

Crap. Maybe I don't like this. Am I in trouble? Like more than spanking trouble? I don't want to be in ass fucking trouble, not when I didn't bring any plugs to stretch me out on this trip.

"So, yeah, they're dead. You win. Yay," I spin an imaginary victory flag in my hand, but Tyler grabs it and pins it to my side.

I smile when he kiss attacks me, biting savagely at my neck, letting his teeth scrape over my pulse.

"The only thing I fucking care about winning is *you*."

That's one thing I'm happy to let him win.

26

GOING NUCLEAR

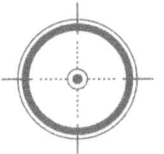

August 23
12:03 p.m.
Outskirts of Kirkuk, Iraq

Royal

We board a private jet Man sent to take us home, and I nearly sigh with relief. The reunion with my guys has been great—a huge mess of tears and sex. But I'm so ready for some fried chicken that I've been staring longingly at every damn one I've seen clucking on the street.

'Merica, here we come.

I'm also a little excited to introduce the guys to Man and my sisters. Fingers crossed that goes well. You never know with my family.

A blond stewardess dressed in pastel blue smiles at each of the members of Triple X as they step into the plane, which is all decked out in brass trim and white leather. I'm last in line, and while I totally can understand and sympathize with her appreciative glances at my guys, I do clear my throat so she'll look at me.

"Hi, I was just wondering if you have any earplugs or sleep masks available?" I say as I pull off the headscarf I wore outside.

She gives a stiff professional smile to me as she reaches for a cabinet and the latch clicks open. "Of course. It's a long flight." She easily pulls out the requested items and attempts to hand them to me.

I push them back toward her. "Yeah it is. I'm so glad those are in stock. I'm gonna need you to wear both of those for me the whole time, okay?"

She blinks, a little startled, because this is clearly the first time she's had an unusual request from a passenger. Maybe she needs a little explanation.

I lick my lips before saying, "Yeah, I'm about to have my first foursome and join the Mile High Club. And while, one day, I might be cool with spectators, I don't think today's that day." I stride past her, fully enjoying the way her jaw is hanging open.

Avery's chuckling from the window seat he chose. Heading over, I toss aside my purse and sit right in his lap, wrapping my arms around his neck.

"You're so funny," he comments, hands coming around my hips.

"Sweetheart, I'm not joking." I reply as the door to the plane is sealed so that it's airtight and the stewardess wisely disappears.

I glance around at the other members of Triple X, who are wearing hungry expressions.

"As soon as we're in the air, first one to make me orgasm gets to fuck me. The other two will have to settle for a blowjob and hand job. One rule: no killing."

It's kind of an essential rule when you're laying out challenges for assassins.

The three friends glare daggers at one another. It's clear there's about to be savagery and brutal violence—my favorite things. and I've never been more excited for an orgasm in my life.

But then, their expressions morph to amusement. Tyler chuckles at me from where he stands in the middle of the plane, hands in the pockets of his gloriously hot suit. "You think your first foursome with...what was it you called us in Morocco ... your harem? Do you really think the first time we all take you, possess you, own every inch of that sweet body that we're going to let you be in charge?"

Fuck.

Ok.

Change of plans.

He can so be the boss of me.

Tyler unbuttons his suit jacket and slowly strips it off and somehow that simple movement has me panting on Avery's lap. My eyes dart over to Colt, to see what he thinks.

"We've had this planned for weeks. Not on a plane, but the sooner the better, in my opinion." His green eyes sparkle with a kind of mischievous naughtiness that I've never seen before. I love it.

Avery's hands come up and wrap around my wrists, pinning them as his lips descend from behind to nuzzle my neck. He holds me in place and I melt against him for a moment when he tongues my pulse. He gets me nice and hot before releasing my wrists and shoving me up to my feet with a curt order, "Up," that doesn't fit his submissive personality at all.

What's going on here?

Avery goes to stand next to Tyler and Colt moseys over casually so that the three of them are all lined up.

Colt produces two sets of handcuffs from the pockets of his cargo pants. He hands one set to Tyler and tosses the other set to me.

I catch the metal rings in my right hand as Tyler steps forward, licking his lips as his eyes scan me from head to toe, devouring me.

"You have one minute to try and cuff one of us. But if we cuff you first, you're ours."

Shit.

I just ruined these panties.

I rub my thighs together in delicious anticipation as I share an eager look with each one of them, filled with a hungry, wild anticipation that sends vibrations through my belly.

I swing the cuffs around on my finger for a second before I quickly clap them on my own wrists. "Oops. You win."

And then my wolves descend.

EPILOGUE

Royal

"Woohoo! Christmas Vacation!" I declare as Triple X and I step off our private flight to Jakarta.

Though I have a rain slicker ready for possible weather, I'm pleasantly surprised to see that the sky, what I can see of it between the giant glass skyscrapers, is clear today. It's a million times warmer here than our farm in Kansas and a zillion times warmer than Man's mansion in Colorado. We've been splitting our time between the two because so many of my sisters have been either moving out or gone on missions that I've been worried about my dad being all alone.

But this trip here?

This is just for us.

Just a luxurious, no murders, no expectations other than hot sex, true-blue vacay.

I've never had one of those before.

I'm like double-fudge, extra cherry, chocolate sundae excited.

I'm pretty sure the guys are too. They keep sharing glances and smiles. Maybe they'll finally give into sword crossing. I keep asking if they're up for it. Hasn't happened yet but like … it would be hot.

I dance around on the tarmac in my ankle-length, electric purple maxi dress, not caring how people stare. I've been so happy for the past four months that I feel like an entirely different person.

The guys grab our suitcases, and we walk toward the terminal, which also has a bunch of commercial flights coming in. There is a private airport nearby for jets, but the guys insisted this one is closer to all the touristy things we're going to do.

We enter the oversized building, and the guys quickly form up around me like guards so that no one in the crowd can touch me. I feel like a princess or a President as they beam out threatening looks in every direction.

Of course, I have to try to mess with the hot vibes a little, because otherwise, I'll be way too close to orgasming in public. I love it when they get all macho overprotective.

I goose Colt first. Then Avery.

Tyler growls, "I will put you over my knee in public."

"Promises, promises," I tease.

We navigate past several gates, down the massive, five-story tall structure with floor to ceiling windows and an industrial chic vibe that's not nearly quirky enough for me. The guys steer me toward the baggage claim, stopping in front of a carousel that's just started spitting out bags like they're multicolored little watermelon seeds.

"Um. Guys. Did you forget? We already have our bags." I point out helpfully, just in case their brains forgot what's connected to their hands.

"Just watch," Tyler orders and he and the rest of the guys seem to scan the crowd, but not with that angry energy anymore. More like they're searching for something.

My heart rate picks up as I start to scan too, but I don't know what we're looking for. "This isn't a fair game if I don't know the rules. What are we trying to spot?"

A knot of people break free from the crowd, a family of four with a daughter and a son. They're dressed raggedly and have huge bags under their eyes, not the look you'd expect for people getting back from vacation. The little girl is painfully gaunt.

A vague intuitive tingling starts up at the back of my skull and my stomach starts to float up inside my belly.

As soon as the family emerges from the crowd, they're swarmed by another group. A cluster of people who'd just been standing and—I assumed—waiting for bags. It turns out, they must have been waiting for this little foursome to arrive. There are shouts and hugs and kisses and crying ... so much crying.

I don't know if I'm just a sympathy crier or what ... but a tear starts to form in the corner of my eye as I watch what is clearly a very sweet family reunion.

Colt clears his throat and takes my hand softly, his big palm wrapping around mine. I turn to look up into his bright green eyes and am surprised to find he's teared up too. His tone is thick as he says, "Remember that family Babanin sold?"

No!

No!

Oh my God.

My hand flies to my mouth and the tear in the corner of my eye erupts into a fountain, a waterfall, a cascade of this intense otherworldly feeling. I sob. I wail, right along with that family, making a scene in public and not even caring.

Each of the guys puts a hand on me, comforting me, holding me up when my knees threaten to buckle.

"Merry Christmas, Royal," Avery says softly.

His words only dredge up more tears and I choke, I gasp. I can't stop crying.

I fell in love with murderers. But love's turned them into heroes.

ACKNOWLEDGMENTS

To the hubby who inspires me and helps me format every single one of these suckers, thank you. I'd never have written without your support.

Thanks to RK and Ivy for being the best friends ever and being my safe space for my chaos. Thank you to Lysanne for reading and encouraging me. Thank you Lori for word-smithing me up to sound better than before. Thanks to Jodie at Jodielocks Designs for the beautiful cover.

And thank you to all my readers who trust me to give you a good experience even when I genre hop. You're an amazing group and I'm so happy to have found you.

ABOUT ME

I'm a shy lady who has always been obsessed with reading, travel, and live theater. I've lived in five states and currently reside in Maryland.

I have two of the world's cutest children, a ten-year-old dog and a pug puppy, along with two guniea pigs, and an amazing husband who is my total opposite, meaning he actually loves talking to people in real life.